IN THE DOGHOUSE

For a moment, there was silence.

And then the growling started again.

Gus tried not to let the images of feral hounds feasting on human flesh completely shut down the logic centers of his brain.

"Anyway, we should look on the bright side," Shawn said.

"We're about to be mauled to death and possibly eaten unless we come up with a magic word, and you think there's a bright side?"

"There's always a bright side."

"And in this case it would be . . . ?" Gus asked.

"That I was right and you were wrong," Shawn said.

"Wrong about what?"

"You said that growling was a dog."

Gus could hear long nails clicking on the pathway below them. "And I was *wrong*?"

"Without a doubt," Shawn said. "That's at least four dogs."

psych

MIND OVER MAGIC

William Rabkin

AN OBSIDIAN MYSTERY

OBSIDIAN

Published by New American Library, a division of
Penguin Group (USA) Inc., 375 Hudson Street,
New York, New York 10014, USA
Penguin Group (Canada), 90 Eglinton Avenue East, Suite 700, Toronto,
Ontario M4P 2Y3, Canada (a division of Pearson Penguin Canada Inc.)
Penguin Books Ltd., 80 Strand, London WC2R 0RL, England
Penguin Ireland, 25 St. Stephen's Green, Dublin 2,
Ireland (a division of Penguin Books Ltd.)
Penguin Group (Australia), 250 Camberwell Road, Camberwell, Victoria 3124,
Australia (a division of Pearson Australia Group Pty. Ltd.)
Penguin Books India Pvt. Ltd., 11 Community Centre, Panchsheel Park,
New Delhi - 110 017, India
Penguin Group (NZ), 67 Apollo Drive, Rosedale, North Shore 0632,
New Zealand (a division of Pearson New Zealand Ltd.)
Penguin Books (South Africa) (Pty.) Ltd., 24 Sturdee Avenue,
Rosebank, Johannesburg 2196, South Africa

Penguin Books Ltd., Registered Offices:
80 Strand, London WC2R 0RL, England

First published by Obsidian, an imprint of New American Library,
a division of Penguin Group (USA) Inc.

First Printing, July 2009
10   9   8   7   6   5   4   3   2   1

This one is for Carrie, too

Prologue

1988

The criminal justice system was a farce. Millions of lawyers fought in thousands of courtrooms, and the result was almost always the same. Criminals walked free and victims were hurt all over again.

Henry Spencer had been fighting this realization for all the years he'd been a member of the Santa Barbara Police Department. He'd had to, because if he had ever acknowledged it, he'd never have been able to put on his blues in the morning.

But as of today, there was no longer any way to deny the truth. The court had jammed his face in it as surely as if he were a puppy that had left a mess on the living room carpet.

Six months Henry had been tracking a bunko crew. Six months he had interviewed the little old ladies whose life savings had been scammed away by these sleazebags. Finally he'd been allowed to set up a sting and the creeps walked right into it—caught on tape, caught with the cash, caught with no doubt.

Except to the United States criminal justice system, that was. For them, there was plenty of doubt. Reasonable doubt, they called it, but it was only reasonable if you could bring yourself to believe that the crooks accidentally switched a bag full of scrap paper for the one holding their victim's life savings, and then accidentally used her money to buy first-class tickets to Antigua.

Henry slammed through his front door and kicked it shut behind him. He should be at the station right now, finalizing the paperwork on a burglary case that was going to arraignment tomorrow, but what was the point? Even if he did everything perfectly, the defense lawyer would argue that the defendant thought he was entering his own house, and that he only crowbarred open a second-story window because he'd misplaced his keys. And the idiot prosecutor would be unable to come up with a way to argue the point.

Henry tossed his gun in the safe and banged it shut, spinning the combination lock. He didn't want the feel of the weapon against his thigh; he didn't need any more temptation—especially since he had a sixer of Anchor Steam in the fridge and no one he needed to share it with.

He pushed his way through the swinging door into the kitchen and froze. Where he had left breakfast dishes scattered over the table, there now arose an enormous tiered edifice of white frosting with a small plastic bride and groom standing on top.

"Shawn!" he shouted. "Get down here."

Two small faces appeared on either side of the wedding cake. Henry was pretty sure they belonged to his son Shawn and Shawn's best friend, Gus, but both were so completely smeared with white, they could have been snowmen.

"Hi, Dad," one of them said in Shawn's voice. "Want some cake?"

"I want you to tell me where you got this," Henry said. "And then I want you to tell me exactly how much trouble you're in."

"It's our cake, Dad," Shawn said.

"Which I'll believe as soon as you show me the ring on Gus' finger," Henry said.

Gus lifted both hands and waggled his fingers. No rings. "We went into the bakery and Shawn asked for the biggest, best cake they had. And they had this, because someone had ordered it and never picked it up."

"Poor Kathleen," Shawn said. "If only she'd listened to her father. He knew Steve was no-good, that lousy two-timer."

Henry could feel the blood vessels under his scalp constricting. His day had been bad enough already without having to deal with his own son's malfeasance.

"Even accepting that this ludicrous story is true," Henry said, "where could you have possibly gotten the money for a cake like this?"

"They gave us a big discount," Gus said. "Apparently there isn't much of a market for used wedding cakes."

"I'm sure you're right," Henry said. "But you went into the bakery and asked for the biggest, best cake they had. And I want to know where did you get the money for that?"

Shawn shrugged innocently. "Oh, you know," he said. "Around."

Henry briefly considered his alternatives. He could get the gun out of his safe, but Henry had long felt that if the imposition of discipline required the threat of deadly force, you'd probably lost the moral authority needed for good parenting. He played with the notion of putting Shawn across his knee and waling on him, but deep down Shawn was Henry's son, and physical punishment would only make him more stubborn.

No, Henry wasn't going to get anything out of Shawn. The kid just didn't seem to have a conscience—at least not an internal conscience. Fortunately, the external model was tiptoeing toward the door, his face still covered with frosting.

"Gus," Henry said softly. "Son. Tell me. Where did the money come from?"

Gus froze. "I've got to be getting home now," he said. "My folks are probably waiting for me."

"I'm sure they are, Gus," Henry said. "Say, why don't I give you a ride?"

"Uh, no, thanks, that's okay," Gus said.

"It's really no problem," Henry said. "I'll just run you over to your house. Of course, I should probably walk you to your front door, just to make sure everything's okay."

"Honestly, you don't have to do that," Gus said.

"Really, Dad," Shawn said, "Gus has walked up his front steps lots of times."

"That way I can say hello to your folks," Henry said. "Lovely people, so proud of their son. I'm sure they'll be dying to hear how their talented boy made so much money in one day."

Gus stared at Shawn, who glared back at him. Then he turned back to Henry. "Shawn did it," he said. "He was playing spot the lady."

"Spot the lady?" Henry said. "That sounds like fun. Do you think I could play?"

Shawn sighed—caught. "Costs a dollar."

Henry reached for his wallet, then pulled his hand away. "I think we should play one round for free."

Shawn shot one last glare at Gus. He wiped his hands on his shirttail to get the icing off, then wiped them again on Gus' shirt to make sure they were clean. Then he dug in his shirt pocket and came out with three playing cards. With great effort he shoved the wedding cake to the edge of the table to clear off a space, then put the three cards down with their faces up. There were two numbered clubs and the queen of hearts.

"It's a card game," Henry exclaimed. "Why don't you show me how to play."

"It's really easy," Shawn said. "I shuffle the cards around. You pick out the queen and you win."

"My, that does sound easy," Henry said. "Let's try."

Shawn flipped the cards over and smushed them around on the table. Henry pointed to the card in the middle, and Shawn turned it over. It was the queen.

"Congratulations, you win," Shawn said. "Now I'm tired. I think I should go to bed."

"Not quite yet," Henry said. "I want to see you play it for real."

"That was for—"

"For real."

Shawn started to move the cards around the table again. This time he moved them quickly and kept up a fast patter. "Okay, find the lady, find the lady, she's looking for you, only one dollar, be a man."

Shawn separated the three cards and stepped back. Henry pointed at the center card. Shawn flipped it over. A club.

"Sorry, Dad, you lose," Shawn said. "You can just add the dollar to my allowance."

Shawn started to collect the cards, but Henry was faster. His hand slammed down on the table and before Shawn could stop him, he turned over the other two—also clubs.

"Where's the queen, Shawn?" Henry growled.

"That's what you're supposed to figure out," Shawn said. "That's what makes the game fun."

"Who taught you how to do this?" Henry said, his voice full of menace.

"What's to teach?" Shawn said. "It's a little game I made up."

Henry turned to Gus. "Who?"

Somehow the icing on Gus' face seemed to get even whiter. "It was Count Orloff!"

"Count who?" Henry said. "Is that some comic book character? Do I have to start previewing your reading material?"

Shawn shot Gus a disgusted look. "You should remember. You're the one who dragged me to the Fortress of Magic. He was some guy in a cape with a deck of cards."

"What did I tell you about talking to strangers?"

"He was talking to me," Shawn said. "And you were right there. Even though you did seem to be preoccupied with the lady magician with the big . . . feathers."

Henry fumed. Then he grabbed Shawn's arm and pulled him to the door.

"Where are we going?" Shawn said.

"First, we're going to find everyone you swindled and give them their money back," Henry said. "And then we're going back to the Fortress of Magic. I've got a trick or two to teach Count Orloff."

Chapter One

Shawn and Gus were halfway up the hill when the growling started.

Gus froze. "What was that?"

"It was nothing."

"It definitely was not nothing. It was something. Something with teeth."

The growling came again, closer this time. Gus wheeled around, searching for its source. The switchback path was illuminated by dozens of ankle-high lights; the landscaped hillside on either side was lost in the black of night. Anything could be out there.

"Let's go home," Gus said.

"We just got here," Shawn said. "In fact, technically we're not even here yet. We're not going to be here until we get to the top of this hill."

There was another growl, and this time Gus could tell it was getting closer. Somewhere beyond the reach of the path lights, bushes rustled.

"I know what that is," Gus said. "That's a dog. A vicious, angry, bloodthirsty guard dog."

"Why would there be a guard dog out here?"

"I don't know," Gus said. "Maybe to guard the place?"

"From us? We're invited guests."

"Maybe you can show Fido our invitation before he rips our throats out."

"Good thinking." Shawn pulled a printed card out of his shirt pocket. Across the top, bloodred letters read ONE LAST NIGHT OF LIFE — JOIN THE WAKE AT THE FORTRESS OF MAGIC. Shawn knelt down to read the invitation in the glow of the path lights.

"Uh-oh," Shawn said.

"Uh-oh?" Gus said. "*Uh-oh?* What's that supposed to mean?"

"It's a common expression of concern, generally uttered on the discovery of information that presages disaster."

"I know what it means," Gus said.

"Then why did you ask?"

There was a snarl from the hill to the left of the path. Gus desperately tried to shift his eyes to night-vision mode, just in case he was actually an android sent from the robot-ruled future to hunt down and kill the future mother of the leader of the human resistance and he'd simply forgotten about that. But his nonbionic eyes refused to illuminate the hillside in a green glow.

"Because I want to know what disaster you were presaging," Gus said. "And since when did you start using words like 'presaging,' anyway?"

"I thought 'augur' would seem pretentious," Shawn said. "Am I wrong?"

There was another growl, this time from the right. "Maybe we can find out when they put it on our gravestones," Gus said.

"In that case, I'd definitely go with 'augur,' " Shawn said. "Those chiselers charge by the letter. In fact, we'd probably want to switch to 'bode' and save a couple of bucks."

"Shawn!"

"Okay, there is a small problem." Shawn handed the invitation to Gus, who struggled to make out the words in the dim light.

"What? It's the right date, the right time, the right place. What's wrong?"

Shawn tapped the block of type at the bottom of the card. "Did we get anything along with this invitation? A note or a letter?"

"You know we didn't. Why?"

"Funny little thing in small print at the bottom here. Apparently if you wish admittance to the Fortress, you must say the magic words, else all is four feet."

"Four feet?"

"Although I think you can't really say it's *all* four feet. Four feet and fangs, more like."

"That doesn't make any sense at all." Gus snatched the invitation and squinted to read the tiny print.

"Neither does siccing a pack of vicious dogs on your guests. Although I've been to a couple of parties where it wouldn't have been a bad idea," Shawn said.

The letters danced in front of Gus' eyes, finally resolving themselves into one recognizable word.

"Not four feet," Gus said. "*Forfeit*. Else all is forfeit."

A growl came from the darkness directly in front of them. Gus moved behind Shawn, just in case.

"Okay, Mr. Night Vision," Shawn said. "What are the magic words?"

Gus desperately scanned every centimeter of the invitation.

"It doesn't say."

There were growls all around them now. Brush rustled in every direction.

"Abracadabra!" Gus said loudly.

"You're kidding."

"It's a magic word," Gus said.

"To a five-year-old."

"Do you have a better one?"

"I know the magic word that opens all doors, rights all wrongs, and grants all favors," Shawn said.

"Oh, please."

"Exactly!" Shawn pulled himself to his full height, took in a deep breath, and spoke in his deepest, most authoritative voice. "Please."

For a moment, there was silence.

And then the growling started again.

"That's funny," Shawn said. "My father always said that was the magic word."

Gus stared out into the darkness. "Shazam! Open Sesame! Alakazam!"

The growling got closer. Gus tried not to let the images of feral hounds feasting on human flesh completely shut down the logic centers of his brain.

"Anyway, we should look on the bright side," Shawn said.

"We're about to be mauled to death and possibly eaten unless we come up with a magic word, and you think there's a bright side?"

"There's always a bright side," Shawn said.

"And in this case it would be ... ?"

"That I was right and you were wrong," Shawn said.

"Wrong about what?"

"You said that growling was a dog."

Gus could hear long nails clicking on the pathway below them. "And I was *wrong*?"

"Without a doubt," Shawn said. "That's at least four dogs."

Furious, Gus turned to look at Shawn's face one last time before he bashed it into butter. But as he tried to catch one last glimpse of that insufferably smug grin, Shawn's face winked out into darkness.

"Shawn? Are you there?"

"I'm here." Gus could feel Shawn's breath in his ear.

"Are you ... invisible?" Gus said hopefully.

"I don't think so," Shawn said. "But it's kind of hard to tell, because all the lights just went out."

Gus looked up and down the path. At least he assumed that's where he was looking. The night was so black, he could have been staring at Jessica Alba modeling Victoria's Secret and he wouldn't have known.

All around them, the dogs started to howl.

Chapter Two

There are some mornings when you get out of bed and you know you're going to end up being eaten by dogs. For Gus, this hadn't been one of them. In fact, just hours before, he'd thought this was going to turn out to be one of his best days in ages.

He'd spent the morning on his other job, driving his route as a salesman for Central Coast Pharmaceuticals, and every stop had been better than the last. The company had introduced a new version of its popular cholesterol drug, and while the pill was different from its predecessor only by virtue of its higher price tag, it came with an entirely new set of pens, notebooks, tote bags, T-shirts, and miscellaneous logo swag to distribute. Which meant that even when he couldn't get in to see a doctor, every nurse, admissions clerk, and parking attendant acted as if he were their best friend in the world. Gus knew that people were only treating him so well because they were desperately excited to get their hands on a stainless steel commuter mug with ZOMBIA emblazoned across it, but it still made his morning rounds a happy occasion.

By the time he returned to the Psych office with his Santa bag empty and his samples already speeding their way through the bloodstreams of Santa Barbara's cardiac-challenged elites, he was thinking it was time to pack it in and head to the beach. Nothing else that happened was going to top his morning.

But just as he was slipping into a Zombia T-shirt, shorts, and flip-flops—if Gus had not dedicated himself to the art of natty dressing, he could have easily made his entire wardrobe out of logo-encrusted freebies—the office phone rang. Gus picked up on the third ring.

"Psych Investigations, Burton Guster speaking," he said jauntily.

There was silence on the receiver.

"Psych, this is Gus," he said, adding a touch of steel to the jaunt, in case this was a prank.

There was another moment of silence, then a single word, rasped out in a choked whisper: "Help." And then a click as the connection broke.

Someone was in trouble. More to the point, someone was in trouble and he—Gus was pretty sure the voice had been male—had turned to Psych for help. This was more than a job; it was a moral duty. He hit the caller ID button.

Nothing came up. The number was blocked.

That might have been a problem for a civilian, Gus knew, but he was a private detective, the nonpsychic half of Santa Barbara's premier psychic detective agency. Better than that, he was a self-taught private detective, so he wasn't burdened with the by-the-book thinking of your average private detective school graduate—that is, if there were private detective schools and if they used books. The point was, Gus was a man of action. He tensed up his entire body, took a deep breath, and pounded his index finger against the buttons marked star, six, and nine.

An electronic siren screeched out through the phone. Apparently, call return was blocked as well. This was going to be harder than he thought. But hard was what Gus was all about.

Gus' first thought was to call a friend on the force and get him to run a trace on the number the way the classic dicks of yore would have done. But since neither Shawn nor Gus had ever gotten around to saving the life of a future police detective in the jungles of 'Nam, thus earning his undying loyalty, there weren't a lot of cops who would donate their morning to the agency.

Fortunately, Gus didn't need police help to track this number. He could use his own mastery of technology. Snatching the receiver back up, Gus punched in the three numbers that would summon aid directly from the phone company. As soon as he heard the click of the connection, he let them know what he needed them to do.

"This is Burton Guster from Psych Investigations, and this is an—"

A soothing female voice interrupted him. "*Para ayuda en español, oprima el numero dos*," she said.

Before Gus could respond, there was a loud beep on the line. He knew the sound. There was another call coming in. He hit the TALK button.

"Psych, talk to me," Gus said.

"Please, please help." It was the same raspy whisper,

but it sounded even more desperate this time. "He's going to—" A loud click cut the connection.

"No!" Gus wasn't going to lose this man again. He slammed his finger against the TALK button, praying that the phone company representative was still on the line. "I need to have that call traced, right now."

"Please listen carefully, as our menu choices have changed," a chipper man intoned on the line. "For repairs, say 'repairs.' For billing, say 'billing.'"

"This is a matter of life and death," Gus said.

"I'm sorry, I don't recognize that option," the voice said. "For account status, say 'account status.' For—"

"Help!"

"Okay," the voice said.

Gus breathed a sigh of relief. He could hear circuits switching as his crucial call was sent to a specialist.

"For help with your account status, say 'account status,'" the voice said. "For help with repairs, say 'repairs.' For help—"

Gus slammed down the receiver. There was no time to waste with a phone company computer. He had to help. The fact that he didn't know whom he was helping, what he was helping him with, or where the help was needed wasn't going to stop him. He punched in a series of numbers that would send any calls directly to his cell phone and grabbed his car keys. At least he'd be out stalking the mean streets when the next call came, and he could swoop down wherever he had to be.

He was just heading toward the door when it swung open and Shawn ambled into the office, bouncing a small, hard rubber ball.

"Where have you been?" Gus demanded.

"In this time of technological miracles, it's easy to

think that everything has been invented," Shawn said as he tossed the ball against the far wall. It flew back into his hand. "And then some fresh genius comes up with something brilliant like Extreme Handball."

Shawn took careful aim and hurled the ball across the room. It bounced off the floor and ricocheted into a framed picture of Gus shaking hands with Santa Barbara's mayor, then flew back to Shawn in a shower of glass.

"We've got to go right now," Gus said, grabbing Shawn as he came through the door and pushing him back out.

"No hurry," Shawn said. "The quarterfinals don't start for another hour."

"We have a case," Gus said. "High priority. Completely urgent."

"It can wait," Shawn said. "Headhunter Hank is going down today."

"Headhunter who?"

Shawn stared at him as if he'd just said he couldn't name all the Goonies. "He's only the reigning champ of Extreme Handball in all of Santa Barbara. And I'm playing him next. Do you know what this means?"

"That you're going to miss your game," Gus said. "This is life and death."

"You think Extreme Handball isn't?" Shawn said, hurling the ball against the wall, where it dislodged three pictures and a clock before returning to his hand. "It's a desperate struggle between two men, an existential battle on a concrete court. Kill or be killed. And by killed, I mean these things really sting when they hit. Headhunter Hank Stenberg is going to feel like he's the guest of honor at a jellyfish convention by the time I'm done with him."

"Headhunter Hank can—" Gus broke off, finally recognizing the name. "Hank Stenberg? You're going to play against Hank Stenberg?"

"Someone's got to take that killer down."

"You mean the kid who lives down the street from your dad? I doubt he's even twelve years old."

"That's what they said about all those Chinese gymnasts, and they still walked off with the medals," Shawn said.

"We have work to do," Gus said.

"That's for sure," Shawn agreed. "My serve is strong, but there are a couple of moves I haven't quite mastered yet. I was thinking we could head down to the handball courts and I could try them out on you."

"We are not going to the handball courts."

Shawn glanced around the office. "I guess we could do it here, but it's going to be dangerous with all this broken glass lying around."

"We are not going to the handball courts because we have a case," Gus said. "It might be the biggest, most exciting case we've ever had."

That got Shawn's attention. He stopped bouncing the ball. "The biggest?"

"It might be," Gus said.

"Got it," Shawn said. "Who died?"

"No one, if we can get there fast enough."

"Get where?"

The phone rang once. Then Gus' cell started ringing as the call forwarding kicked in. "There."

Shawn snatched the cell out of Gus' hand and hit the SPEAKER button. "Psych Investigations," he said.

"Help, he's killing me," the rasp whispered harshly. But not quite as harshly, or as whispery, as it had be-

fore. There was a hint of tone, a smidgen of voice—
not a lot, but enough for Gus to realize he knew the
speaker from somewhere.

Shawn stared at the phone. And then spoke one syl-
lable that chilled Gus to his liver.

"Dad?"

Chapter Three

The drive from the Psych offices usually took fifteen minutes, twice that at rush hour. But Gus kept his foot jammed down on the gas, blasting through stop signs and red lights, screaming around traffic, and violating every precept of the state vehicle code that didn't involve the transportation of livestock. In the passenger seat, Shawn desperately dialed and redialed his father's number, but every call went direct to voice mail.

As he hurtled past a bus full of nuns on their way to a local convent, Gus cursed himself. How could he have failed to recognize Henry Spencer's voice? He'd heard it almost every day of his life since he was in single digits. He knew it as well as his own voice—better, actually, since he always covered his ears and hummed loudly whenever he was forced to listen to a recording of himself.

Logically he knew that part of the fault was Henry's. If he'd only identified himself, or even just engaged a little more of his vocal cords, there's no way that Gus wouldn't already have been there to help him. But that only made Gus worry more. Henry had been a cop for decades. He knew better than anyone how important it was to identify yourself clearly in an emergency. That meant there was only one reason he didn't—because he couldn't. Whatever danger he was facing, it was bigger than anything Gus could imagine.

Gus took his eyes off the road for one second to sneak a glance at Shawn. His best friend was ashen faced as he listened to his father's voice on the outgoing message.

"Shawn, I'm so sorry," Gus said for what must have been the hundredth time.

Shawn shook his head tightly. No need for apologies. He knew how much Gus cared about Henry.

Gus yanked the wheel hard and felt the Echo rise up on two wheels as it screamed around a corner. The car slammed back down on all fours and Gus jammed the gas pedal even harder. He could see Henry's house straight ahead.

Two more seconds and they were out front. The Echo screamed to the curb and Shawn and Gus leapt out, tearing up the walkway to the front door. Shawn twisted the knob. It was locked.

"Stand back," Shawn said, raising his leg to kick the door in.

"Hey, I just painted that!"

Gus and Shawn wheeled around to see a man emerging from the garage. It took Gus a moment to realize that this was indeed Henry Spencer, because he'd spent the last eight minutes visualizing him covered in blood, his ears and hands cut off, and set on fire. The fact that he was dry, intact, and completely unflamed simply didn't make sense.

"Dad?" Shawn's face seemed to be torn between relief and disbelief.

"We got here as fast as we could," Gus said.

Henry checked his watch. "Did that include a stop for doughnuts along the way?" he said. "Because if it didn't, eight minutes is pretty pathetic."

He walked past them to a corner of the house where red paint was beginning to peel after simmering through another summer of Santa Barbara sun.

"You said it was an emergency," Shawn said.

"Good thing it wasn't," Henry said as he pulled a paint scraper out of his back pocket. "Three phone calls before you guys figured out who I was? I could have been murdered a dozen times over."

"The day's still young," Shawn said, relief turning to anger.

"Wait a minute," Gus said. "This was all some kind of test?"

"Not exactly," Henry said. "I do need help."

"You want us to scrape the paint off your house, you call like a normal human being and ask politely," Shawn said. "That's the way human beings do it."

"If I called and asked you politely to scrape the paint off my house, you'd invent some ludicrous excuse for not coming over immediately, promise to drop by in a couple of days, and then I wouldn't hear from you until the rainy season started," Henry said.

"Exactly," Shawn said. "That's the way human beings do it." He turned and headed back toward the Echo. "Come on, Gus."

Gus was frozen, if only by the desire to find exactly

the right parting shot for Henry. Finally he realized there was nothing he could say that would sum up everything he was feeling. He gave Henry a look he hoped would convey a bevy of emotions, then turned and followed Shawn.

"Okay, hold on," Henry called after them. "I'm sorry if I scared you two little girls."

"Way to apologize, Dad," Shawn called over his shoulder.

"But I really do need your help," Henry said. "And it doesn't involve scraping paint, and it is kind of an emergency."

"What kind of emergency?" Shawn said.

"The kind that's best discussed over pizza," Henry said. "Fortunately, Giuseppe's took a lot less time to get here than you guys."

By the time the three of them had finished two large pies, a family-size chopped salad, and a side of buffalo wings, Gus found his anger had been drowned in a sea of carbohydrates. That's when Henry consented to discuss the nature of his crisis.

"It's about Bud Flanek," Henry said.

"What is that, some kind of skin disease?" Shawn said. "Because if you're hoping I'm going to donate my flesh to you, I'm still using it."

"Bud Flanek," Henry said irritably. "You remember him. He was on my bowling team years back. Tall guy, one shoulder lower than the other, always wore bib overalls."

"Let me guess," Shawn said. "He's been accused of a crime against fashion, and you want me to get him off. Sorry, Dad, I don't think I can help."

Gus admired the way Shawn could continue to hold

his grudge even when he was stuffed with pizza, because he couldn't fight against the warm feelings his
digestive system was sending through his body.

"Is your friend in trouble?" Gus asked.

"In ways he can't begin to imagine," Henry said. "He's
about to get married for the first time at sixty-two."

Shawn stifled a bored yawn. "And you want us to investigate his fiancée and prove that she's actually some
floozy who's going to steal all his money and break his
heart."

"Why would I want that?" Henry said. "I think it's
great that Bud's finally found someone who makes
him happy. And she hardly needs his sewer department pension. She manages a very profitable bakery
in Summerland. Not bad for a recent immigrant from
Eastern Europe."

"Then what do you need us for?" Shawn said. "Or
did you drag us up here just to make us listen to the
joyous news about one guy I barely remember mar-
rying some woman I've never met? Because if that's
what's going to make your life worthwhile, you should
start a blog, and then you can bore complete strangers,
too."

Henry pushed off from the table and wandered out
of the room. When he came back, he was carrying a
brightly wrapped box about the size of a mediocre dic-
tionary. He tossed it on the table in front of Shawn.

"That's really special, but didn't you get anything for
Gus?" Shawn said.

"It's not for you," Henry said. "I'm in charge of Bud's
gag gift. I need you to deliver it to his bachelor party
tonight."

Gus and Shawn stared at him, not understanding.

"That's the emergency?" Shawn said finally.

"Maybe 'emergency' was a little strong," Henry said. "But it's important to me that Bud get this tonight."

"Just not important enough that you would bother going to his bachelor party."

"I have my reasons," Henry said.

"Like what?" Shawn said.

"When a man is preparing to declare lifelong fidelity to one woman, it seems morally wrong to celebrate that by spitting in the face of those vows," Henry said.

"First of all, vows don't have faces," Shawn said. "You're thinking of cows, which do have faces, but you really don't want to spit in them, because they can spit back."

"Those were llamas," Gus said, remembering that one long afternoon when their elementary class field trip had taken them to a farm. "And the teacher warned you about five hundred times not to taunt them."

"Second," Shawn said, "I can't believe I'm hearing this from a man who organized a bachelor party in Vegas for Earl Mountlock that was so insane the wedding had to be postponed for a week because the judge refused to let the groom out on bail."

"That was before I started listening to Dr. Laura," Henry said. "She has a lot of wisdom on the subject. Are you going to do this or not?"

Gus recognized the look on Shawn's face. He was trying to figure out what was really going on here.

"See, if you gave me this present and asked me to carry it onto an airplane for you, I'd understand that there was a bomb in it and you wanted to make your insane political point without dying in the process," Shawn said. "But you're handing it to me and asking me to carry it into a trendy nightspot filled with naked women pouring free drinks, and I can't see the rationale behind it."

Henry pounded the table in frustration. "Can't you just do me this one small favor without turning it into some grand inquisition?" he growled. "I can't go to the party. I'd like Bud to open his gift in front of his friends. It's not that big of a deal. And there aren't going to be any naked women. It's a cash bar, and no one would use the word 'trendy' to describe the Fort—"

Henry broke off in midsyllable, his face reddening.

"What fort?" Gus asked. "There's no fort in Santa Barbara."

Henry sat still, grim faced. Baffled, Gus glanced over at Shawn to see if he had any idea what his father was talking about. Apparently he did, because his face was split by a wide smile.

"Please, go ahead and finish your word, Dad," Shawn said, taking a pleasure that Gus couldn't begin to understand.

"Look, if you don't want to help me, you don't want to help me," Henry said. "I'll ask one of the guys to drop the present off."

"Drop the present off where, I wonder," Shawn said. "Oh, yes. The Fort. Which I believe is an abbreviated version of a longer word. What would that be again?"

"Fortress?" Gus guessed.

"Don't worry about the dishes," Henry said, stacking the plates on top of the empty pizza boxes. "I can take care of them on my own."

"Ah, yes, *fortress*," Shawn said. "As in Fortress of Magic. Would that be where Bud Flanek's bachelor party is being held?"

"It wasn't supposed to be," Henry grumbled. "But the damn health board shut down the Beef 'n' Fish Barrel two nights ago, and Bud's best man, Lyle Wheelock, managed to book that dump."

"And I guess he didn't ask you first." Shawn beamed. "Or maybe he did, and you were just too embarrassed to tell him the truth."

"What truth?" Gus asked.

"Dad can't go to the Fortress of Magic," Shawn said. "Not since he took me there when I was a kid. He was banned for life."

"But that was twenty years ago," Gus said. "They can't possibly still—"

"They renewed the restraining order six months ago," Henry snapped, then turned to Shawn. "Are you happy now? Have you humiliated me enough?"

"Not nearly enough." Shawn picked up the package and spun it around in his hands. "Not to make up for what you did to us today. But once I tell everyone at that bachelor party exactly why it is you're not there, I think we'll be even."

Henry glared at Shawn. Then he marched the plates and pizza boxes into the kitchen. When he returned, he slammed a printed invitation on the table in front of his son.

"Really?" Shawn cast a quick look at the invitation to make sure it was what he thought it was. "You still want me to go, knowing what I'm going to do?"

"More than ever, son," Henry said through clenched teeth. "Because I'm sure now that you're an adult, you'll do something that will get you banned for your grandchildren's lifetimes."

Chapter Four

The black night was filled with howls and growls of a pack of vicious dogs. Gus moved closer to Shawn. At least he tried to, but since he couldn't see his friend in the darkness, he might just as easily have been moving away. Something brushed his ankle, and Gus leapt away. He could practically feel the hot breath through his socks.

"How many do you think there are?" Gus said, trying to differentiate between dozens of dog sounds.

Shawn listened for a moment. And then for another moment. And another. "I don't have to think," he said finally. "I know exactly how many."

At first, Gus thought Shawn was cracking under the strain of their impending, and very unpleasant, death. But he quickly realized that what he heard in Shawn's voice was not a tremble of fear, but a poorly repressed chuckle.

"And that's funny somehow?" Gus said.

"It is if you know the number," Shawn said. "What did the invitation say again?"

"It said we needed to know the magic word, or we'd be eaten to death," Gus said. "Or words to that effect."

"I don't care about the effect. I need to know the exact words."

Gus called up the image of the small red type in front of his eyes. Even in this remembered state it was hard to read. "If you wish admittance to the Fortress, you must say the magic words, else all is forfeit."

"Okay then, let's say the magic words."

"We don't know them!"

"Don't we?"

"No, Shawn, we don't. That's why we're standing in the dark, surrounded by vicious hell hounds."

Gus could almost hear Shawn's smirk. "My friend, you are wrong on every count."

"Then if you're so smart, you go ahead and say the magic words."

"I don't think you want me to do that."

"To save our lives? Say the words."

"You're going to be mad."

"Because you figured it out first? I'll live—if you say the words."

"Fine, I will," Shawn said. He took a long, dramatic pause, and then let his voice ring out over the hillside. "The magic words!"

Gus felt his heart sink in his chest. At least it would be harder for the dogs to get to it that way, he thought. He had actually allowed himself to hope that Shawn knew what he was doing, that they might get out of this alive. He squeezed his eyes shut and tried to prepare himself for the first fangs to penetrate his flesh.

After a moment, he realized there were no fangs.

There weren't even any growls. The dogs seemed to have disappeared. Cautiously he opened his eyes just as the entire hillside erupted in a blaze of landscape lighting. There wasn't a bared tooth anywhere, unless you counted the ones in Shawn's broad smile.

"The magic words?" Gus sputtered. "That's it? That's the dumbest thing I've ever heard."

"Told you you were going to be mad."

Gus realized he was. Relieved, yes, at no longer facing a hideous, drooling death. But also annoyed at the simplicity—in fact, the stupidity—of the clue.

"How did you figure it out?"

"You've just got to know how magicians work," Shawn said.

"How do they work?"

"Mostly as waiters," Shawn said. "It's convenient for them because they can use the tux for both jobs. Shall we head on up to the Fortress?"

Shawn waved Bud's present up the now brightly illuminated path to a grand craftsman manor that sat on top of the hill.

"But where are the dogs?"

"Same place they always were." Shawn pointed to a spot a foot away from the path where a small speaker was staked between two lavender bushes. Gus could see several other speakers hidden in the landscaping.

"How did you know?"

"Magic."

"Exactly what kind of magic?"

"The magic of the human ear," Shawn said. "Do you realize how complex that organ is?"

Gus glared at him and waited for him to continue.

"The dog growls were on a tape loop," Shawn said.

"After the fourth dog joined in, there was a tiny blip where it was spliced together. And since it seemed unlikely that the canines were doing the editing job themselves, I figured out that there were no dogs anywhere around."

Shawn headed up the path to the Fortress. Gus chugged behind him until they reached the front door, a mammoth slab of green painted oak with a sign across it reading REALITY ENDS HERE.

"I'll say," Shawn muttered as he pushed the door open.

Inside, the old craftsman had been skillfully transformed into something that looked like the haunted house at a middle school carnival. Plastic skeletons dangled from the ceiling, their formerly white limbs encased in gray dust, and the fake spiderwebs that had been sprayed in the corners had all been covered with real ones. A banner hand-painted in red tempera on butcher paper welcomed Bud's bachelor party to the Fortress.

Gus looked around the room, dismayed. He had spent much of the afternoon reading up on the Fortress of Magic, and until the attack by imaginary dogs, he'd been looking forward to seeing it. Founded in the late twenties by a group of professional magicians, the Fortress was a place for "the peers of prestidigitation" to "practice their dark arts away from the prying eyes of the public." In its heyday, every great stage magician stopped by whenever they passed through Santa Barbara, and many made the trip west specifically to visit. It was a place where they could talk about their craft and test their new illusions on the most demanding audience of all.

Over the years, the Fortress had gained a certain mystique, mostly because only members were allowed in, and only professional magicians could become members. Of course, that mystique had diminished as the small group of magicians who sat on the Fortress' board started to rent the place out for parties to bring in a little money for operating expenses. Apparently there had been a fierce controversy over the idea of allowing nonpros in to see the magicians' sanctum sanctorum, but when the board insisted that they needed money to stay in business, and the only two options were to open the place to outsiders or raise prices at the bar, the membership quickly fell in line.

Now the Fortress was an exclusive club open only to members—and to anyone who held an invitation for a fundraiser, a book club meeting, or a bachelor party. Still, the magicians who attended continued to act as if they were in their own private preserve, testing out their new illusions on each other while making sure their business cards ended up in the pockets of anyone who looked like they might be hiring.

From the descriptions Gus had read online, he'd expected the Fortress to be a grand, Gothic spectacle, a step inside a private world few would ever have the opportunity to experience. Instead, he saw a run-down mansion with wobbly furniture, threadbare carpets, and a smog of desperation hanging over the small crowd that populated it. He was momentarily surprised that none of the Web sites he'd checked out had described the place as anything but a palace of wonders. But he quickly realized that the illusion of exclusivity was stronger and more appealing than anything reality had to offer—what was the point of gaining admittance to this fabulously private place, only to describe it as a dump? If the writer's privilege was to mean anything, the Fortress had to be portrayed as something, well, magical.

What it felt like more than anything else was the headquarters of an Elks lodge that hadn't recruited a new member since Nixon resigned.

"This is some rocking party," Shawn said. "My father doesn't know what he's missing."

"So when are you going to tell me what he did that was so bad, they banned him for life?" Gus said.

"It was a little misunderstanding, that's all," Shawn said. "They thought they should be able to practice their craft in their own building. He disagreed."

"Let's just find this Bud Flanek guy and get out of here," Gus said. "This place is depressing."

"If there's one thing that professional magicians and aging bachelor partyers have in common, it's their choice of location," Shawn said. "We'll find him in the bar."

A burst of laughter from down the hall strongly suggested where that bar might be found. But when they turned to head in its direction, Gus nearly tripped over an enormous lump on the floor. Looking down, he saw a crown of bald scalp laurelled with graying ringlets that resolved into a greasy ponytail. Fleshy hands scrabbled over the carpet, scraping together a mound of playing cards.

The lump looked up and Gus found himself peering into the cherubic face of a Quattrocento *putto*—or at least what such a cupid might have looked like if he'd spent his thirties and forties trapped inside a bottle of vodka.

"Knew I shouldn't have tried the Brazilian shuffle in public yet," the *putto* said sheepishly as he gathered the rest of the cards into a neat block and scooped them into one hand. He used the other to push himself up to his knees, and from there up to his feet. Once he was standing, he adjusted the cummerbund on his too-tight tuxedo to cover the stomach-revealing gap in his shirt. "Darn cards keep getting away from me. Speaking of which . . ."

The *putto* fanned the deck clumsily and thrust it under Gus' nose. "Choose a card."

Gus' hand reached up reflexively, but Shawn pulled it back down.

"We'd prefer not to choose," Shawn said. "We like them all equally."

"No, really, this is good," the *putto* insisted. "I've practiced it a lot." His face blazed red as he screwed up his mouth in embarrassment. "I mean, it will astonish and amaze you. You like being astonished and amazed, don't you?"

Gus had to admit he did. He reached out for a card, but again Shawn pulled his hand away. "You're just encouraging him."

"What's the problem?" Gus said. "All he wants is to do a trick for us."

"Sure, that's how it starts," Shawn said. "But then he's going to follow you home, and you're going to want to take care of him. You'll promise to feed him and clean up after him and take him out for walks—"

"It's a card trick," Gus said. He reached for a card and waited until Shawn knocked his hand away. Then he reached out with his other hand and snatched a card out of the deck. "What do I do now?"

The *putto* looked confused. "I'm trying to remember. It's been so long since anyone actually said yes."

"Come on, Gus," Shawn said. "Let's find Bud Flanek and get out of here."

"Wait, wait! I remember," the *putto* said. "You look at the card. That's right. You look at the card and then put it back in the deck."

Gus glanced at the card. It was the five of hearts. He slipped it back into the deck, which the magician had helpfully shoved back under his nose. The magician gave the deck a couple of sloppy shuffles, then proudly pulled out one card.

"This is your card!" the *putto* pronounced, holding up the two of spades.

"That's right, that's amazing, that's astonishing," Shawn said quickly. "If only there was a tip jar."

Shawn pulled Gus away toward the bar as the *putto* gaped after them.

"You know that wasn't my card," Gus said.

"And so did he."

"So, what, you were trying to spare his feelings?"

"I was trying to spare us another fifteen minutes watching him pretend to be a bumbling idiot while he worked you over," Shawn said. "You still have your watch, don't you?"

Confused, Gus checked his wrist. The Fossil was firmly in place. "I don't know why you say he was pretending," Gus said.

"Why are you limping?"

"I'm not." Gus stopped, realizing that he was. He pressed his left foot down on the floor. "I think there's something in my shoe."

"Maybe you should take it out."

Gus sat on an overstuffed couch, fighting a sneeze as dust motes flew up around him, and pulled off his left oxford. He peered under the tongue. "Nothing there."

"Try the sock," Shawn said.

Gus pulled the Gold Toe Executive Stretch off his foot. As it cleared his arch, something fluttered out. Gus picked it up and stared at it.

The five of hearts.

"Is this your card?" Shawn said wearily.

"But he was . . . ," Gus started, casting a glance back to where the *putto*, apparently failing another attempt at the Brazilian shuffle, knelt on the floor, scraping up cards in front of a young couple clearly here for a function more glamorous than Bud Flanek's bachelor party. "How did he? And how did you?"

"You don't want to know," Shawn said. "It's just going to make you mad."

"That's the second time you've said that," Gus said.

"And I was right the first time, wasn't I?"

Gus had to admit it was true. "But why?"

"This is how stage magic works," Shawn said. "They do a trick. You're amazed. You can't imagine how they pulled off something so miraculous. You're dying to know. But they'll never tell you."

Gus slipped his sock over his foot, then stood into his loafer. "Because if you know the trick, then the illusion is ruined."

"But why would that be?" Shawn said. "If they were really communing with the spirits or reading your mind or dancing with dragons, wouldn't they want you to know?"

"Sure, but they're not."

"Obviously," Shawn said. "But even if what they

were doing was so difficult, so complicated, so challenging, knowing how they did it would only make you respect them more."

"Yeah."

"So why don't they want you to know how they do it?"

Gus thought it through, but he still couldn't see where Shawn was going with this.

"Just watch him." Shawn pointed at the *putto* collecting his cards on the floor.

"What am I watching?"

"That."

It was just a flicker of movement. If Gus hadn't been staring so hard at the magician's hands, he never would have noticed it. But while the *putto* was down on the floor gathering his deck, one hand shot out and slipped a card into the shoe of the young man whose way he had blocked. Unlike every other one of the magician's fluttering movements, this one was sure, direct, and clean.

"Hey!" Gus said. "Did he do that to me, too?"

"What do you think?"

Gus tried to recreate the first moment he saw the man kneeling on the floor. Had he felt something brushing at his ankle? He couldn't remember.

"But even if he could get a card inside my sock—"

"Which he did."

"Okay, even after he got a card inside my sock, what if I had chosen the nine of clubs?" Gus said, trying to work out the trick. "He'd look pretty stupid."

Shawn let out a heavy sigh. "Which is why he didn't give you a choice of which card to choose. If you could get that deck away from him, I bet you'd find that every other card is the five of hearts. And he knows how to force the right one on you."

Gus stared as the magician climbed to his feet and thrust the deck of cards into the young man's face. "So it's not that he made the card I chose end up in my shoe. . . ."

"It's that he made you choose a card identical to the one he'd already stuck down your sock," Shawn said. "Feeling mad yet?"

"Yeah," Gus said. "But I'm not exactly sure why."

"It's the one thing that all magicians share," Shawn said. "No one ever figures out the secrets to their tricks, not because they're so complex, but because they're so obvious. And when people find out the truth, they get mad because the entire illusion depends on the audience behaving like idiots. When they figure it out—if they ever figure it out—they get mad."

Gus thought that over. And then he got mad all over again. "Let's go."

"After we deliver the present."

"No, let's go back and expose that fake," Gus said, staring hard as the chubby magician forced the five of hearts on the young couple.

"Don't bother," Shawn said wearily. "These guys are pros. They're ready for hecklers."

"He's not ready for me."

"Gus, Gus, Gus," Shawn sighed. "Didn't you learn anything from *War Games*?"

"If you mean not to turn complete control of your nuclear arsenal over to computers on the grounds that they're more logical and less likely to act out of emotion or error, I had already learned that from *Colossus: The Forbin Project*," Gus said. "And if it's that sentient computers find Ally Sheedy irresistible, *Short Circuit* is much more believable on that score."

"I mean the lesson that WOPR has for all of us," Shawn said. "The only winning move is not to play."

"I don't want to play. I want to expose that fraud."

Shawn sighed. "Look, if I wanted to shoot a bear—"

"Why?" Gus interrupted, his eyes laser focused on the fraud crawling around on the ground.

"Why what?"

"Why would you want to shoot a bear? Remember what happened that time you borrowed Eli Messenger's BB gun and accidentally winged a squirrel? You were a wreck for weeks."

"First of all," Shawn said, "I didn't 'accidentally wing' the squirrel. I tracked it to its lair, waited until I could see the whites of its eyes, and then, reenacting the primordial battle of man against beast—"

"You dropped the gun. It went off and hit another squirrel that was watching you from a branch above," Gus interrupted. "And even though it was just a flesh wound, you climbed up that tree every day for a week to bring your victim a bowl of Screaming Yellow Zonkers. Which even you have to admit was a strange choice, since of all the sweetened popcorn-based snack foods, Zonkers is the only one that doesn't contain peanuts."

"It was a young squirrel, and it might have had an allergy," Shawn said. "Anyway, I wasn't actually proposing that we go out in the woods and hunt a grizzly. What I was saying was that *if* I wanted to shoot a bear—" He broke off, making sure that Gus wasn't going to interrupt again. Assured that he wouldn't, Shawn continued. "If I wanted to shoot a bear, I wouldn't do it in a den full of other bears."

"Thank you for this moment of folksy wisdom," Gus said. "Now, can we go expose that fraud?"

Shawn took Gus by the shoulders and turned him so he was facing the fireplace. "Tell me what you see."

Gus glanced across the room and saw a sixtyish man, sporting a shiny red suit and an even shinier red nose, pulling miles of colored scarves out of one sleeve. By the front door, an aging hipster in a gold lamé jumpsuit was crashing metal rings together. Shawn pointed to the fireplace and Gus saw a woman with close-cropped hair, black slacks, and a black vest over a vividly patterned blouse lift a pair of daggers and drive them into her eyeballs, then wander off with the hilts sticking out of her sockets as the two people who had been paying attention stared in horror.

"People who make us look cool," Gus said.

"Exactly," Shawn said. "And if we go after one of them, they'll all put aside their differences to fight back. Just like the bears in the den. So instead of exposing anyone, how about engaging in a little fraudulent behavior of our own?"

Shawn headed off down the corridor toward the noisy bar. Gus shot one last glance across the room, just in time to see the young woman squealing with delight as her boyfriend removed a playing card from his shoe. Then Gus followed Shawn down the hall.

The pub was clearly the most used room in the Fortress. The walls were clean and cobweb free; the carpet between the door and the bar had been worn down to threads. There were clearly several different events being held here tonight, and the room was clustered with tight knots of partyers.

"So, which one is Bud Flanek?" Gus said.

"Look for a guy wearing bib overalls."

Gus scanned the crowds, but saw no one dressed as a farmer or train engineer. "We don't even know which is the right party," he said.

"Shouldn't be that hard to figure out," Shawn said. "Just look for wide ties and wider lapels."

Gus wasn't sure what Shawn meant by that, until he noticed a group of graying and balding men standing by a flickering fireplace. Each one wore a single-breasted suit fashioned out of some material nature had never intended, with lapels so wide they nearly touched at their wearer's spine, and a tie that practically obviated the need for a shirt.

"How do you know that's them?" Gus asked.

"Dad's bowling group was all blue-collar guys," Shawn said. "Sewer workers, garbage truck drivers, mechanics—not exactly jobs that require a coat and tie. They wear a suit only once or twice a year to weddings or funerals, which means the first one they bought is still in great shape. So why should they ever buy a second?"

A roar of laughter came from the bachelor party as Shawn and Gus made their way over to them. When the hilarity over what was evidently a bit of clever wordplay involving the names of various items of the female anatomy subsided, Shawn stepped forward with the present.

"Mr. Flanek?" Shawn said to a tall, stooped man in the center of the crowd.

Bud Flanek studied Shawn carefully, trying to place a face he seemed certain he'd seen at least once before. "Do I know you?"

The man whose joke had been the cause of the recent merriment pushed his way out of the crowd and grabbed Shawn by the shoulder. He was shorter than Bud and almost completely bald except for a few strands of gray hair combed over his scalp and pasted down with spray. There was something about the way he moved that told the world he was to be the center of attention in any circumstances.

"This is the stripper we got you, Bud," the man barked. "Sorry she's so ugly—best we could afford." He dissolved into gales of laughter over his own witticism.

Gus realized that the man was Lyle Wheelock, Bud's best man and the evening's host.

"I think we met once," Shawn said. "My father is Henry Spencer. He asked me to—"

"Henry!" Lyle interrupted. "That old goat! What's his problem that he can't even bother to show up to the most important night in Bud's life?"

"Second most important," another man shouted from the crowd. "I think the wedding night is number one."

"Not if this party goes the way I think it will!" Lyle roared, then, as the men erupted in laughter, turned back to Shawn. "So what's Henry's story? Is he afraid I'm going to tell everyone about that time in Reno?"

"Why isn't Henry here?" Bud asked. "I was there for his bachelor party."

This was Shawn's moment: maximum humiliation of his father for minimum effort, a perfect revenge not only for this morning's scare, but for years of similar scores. He was about to launch into the story of just why Henry would never again be allowed on the steep walkway to the Fortress of Magic, when he realized something was wrong. Henry had sent him here for a reason. He could just as easily have used a courier service, or dropped off the gift with the doorman. Henry was setting Shawn up for something, and while Shawn didn't know what it was, he was pretty sure it was going to be some kind of lesson he wouldn't enjoy learning.

"He's in bed with a bad cold," Shawn said.

"I know who you are," Lyle bellowed. "You're that psychotic kid."

"Psychic," Shawn said.

"I'm pretty sure I heard Henry say psychotic," Lyle said. "Go ahead, tell my future."

"I don't tell futures," Shawn said.

"And we've really got to be going," Gus said, trying to pull Shawn away. "Give Bud the present and let's get out of here, Shawn."

But Lyle Wheelock placed himself directly in front of them. "Come on, brain boy," he taunted. "We need some entertainment at this party. Do your trick."

"I don't do tricks," Shawn said. "Talk to any of the magicians here. I'm sure they'll be happy to help you out."

"I knew you were a phony," Lyle shouted. "You couldn't read my mind if I took it out of my skull and handed it to you."

"You tell him, Lyle," Bud said.

"Come on, brain boy," Lyle said. "Do something psychotic. Tell me something about myself nobody knows."

Shawn pressed his fingers to his forehead and doubled over as if in pain. Then he straightened suddenly. "You are . . ."

"I am what?" Lyle said.

"Not nearly as funny as you think you are."

A voice came out of the crowd. "He said tell him something no one else knows!"

Lyle's face burned red as Shawn turned to go. "Come on, I want you to read my mind," he said, grabbing Shawn's arm. "I'm not letting you go until you tell me something amazing."

Shawn sighed and took a hard look at Lyle Wheelock. And he *saw*. Saw a fine white powder on his shoulders—powder that might have been dandruff, except that Lyle didn't have any hair. Saw a film of yellow grease under his fingernails. Saw the small tear in his shirt that had been amateurishly stitched together. Saw the bare white band on his ring finger.

Shawn's hands dropped away from his forehead. "I'm not seeing anything," he said, then turned to Gus. "Let's go."

"Just tell him something so we can get out of here," Gus hissed in Shawn's ear.

Shawn sighed again. "If that's what everyone wants . . ."

Shawn leaned close to Lyle and whispered into his ear. Gus couldn't hear what Shawn said, but he could see the reaction. Lyle dropped Shawn's arm, his face turning red.

"Let's go," Shawn said, turning toward the door. But before they could take a step, Lyle let out a howl.

"How dare you come to this party and tell everybody I'm sleeping with my best friend's fiancée?" Lyle shouted.

Behind Lyle, Bud Flanek turned pale. The other members of the party looked like they'd been struck with hammers.

"I didn't," Shawn said. "You just did."

Lyle leapt across the room and grabbed Shawn by the throat. "Shut up! Shut up!"

Shawn gasped for breath, but Lyle was squeezing too tight. Gus tried to pry his fingers off, but they were like steel bands. Shawn could feel himself beginning to lose consciousness, when a scream echoed from the front room.

"What was that?" Lyle said, releasing his grip on Shawn's throat and letting him drop to the floor.

Every head in the bar swiveled toward the door, and for a moment, the entire crowd stood frozen. And then the scream came again.

"This way," someone shouted, and the entire crowd drained out of the room.

"Can't see why my father doesn't like this place more," Shawn said, rubbing his neck.

Chapter Five

The Fortress shook as if someone had slammed a wrecking ball into it.

"Earthquake!" Gus shouted as he followed Shawn into the main parlor.

"I don't think earthquakes usually hit at two-second intervals," Shawn said.

Shawn and Gus pressed into the room, but all they could see were the backs of the people who'd gotten there before them. The Fortress shook again.

"Then what's going on?"

Shawn scanned the room. Then he pointed above the crowd toward the entrance. "I think it may have something to do with that."

Gus craned his head around a tall man in a cheap tuxedo, looking to see what Shawn was talking about. And when he did, he wished he'd never opened his eyes. It wasn't the fact that there was a head bobbing above the crowd that bothered Gus, even though its bald crown must have been more than seven feet off the ground.

It was the fact that the head was green.

The Fortress shook again. The head moved through the crowd like a shark's fin cutting through the waves, and Gus realized what was rattling the building: It was the green creature's footsteps.

"What is it?" Gus whispered to Shawn.

"A product of global warming, I'm thinking," Shawn said.

"What?"

"Don't you remember *Frankenstein: The True Story*?" Shawn said. "At the end, Victor Frankenstein is chasing the monster over the North Pole, and they both get buried by an avalanche. Clearly, global warming has melted the ice enough to set the monster free."

"That was a movie, Shawn," Gus said. "It didn't really happen."

"It's the *true story*," Shawn said. "It said so in the title."

"That doesn't make it real," Gus said.

"Really?" Shawn said. "I thought there was a law."

The room shook again as the creature took another step. Somewhere in the crowd, a woman screamed.

"What's it doing?" Gus said, jumping up to see over the crowd.

"The last thing you want it to do," Shawn said. "Coming this way."

Shawn was right. The head had turned and was now moving directly toward them. Up ahead, Gus could see the crowd falling away to make room for the creature.

"Do you think it eats people?" Shawn said, edging back a little. "Because if so, I think Lyle would make a tasty treat."

The crowds parted as the stomping footsteps got

closer. The two men blocking Shawn's view fell aside, and the creature stood directly in front of him.

Its enormous feet were encased in heavy black boots. On its bald head it wore a thick gold band as a crown. Its midsection was wrapped in a black loincloth. The rest was rippling muscles covered only by bare flesh.

Bare *green* flesh.

Gus stared up into the creature's face. If he ignored the coloring and the razor-sharp teeth, he could imagine he was looking at a normal human. Of course, if he could ignore the coloring and the razor-sharp teeth, he could imagine a great white shark was a goldfish, but that wouldn't keep him from being digested as a snack.

The creature stared down at Shawn and Gus, arms crossed over his mammoth chest. "Puny humans, tremble before P'tol P'kah," his voice boomed down at them.

The creature pushed between Shawn and Gus as it stomped toward the back of the building. Before Gus could decide between following the green monster or collapsing into a dead faint, a thin, reedy voice came from behind him.

"Fellow magicians," the voice said, "P'tol P'kah has come here to meet your challenge."

Gus turned to see a tiny man following in the open aisle the creature had created. His salt-and-pepper hair was razor cut; his designer suit hugged his body. Aside from the fact that the top of his head didn't quite skim the five-foot mark, he could have been Mitt Romney.

"Now, who here has dared call P'tol P'kah a fake?" the small man said.

There was a concerned murmur in the crowd before

a heavyset man in a worn tuxedo pushed his way up to the speaker, his face twisted in scorn.

"I dared," the man spat. Gus was certain he'd seen the angry man before, but couldn't quite place him. "If I could build my own Vegas showroom and never let anyone backstage, I could perform miracles from beyond the wonders of space, too."

"Of course you could, Balustrade," the small man said patiently. "And all of America would flock to Vegas to see you practice your card tricks."

Now Gus realized who the heavyset man was—the same magician who had slipped the five of hearts into his sock. But the cherubic look was completely gone, replaced by a visage of pure fury. He looked like a different person. He was, Gus realized, a much better performer than he had given him credit for.

The man in the red suit pushed his way to the front of the crowd. As he got closer, Gus could see that the suit wasn't just shiny; it was made of vinyl.

"At least we perform our illusions honestly." The red-suited man shouted his words over the other man's head, which wasn't hard to do.

Gus caught a glimpse of gold out of the corner of his eye and turned to see the man in the jumpsuit standing at the edge of the crowd. "That's right! I don't use computers and video screens and high-tech gadgets to fool a gullible public into thinking I have talent."

"There's no computer in the world that's that good, Sludge!" a drunken voice called out from the back of the room.

A wave of laughter passed through the room, which only infuriated the laméd man further. "It's *Rudge*," he shouted. "You all know it's Rudge. Barnaby Rudge."

Rudge jolted forward as if to take on the green giant in a fistfight, and the crowd whooped in anticipation of a bloody, if extremely short, fight. But he quickly dived back into the crowd, and Gus could see that the only reason he'd stepped forward was because he'd been pushed. It took Gus a moment to realize where he'd seen the woman who'd shoved Rudge, because he didn't immediately recognize her without knife handles protruding from her eye sockets. Now that he was closer to the woman, he could see that she wasn't wearing a brightly patterned blouse after all. She had on a simple black vest; the colors that ran up and down her arms and covered her upper chest were all tattooed there. And they weren't just colors—they were snakes and lizards and, Gus was pretty sure, slugs.

"Isn't anyone going to stand up for our art?" the woman called to the crowd. "Or are you all going to take little Benny Fleck's side because he's rich and you think he'll stake you to a show when his pretty boy flames out?"

"Pretty boy?" Gus whispered to Shawn.

"It's all relative," Shawn said. "Consider who's talking."

"P'tol P'kah does not flame out," said the small man, who Gus realized must be Benny Fleck, whoever that was. "Unless you are referring to his newest illusion, in which he will be consumed by a pillar of fire, transforming himself into a cloud of smoke. The cloud will then rain down on the stage and the puddle of rainwater will then rise up in the unmistakable form of P'tol P'kah, the Martian Magician!"

An excited buzz ran through the crowd, and members of the Fortress began to shout out questions. Mostly the magicians wanted to know when this new trick was going to premiere, but at least two were asking how they might buy tickets.

"And he'll do that on a stage fifty feet from the nearest member of the audience so no one can see what a fake he is," Balustrade said. "Real magic isn't like going to see *The Matrix* at a movie theater. It's up close. It's personal. It's real."

"It's three shows a night at the Budget Buffet Dinner Theater," Fleck said. "That's what you mean, isn't it? Real magic is what you do, the way you do it, and nothing else counts?"

Another wave of laughter rippled through the crowd. Balustrade's face was getting redder by the second. He sputtered and spit, but he was so enraged, his tongue couldn't form words.

The tattooed woman didn't have the same problem. "We all know what stage magic is supposed to be, and we know where the art of it lies," she shouted to the crowd. "All of you, fellow magicians, have spent years perfecting your art, mastering your craft, honing your skills so that what you do is seamless. Perfect. So that you can stand right in front of your audience and they will never be able to figure out your illusion. But this man might as well be George Lucas, casting digital shadows on a wall. He is not worthy of your respect, or of the name magician."

Gus looked around the room and saw that the woman's impassioned plea had actually begun to move some of his listeners. Benny Fleck apparently saw the same thing, because he lifted his arms high in the air—high for him, anyway, which brought them roughly to the level of Gus' nose—and spoke in a serious voice.

"P'tol P'kah has heard the complaints of his fellow practitioners, and it has hurt him deeply," Fleck said. "Although he is not a native of this planet—"

"Oh, knock it off for five minutes," Rudge moaned from his new spot deep in the crowd.

Fleck glared at Rudge, then started over. "Although P'tol P'kah is not a native of this planet, as so many of you know, he has adopted Earth as his home. And he feels closer to you, his brethren, than to any other humans. All he desires is your respect."

"And the hundred K a week he pulls down at the casino," the man in red vinyl muttered.

"For many, many months he has heard these complaints," Fleck continued. "That he performs too far from the audience. That somehow he cheats with technology. That he is not a real magician. And his desire for privacy has only inflamed the rumors. But tonight, he has come here to put all this to rest. Tonight, P'tol P'kah has come to the Fortress of Magic to prove to his fellow magicians that he belongs not only among your number, but at the top of your profession."

"It's a profession now?" Shawn whispered to Gus. "Does that make three-card monte a career path?"

Gus waved him off, fascinated by the argument going on in front of him.

"I got a deck of cards, if he wants to start with a few basic moves," Balustrade said.

"We'll dispense with the sleight of hand," Fleck said. "P'tol P'kah has come to the Fortress of Magic to prove that he does not need a special stage or lighting to perform his miracles. He has come to you tonight to perform for you the keystone of his act."

A woman in the crowd gasped. "The Dissolving Man?"

"The Dissolving Man," Fleck confirmed. "In front of your eyes, P'tol P'kah will immerse himself in a tank of water, and the lid will be locked. And then in front of your eyes, he will become one with the water. He will dissolve into a cloud of bubbles. And then he will rematerialize outside the tank. I tell you all the parts to this performance now so you can watch at every step for chicanery."

A spontaneous burst of excited applause broke out in the room.

"If this demonstration is of interest to you, I invite you to come into the main showroom now," Fleck said. "Or you can stay here and count how many people have the five of hearts in their shoes."

Fleck made a theatrical turn and led the way down the hallway. Chattering excitedly, the crowd of magicians, bachelor partyers, book club members, and other guests followed. Lyle Wheelock was at the head of the crowd, and he was pushing past his guest of honor to be among the first to get into the showroom.

"I don't think your father's present can compete with the Dissolving Man," Gus said, gesturing down at the wrapped gift that was still in Shawn's hand.

"You're right. Let's go home."

Shawn started toward the door. Gus grabbed his arm. "What do you mean 'home'?"

"Generally I mean that place where I keep my clothes and my toothbrush," Shawn said. "Although in this case I think I really meant anywhere that doesn't have magicians in it."

"You don't want to see how a seven-foot-tall Martian dissolves in a tank of water?"

"I've got a package of lime Fizzies in my kitchen," Shawn said. "Probably pretty much the same effect."

"Only if the Fizzie can reconstitute itself into a tablet across your kitchen. Come on, you can't tell me you're not the slightest bit curious about how he's going to pull this off."

Shawn sighed heavily. "Because it's impossible, right?"

"Well, yeah."

"See, that's the problem," Shawn said. "He's telling you he's going to do something that's impossible. Which means he's figured out a foolproof way to make it look like he's doing the impossible, while he's really backstage, making out with a showgirl or something. So who cares?"

"I do."

"Only because you haven't thought it through."

"That could be," Gus said. "But there's something you haven't thought through."

"What's that?"

"I've got the car keys."

Gus turned and followed the last of the crowd down the hallway. Shawn cast a longing glance at the front door, then followed him toward the showroom.

Chapter Six

.

The tank was simple, a glass rectangle ten feet tall and four feet across with steel brackets reinforcing the corners and a metal lid on the top. It towered over Benny Fleck in the middle of an empty stage that was raised three feet above the showroom's threadbare rug.

"As you can see, P'tol P'kah has nothing to hide," Fleck said as the audience crowded the edge of the stage for a better view. "And more important, he has no place to hide. He will perform this astonishing feat directly before your eyes."

Gus and Shawn stood at the back of the room, nearly forced against the rear wall by the crowd of spectators.

"Figured out how he's going to do it yet?" Gus said.

"You really think this is something special, don't you?" Shawn said.

"Five minutes ago you were cowering in fear because the defrosted Frankenstein monster was going to eat you," Gus said. "So don't act like you're better than everyone else here."

"I wasn't afraid," Shawn said. "I saw that you were enjoying the experience, and I decided to enhance the moment with a small performance of my own."

"If your performance was any bigger, you'd have to change your pants."

"It's about committing to the moment," Shawn said. "Now that moment is over, and all that's left is some fugitive from vaudeville who's painted himself green to trick the rubes into thinking he can do magic."

"If it's so obvious, go ahead and tell me."

Shawn studied the tank on stage, examining the way the theatrical lighting refracted through the water in the tank, sending ripples of light across the room.

"All an illusion," Shawn said. "There probably isn't even water in that tank."

The crowd fell silent as P'tol P'kah's heavy boots rocked the stage. He stomped up beside the tank and surveyed the crowd.

"Is there anyone who doubts?" the green man said, his filed teeth bared in a grin that would cause most people to give up any suspicions very quickly. "Is there anyone here who wishes to challenge me?"

Gus nudged Shawn. "This is your chance. Go up and expose him."

"Bear. Den," Shawn said.

"Cow. Ard," Gus said.

"I challenge you, you giant zucchini!" There was a bustle in the crowd and after a moment, Balustrade heaved his body onto the stage. "What are you going to do, throw me off this stage to keep me from investigating your tank?"

"I welcome your attention," P'tol P'kah said. "You may study every inch of it."

"You bet I will," Balustrade said, walking around the tank. As he passed behind it, Gus could see his distorted image through the water. Balustrade finished his circumnavigation and appeared at the front. He rapped on the glass, and the sound was a damp, heavy thud.

"Are you satisfied?" boomed P'tol P'kah.

"Satisfied that you're a fake," Balustrade said.

"Would you like a closer inspection?"

"Do you have to ask?"

P'tol P'kah stomped off stage and came back wheeling out a set of metal stairs, the kind they used at airports too small to build Jetways. He wedged the steps against the side of the tank and motioned to Balustrade. "After you."

Clutching the handrails, Balustrade climbed up the stairs. At the top, he peered down suspiciously at the tank's lid. "I suppose you won't let me open this."

"You may do as you wish," P'tol P'kah said. "Although I warn you, you may not be happy when you do."

"Yeah, I'm the one who's going to be unhappy," Balustrade said. He knelt down on the top step, opened a latch, and, groaning under the weight, pulled back the lid. When he looked down into the tank, his face fell.

"Would you like a closer look?" P'tol P'kah had climbed the stairs behind Balustrade, and now, even standing two steps below the magician, towered over him.

Balustrade suddenly looked nervous. "No, I—"

"I insist," the green man said, giving Balustrade a

shove that knocked him off balance and sent him tumbling into the tank.

Balustrade sunk slowly to the bottom, his ponytail floating up behind him. Flailing desperately, the magician tried to turn himself right side up, but the tank was too narrow to maneuver in. His face reddening, cheeks puffed out with his last breath of air, the magician pounded feebly on the inside of the tank as if he hoped to break through.

The green man put his hands on his hips and let out a booming laugh. "Do you think he's had a close enough look?" he shouted to the crowd.

A couple of people in the audience laughed, but most were silent as they watched Balustrade struggle to bring himself back above the water.

"Help him!" a woman in the crowd shouted. "He's drowning in there!"

The green man peered out into the audience to see who was talking to him, cupping an ear to suggest that he couldn't hear what was being shouted.

"What's he doing?" Gus said to Shawn.

"Proving I was wrong," Shawn said. "There really is water in there."

"There's a guy in there, too," Gus said. "We should help him."

"And mess up the trick?" Shawn said. "I'm shocked."

"This isn't part of the trick."

"Isn't it?" Shawn said.

Shawn pointed to the stage where the green man was reaching his hand up behind the proscenium arch and pulling down a sturdy cable with a noose at the end. He dropped the noose into the water and looped it around Balustrade's ankle. Then he gave the cable a sharp tug and it retracted quickly, like a cheap roll-up window blind, pulling Balustrade straight out of the tank.

Gasping and coughing, the magician hung by his ankle, high above the stage. The green man closed the tank lid, then took the magician gently by the hand and pulled him along as he went back down the stairs. When he reached the bottom, he settled Balustrade on the stage, then unhooked the cable from around his ankle. The magician flopped on the floor, gasping like an angelfish scooped from its tank by a curious kitten.

Benny Fleck emerged from the wings. "Let's have a round of applause for our gracious volunteer," the small man said as he helped the still-coughing Balustrade to his feet. A small spate of confused clapping came from various corners of the room as Fleck led the magician off stage.

"Volunteer?" Gus asked Shawn. "Is that a regular part of the act?"

"I don't know, but I bet the green guy never gets a second heckler," Shawn said. "Besides, it accomplished its purpose."

"To humiliate Balustrade?"

"That was a bonus," Shawn said. "It was to keep you watching Balustrade so you wouldn't pay attention to whatever the green giant was doing."

"What was he doing?"

"Something he didn't want you to notice."

Gus waited for more details, but Shawn didn't have any to offer. He turned his attention back to the stage, where the green man had climbed back up the stairs and reclosed the hatch, bolting it shut. He faced the audience, hands on his hips.

"Ladies and gentlemen, this is the moment where we must take our leave from each other," he said. "If all goes according to plan, I will see you shortly. In fact, I will be right there."

He pointed to a spot exactly in the center of the showroom. Unconsciously, the crowd edged away from his destination, in case he was planning to materialize inside of them. The three nondampened magicians who had challenged the green man in the lobby all moved a little closer.

"But it is possible that I will not return at all," the green man continued. "To dissolve one's molecules is difficult, but to reintegrate them is much harder. If I fail, then I will forever remain a cloud of dust suspended in a tank of water. And if that is to be my fate, then so be it!"

The green man took a deep bow, then unlatched the lid and threw it open. He stretched to his full height and stepped off the platform. Weighted down by the heavy boots, the Martian Magician sunk to the bottom of the tank. For one long moment, he stood absolutely still, staring out through the glass at the audience.

Gus knew this was a trick. He understood that everything Shawn had said was right. But as he watched the green man standing patiently at the bottom of a tank of water, he could feel the pounding of his heart, the thin trickle of sweat on his palms. His lungs began to ache for air, and he realized he'd been holding his breath since P'tol P'kah slipped under the water.

"This can't be part of the trick," Gus whispered to Shawn. "There's got to be something wrong."

"That's what you're supposed to think," Shawn said.

"Well, I'm not the only one here who's good at taking instruction." Gus gestured at the crowd of bachelor partyers. They were staring, transfixed, worry on their faces. Even some of the magicians in the room were beginning to look concerned.

"We should do something," Gus said.

"You're right," Shawn said. "If we left now, we could beat the rush to the parking lot."

Before Gus could respond, there was a gasp from the audience. He turned back to the stage to see that the water in the tank had changed. Before it had been perfectly still. Now it bubbled and frothed like a glass of cheap champagne. As Gus stared, he realized that the bubbles were coming from the green man's body.

P'tol P'kah raised his hands over his head, sending a storm of froth rising to the surface. As the bubbles flew from the green fingertips, Gus saw with a shock that the fingers were shrinking. No, *dissolving*. Within seconds, they were gone down to the first two knuckles, and quickly the hands were reduced to clublike stumps.

The green man lowered one deformed hand to touch his stomach, and immediately the bubbles began fizzing out of his abdomen. But they didn't rise to the top of the tank. They spun around, as if caught in a whirlpool. And when they cleared, Gus could see they had eaten a hole clear through P'tol P'kah's midsection.

This has to be a trick, Gus told himself. *Shawn must be right*. But he didn't see a trick. What he saw was a giant man dissolving like an Alka-Seltzer tablet. Where moments before there had been rock-hard green abs, now there was a void. And it was growing in all directions, devouring his chest, his hips, his shoulders. His arms, eaten from both sides, fell off his body and dissolved into bubbles before they hit the tank floor. All that was left was the grinning green head floating seven feet over the enormous black boots.

The bubbles were working on P'tol P'kah's chin now. Before they could reach any higher, the green man opened his mouth as if to speak—or to scream. But what came out wasn't just a blisteringly loud roaring sound. It was light, a blast of pure white light that lit up every corner of the showroom, blinding Gus temporarily—but not before he could see the stunned faces of everyone in the audience.

Then the light went out, and the room was plunged into darkness.

For a moment the room was so silent, Gus thought he might have been struck deaf as well as blind. And then he heard a sound from across the room. He was so stunned by what he had just seen, it took his brain a few seconds to understand that what he was hearing was the clapping of hands. At first, it was just one person, but soon the entire auditorium had erupted into wild applause and cheers.

Gus knew exactly what he should be doing at this very moment. He should be constructing the perfect pithy phrase to shoot at Shawn, something that would take all his friend's premiracle jibes and throw them back in his face

But Gus didn't feel like lording it over Shawn. He didn't want to win an argument or grab a few well-deserved points. All he wanted was to luxuriate in the moment. Before he even started the inevitable—and inevitably futile—process of trying to figure out how P'tol P'kah had achieved this impossibility, Gus wanted to replay the moments in his mind and marvel over the vision.

As the cheering started to subside, the houselights flickered on. Gus turned instinctively to the spot in the crowd where P'tol P'kah had promised to materialize. He wanted to see the giant take his much-deserved bows.

But P'tol P'kah wasn't where he said he would be. No one was. The magicians surrounding the spot had kept it clear, just in case, and the entire audience was staring at the empty hole in the crowd, but the giant hadn't materialized. The applause faded away to a confused muttering.

Gus tried to ignore the minor disappointment. After all, the Martian Magician had dissolved in a tank of water. If he didn't stick the landing, that didn't take anything much away from the rest of the performance. But he knew that Shawn was going to start mocking the show any minute now.

"If you've figured it out, you can say anything you want," Gus said, not even casting a glance at Shawn. "Until then, I don't want to hear that it was cheap or cheesy or fake. Because I'll know you're not telling the truth."

Shawn didn't answer. Which was odd, because in all the years they'd been best friends, Gus couldn't remember a single time when Shawn didn't answer a taunt. Even when he'd had strep throat and couldn't talk for days, he'd scrawl a response on a piece of paper, or at least hit Gus with a rolled-up magazine.

Gus turned to Shawn and saw that his friend was staring straight at the stage, a look of pure fascination on his face.

"A-ha!" Gus said. "You can't even pretend you're not amazed. That was much better than you thought it would be, and you can't figure out how he did it."

"I am amazed," Shawn said. "But I don't think I'm amazed by the same thing you're amazed by."

"You mean the fact we just saw a giant green man dissolve into bubbles?" Gus said. "That's not what you're amazed by?"

"No."

Even for Shawn this was a ludicrous level of stubbornness. Gus wanted to shake him until the truth dropped out onto the floor. "If you're not amazed by the sight of a giant green man dissolving into bubbles, then would you please be so kind as to explain exactly what does amaze you?"

Somewhere in the auditorium, a woman screamed. "Oh my God, he's . . ."

Gus whirled around and saw that the woman was pointing at the stage. The rest of the crowd was turning to see what she was pointing at. Gus followed them.

The tank was simple, a glass rectangle ten feet tall and four feet across with steel brackets reinforcing the corners and a metal lid on the top. It towered over the audience in the middle of an empty stage that was raised three feet above the showroom's threadbare rug.

On the tank's floor stood a pair of enormous, empty black boots. And at the top of the tank floated a bowler hat. This might have been only of passing interest, except that the hat sat on a head, and that head was attached to a portly body clad in a three-piece suit. And the head and body were both obviously dead.

"That's what amazes me," Shawn said.

Chapter Seven

Detective Carlton Lassiter hated the full moon.

Not the moon itself, of course. The head detective of the Santa Barbara Police Department knew that it was nothing more than a hunk of rock spinning in orbit around Earth, and aside from a moment of weakness during *Apollo XIII* when he shed a tear for the astronauts who were never going to reach it alive, he'd never been able to work up any kind of emotional reaction to it.

It wasn't the psychological effect the full moon had on people that he hated, either. He knew that there was no way that human psyches could be affected by the percentage of shadow Earth cast on its lone satellite in a given time of the month.

What Lassiter hated was the belief shared by so many losers and lowlifes that the full moon had some bizarre power over their behavior. He hated the way they used the monthly lunar phase to justify abandoning the inhibitions they barely managed to hold in check the other twenty-nine or thirty days. And while there was only a relative handful of miscreants who felt compelled to submit to the lunacy, there were far more people who believed that crazy things happened when there was a large orb shining down instead of a thin sliver, so they started seeing them—and worse, reporting them to the police.

To Lassiter, this was all nonsense. And the head detective was one hundred percent No Nonsense. A stern, dogged investigator who worked his cases with the unrelenting rigor of a bloodhound in full tracking mode, he refused to be distracted by anything he considered less than serious. He'd been like this all his life. In his high school yearbook, under a photo of Lassiter wearing his hall monitor sash, he was called the "least likely to put up with nonsense," and his patience with the stuff had only grown shorter over the years.

That meant he was going to be extremely annoyed by the time this night was finally over. It was barely ten o'clock, the full moon was entirely invisible behind a thick wall of fog, and he'd already fielded calls from one citizen who had seen Charles Manson buying yogurt at the Shop King, a homeowner who insisted that the gophers in her lawn were holding a meeting on her front steps and that they kept pointing at her and laughing, and a group of teenage girls who claimed that Shrek was cruising down State Street in a convertible. Two guys had turned themselves in at the police station, begging to be locked up before they transformed into werewolves, and then gotten into a fistfight over the question of which one would lead the pack.

And now, this. On a night when the crazies were all out to play, Lassiter had been called to a crime scene where almost everyone was a nut-job: the Fortress of Magic, or, as he liked to call it, the Kingdom of Clowns. As a rookie officer, he'd been called here innumerable times to break up fights between two self-styled wizards who'd gotten liquored up and started revealing the secrets of each other's illusions. This wasn't hard, because there were apparently all of three unique magic tricks in the world, and everything else was a variation of one or another.

And now he'd been dragged out again, this time to investigate a drowning—some investigation. As he strode determinedly up the steep path to the Fortress, he guessed that the only mystery here would be how a grown man could drown in two inches of vodka.

Somewhere on the landscaped hill, a guard dog growled angrily. Lassiter's partner, Detective Juliet O'Hara, stopped on the path, her hand instinctively reaching for the gun in her purse.

"Did you hear that?" she said, trying to peer into the darkness.

Lassiter sighed wearily. There were many things he admired about his partner. Although she was the youngest detective on the Santa Barbara force, she was also one of the smartest cops in the country. She looked like she had just graduated from a high school cheerleading squad, but those looks hid a powerful mind—and she knew how to use her appearance as a key tool in her casework.

The one thing he didn't admire about his partner was her willingness to put up with nonsense. Behavior that Lassiter would simply forbid as foolishness, O'Hara chose to dignify with her attention. To be fair, that often gave her an understanding of human nature that had helped them solve many cases. But it also ate up valuable time Lassiter could use for more serious purposes.

"Keep up, O'Hara. We've got to pull a drunken magician out of a whiskey bottle," Lassiter snapped, not pausing on his way to the top.

The growl was joined by several others. O'Hara's hand tightened on her gun's grip. "There are dogs. We can't just—"

Lassiter didn't slow down. "Turn that thing off or I'll arrest you all for disturbing the peace and interfering with a police officer." The growling stopped. He took a second to cast a glance back at his partner. "You just need to know the magic words."

By the time the detectives reached the entrance to the fortress, uniformed officers had corralled the spectators in the two large parlors.

"We've segregated them into members and guests," Officer McNab volunteered as soon as Lassiter and O'Hara stepped through the door. "The guests were all attending a couple of different parties, and they're in the East Parlor. A lot of them want to know when they can go home. The members are in the West Parlor. They all want to know when they can go to the bar."

"There's a surprise," Lassiter sighed. "Get statements from the guests; then send them on their way. I want your primary focus on the magicians. Find out which ones had a grudge against the victim."

"I've already done that, sir," McNab said. "It seems they all did."

"Of course," Lassiter said. "I'll get to them as soon as I can. See if you can separate the childish, petty grudges from the substantial issues. If you can find any substance. Oh, and track down whoever's in charge and tell him if he doesn't disconnect that dog machine, I am going to spay and neuter it personally."

"Yes, sir."

"Now, where's the body?"

"Still in the tank, sir," McNab said.

"Don't you mean the bottle?"

"Um, no," McNab said. "You really need to see this. But there's one thing you should probably know first."

Lassiter didn't wait to be told. He marched down the corridor as quickly as he could. Detective O'Hara gave McNab a sympathetic smile.

"Don't take it personally," O'Hara said. "Detective Lassiter likes to come into a crime scene cold so his first impressions aren't colored by anyone else's."

"I just wanted to say there's something you're not going to like in—"

O'Hara held up a hand to cut him off, the sympathy gone from her face. "All good detectives like to come into a crime scene cold."

She turned and scurried to catch up to Lassiter, who had slowed enough to let her catch up with him at the closed doors to the showroom.

"You didn't let him color your impression, did you?" Lassiter snapped.

"Not a tint," O'Hara said.

"Good. Let's solve this puppy." As Lassiter threw open the doors to the showroom, he also opened the doors to his mind, letting out all his prejudices and preconceptions, even the well-earned ones about magicians. He was a blank slate, waiting to be filled by the sight in front of him.

What he saw first was an enormous glass and steel tank, filled with water—and with the floating corpse of a chubby man in a three-piece suit and bowler hat. In front of the tank stood a small man, half a step above a midget, dressed immaculately in expensive designer clothes. His arms were crossed angrily, as if he expected somehow to use the force of his will to keep an army of normal-sized people from removing him from his spot in front of the tank.

And it seemed to be working. The night guy from the coroner's office stood next to the near-midget, a pleading look on his face, two uniformed officers lined up behind him. But somehow they couldn't bring themselves to push past the little guy to get to the body.

Something was wrong here; Lassiter could sense it. No, worse than wrong. There was nonsense in the air, and the detective would have none of that. This was a serious business, and he was going to treat it seriously.

Officer McNab appeared in the doorway behind them. "I'm sorry, Detective, but I really thought you should know—"

"That there's nonsense afoot, McNab?" Lassiter snapped. "I can figure that out for myself. And you know I will brook no nonsense."

A cheery voice called out from the other side of the room. "I'll brook no trout, myself. Not that I have any idea what that means."

Lassiter felt every muscle in his body tightening. He had heard that voice so many times, and whenever he did, it guaranteed that the next few hours would be filled with nothing but nonsense. Well, nonsense and occasionally the solution to a crime that had baffled the entire SBPD, but Lassiter wasn't entirely sure that catching a few murderers was worth tolerating such a level of drivel.

"That's what I was trying to tell you, sir," McNab said. "Shawn Spencer and Burton Guster are here."

"I can see why you thought I might have missed that," Lassiter said. "Since they're usually so quiet and unobtrusive."

"Hi, Jules! Lassie!" Shawn strode up to them, Gus following right behind him.

"What I don't understand, McNab," Lassiter continued without even a glance in Shawn and Gus' direction, "is why you felt compelled to admit them to the crime scene."

"He didn't have to, Lassie," Shawn said. "We were already here."

"Saw the whole thing," Gus said.

"Did you now?" Lassiter said. "That's very good to know. If you'll follow Officer McNab, he'll put you somewhere until I can take your statement."

Detective O'Hara stepped in front of Lassiter. "Hey, guys," she said. "So, what's going on here?"

Lassiter was surprised to discover that his muscles could tighten even further than they already had without starting to snap like overstretched violin strings. When he complained that his partner was willing to tolerate nonsense, it was her friendly attitude toward these two that was his primary complaint.

"Not much," Shawn said.

"Unless you count the disappearing Martian," Gus said.

"Oh yeah," Shawn said.

"And the dead guy who mysteriously appeared in that tank," Gus said.

"Good point," Shawn said.

"And the short dude who won't let anyone near the body," Gus said.

"Right," Shawn said. "But aside from that, not much. What's up with you two?"

"We're here to investigate a murder," Lassiter said.

Shawn slapped his forehead. "I knew I forgot something," he said. "The murder."

"What about it?"

"We solved it."

Chapter Eight

Everyone was staring at Shawn. Even Gus.

"Excuse us for a second," Gus said. He dragged Shawn a few steps away and whispered furiously at him. "We solved it?"

"Didn't we?"

"Do you know who the dead guy is?"

"It's the twenty-first century," Shawn said. "How many men wear bowler hats? It won't take long to track them all down, and then we just have to pick him out."

"Do you know how he got into the tank?"

"I know it wasn't magic," Shawn said. "And once you know what it wasn't, you're halfway to knowing what it was."

"That's great," Gus said. "Do you have any idea where the green guy went?"

Shawn thought that one over for a moment, then stepped back to the police. "Small correction, just a tiny point," he said. "When I announced that we had solved this case, what I meant to say—"

"Was that you're completely useless and should get out of my way." Lassiter pushed past him and strode up to the night-shift coroner. "Hey, body snatcher. Why aren't you snatching that body?"

The coroner's assistant was barely twenty-five years old. No doubt a medical student earning near-minimum wage to fill in when the grown-ups were sleeping, Lassiter thought.

"He won't let me," the kid said, pointing at the little man.

"And what's he using to stop you?" Lassiter demanded. "A gun? A knife? A light saber?"

"That." The kid pointed at the short man's hand, which was wrapped tightly around a glowing iPhone.

"So it's an iPhone," Lassiter said. "What's the problem—he's cooler than you?"

"It's not the phone, Detective," Fleck said. "It's what's on the screen."

"The hot new video on YouTube?"

"It's a restraining order signed by Judge Albert Moore of the California Superior Court for Santa Barbara County forbidding any agent of the state to examine, investigate, or in any way come into contact with the secret work product of my client, P'tol P'kah, the Martian Magician, that would expose his methods and practices and thus threaten his career, without the express permission of Mr. P'kah or his duly authorized agent."

Lassiter cast a glance at the corpse in the tank. "If that's your client, I think his career is facing greater threats than anything I can do."

"That's not my client," Fleck said. "I have no idea who he is, or what he's doing trespassing on my client's property."

Lassiter fought the impulse to pick up the little man and toss him in the tank with the corpse. He turned to O'Hara, who was stepping up beside him. "Who is this guy?"

"Benny Fleck," O'Hara said. "He manages, produces, and owns half the top-grossing shows on the Vegas Strip, along with several sports franchises, the nation's largest ticketing agency, and a big chunk of Times Square."

"Fast detective work," Lassiter said.

"One of the meter maids always leaves her *People Magazine* behind in the women's restroom," O'Hara said. She turned to Fleck. "Mr. Fleck, I understand your position here, and I hope you can understand ours."

"Understand yes, care no," Fleck said. "And don't even think about trying to go over Judge Moore's head to void the restraining order. He's not the only member of the bench who's indulged some of his more individual tastes in Las Vegas."

Before Lassiter could respond, there was a moan from the other side of the tank. Reluctantly, he turned to see Shawn clutching his forehead as if in great pain.

"Are you the keymaster?" Shawn groaned, staggering toward Fleck and reaching down to grab his lapel. "Or are you the gatekeeper?"

"I don't know what you're talking about," Fleck said, shoving Shawn away.

"The keymaster!" Shawn howled.

Gus stepped up and pulled Shawn back a few feet, then whispered in his ear. "What are you doing?"

"I'm invoking an ancient mystical text," Shawn said. "All the best psychics are doing it these days."

"Ancient mystical text?" Gus demanded. "That's from *Ghostbusters*."

"And when it was made, the smallest cell phone weighed two pounds, Kings Quest 1 was the greatest computer game in history, and people took Frankie Goes to Hollywood seriously," Shawn said. "I think we can all agree that qualifies as ancient."

Shawn stepped back up to Fleck and grabbed his forehead again. "The keymaster," he moaned.

"Can't anyone get this clown out of here?" Lassiter demanded.

Officer McNab made a move toward Shawn, but before he got there, Shawn bent over double and let out a howl of pain.

"No, not the keymaster," Shawn said. "We need the latchmaster. I see a latch. It's open, then it's closed, and then it's open again. And though it needs to be opened, the latchmaster closes it again before he opens it. Oh why, latchmaster, why?"

Shawn straightened and dropped his hands to his side. Fleck stared at him.

"Who is this?" Fleck said, never taking his eyes off Shawn.

"Shawn Spencer, official psychic to the Santa Barbara Police Department," Shawn said.

"Occasional consultant to the Santa Barbara Police Department," Lassiter corrected. "When he's been called in to consult on a case. Which in this case he has most definitely not."

"I haven't?" Shawn said.

"Absolutely not," Lassiter said.

"You know only the chief has the authority to bring

you on to a case, Shawn," O'Hara said. "And I suspect she might find you more useful as a witness on this one."

"Well, then," Shawn said, "that makes me Shawn Spencer, private citizen. Oh, and psychic detective, available for weddings, bar mitzvahs, and really impossible murder cases."

Fleck eyed him thoughtfully. "So you're a licensed private detective?"

"Licensed?" Shawn said. "You have to ask?"

"I have to ask."

Shawn pulled out his wallet and flipped through the contents. "I've got a license to drive. License to fish. License to use official Microsoft Office software as long as I don't violate the terms of the user's agreement. License to kill."

"You do not," Lassiter said. "There's no such thing."

"The James Bond fan magazine I snipped it from said it was authentic. Oh, according to my father, I've got a license to make a fool of myself," Shawn said, still flipping through his wallet.

Gus stepped up beside him. "Psych Investigations is duly licensed by the California Bureau of Security and Investigative Services, number 06-443672. If you need to see the actual certificate, it's hanging on the wall at our office," he said, hoping that Fleck wouldn't need to see it for at least a couple of days. The framed certificate was one of the things that Shawn had knocked off the wall during his Extreme Handball practice, and it was currently lying on the floor under a heap of broken glass. "I'm Burton Guster, Shawn's partner."

"And you are not currently working for the Santa Barbara Police Department?" Fleck said.

"God, no," Lassiter said.

Fleck studied Shawn carefully, then made a decision. "In that case, I am hiring you to investigate the disappearance of my client, P'tol P'kah, the Martian Magician. We'll work out the terms and conditions when you come to my office in Vegas tomorrow."

"Mr. Fleck, that doesn't help us with the question of the dead man floating in your tank," O'Hara said.

"Actually, it does," Shawn said. "Because P'can P'kie—"

"P'tol P'kah," Gus corrected.

"Right, what he said," Shawn said. "Anyway, he vanished from this tank and the man in question stepped in to take his place. For all we know, the floating fellow is actually the insane genius behind a brilliant plan to abduct the green guy."

"Yes, that would be a brilliant plan," Lassiter said. "I particularly admire the part where he throws the police off his trail by winding up dead."

"I still don't see how that helps us," O'Hara repeated. "We can't do anything as long as that court order is in force."

"You can't, but I can," Shawn said. "Because as a licensed detective, I have a fiduciary duty to protect my client's privacy. Which means that if I were to climb up the stairs and loop the cable that's hanging above the tank around the dead man's arm, then even if I did see something that Benny Fleck didn't want revealed about the workings of the tank, I would be prevented by detective-client privilege from revealing anything about it, even if I were called to testify in a court of law."

"That's not—," Lassiter started, but O'Hara cut him off.

"Wouldn't you like to examine this body, Detective?" O'Hara said. "Don't you think this is a potentially good compromise?"

Lassiter didn't assent, but he didn't finish his objection, either.

"Of course, as a licensed Microsoft Office end user, I have agreed that the software company can share my information with others, such as hardware and software vendors," Shawn said. "But I'm willing to stand up even to Bill Gates to protect my client."

"So, Mr. Fleck," O'Hara said, "can we proceed under these conditions?"

For a moment, everyone in the room held his breath waiting for Fleck's answer, except for the man floating in the tank, who didn't have any breath left to hold—and Shawn, who was quietly humming the theme song from *Ghostbusters*. After a long pause, Fleck gave a sharp nod and the combined exhalation could have filled a weather balloon.

Shawn and Gus climbed up on the low stage and pushed the airplane stairs up to the tank.

"How did you get him to agree?" Gus said as they maneuvered the staircase into place.

"Something I saw when P'teter P'karker—"

"P'tol P'kah."

"Right, that guy," Shawn said. "Anyway, after he gave Balustrade his swimming lesson, he climbed back up here and even though the tank was open, he closed it again, latched it, then unlatched it and reopened it. Why do that?"

"Showmanship?" Gus said.

"If that was all it was, then Fleck never would have blinked and we'd be sitting in a broom closet guarded by McNab waiting for Lassiter to pretend to question us," Shawn said. "What I guessed, and what Fleck has now confirmed, is that flipping the latch did something to the tank that was necessary for the trick to work."

"What?"

"Possibly it turned on the chubby-dead-guy-generator," Shawn said. "Other than that, I don't have a clue."

Gus stepped away and watched as Shawn climbed up the metal stairs. At the top, Shawn peered down into the tank, a look of disgust on his face as if he suddenly realized the particularly unpleasant flaw in his plan.

"I have an idea," Shawn said. "Why don't I deputize a couple of big, strong police officers to be temporary Psych employees. That way they could reach into the tank and fish out the body and still couldn't say anything."

"Unacceptable, Mr. Spencer," Fleck said. "It's you, or he stays in there until we get a ruling from the Supreme Court. And I don't mean the one in Sacramento."

"This was your idea," Lassiter said. "Do it or I'll throw you in jail for obstructing justice."

O'Hara shot her partner a weary look, as if to suggest that he wasn't helping. "What Detective Lassiter means to say is 'please.' "

"That's the magic word," Shawn said. "Unless there are fake dogs involved. Then—"

"Shawn!" Gus yelled up at him. "Stop stalling."

Shawn sighed heavily, then reached up and grabbed the cable. From here he could see that it ran through a series of pulleys and down to a hand-cranked winch on the far side of the stage, which was no doubt useful for bringing heavy equipment such as tanks of water onto the stage, or making heavy objects such as elephants disappear from it.

Shawn lowered the cable into the water and tried to maneuver the noose around the dead man's hand. But of all the carnival games Shawn had ever tried, the ring toss was the one he had never mastered, and this was like that, only upside down. Every time the noose drifted close to the hand, the body drifted away, bounced against the tank wall, then drifted back in a slightly different position.

"It would be a lot easier if you got into the tank," Gus said.

"It would be even easier if *you* got into the tank," Shawn snapped.

"For all I care you can both go into the tank and never come out," Lassiter said. "But I need that body on the ground in thirty seconds or I'm shutting down this charade."

"Fine," Shawn said. Getting down on his knees, he rolled up his sleeve, took a deep breath, and lay down on the platform. He squeezed his eyes as tightly shut as he could, then plunged his hand into the water.

"It would be easier if you opened your eyes," Gus suggested.

Shawn scowled, but when he followed his partner's advice he discovered that the noose was at least four inches from the target and moving in the wrong direction. He shifted the cable and maneuvered it around the dead man's wrist, then yanked it so it slid up to his armpit. Jumping to his feet, he gave the cable a yank, just as the Martian Magician had done when Balustrade was on the other end. Only this time nothing happened.

"Gus, go man the winch," Shawn said.

"I'm not sure Mr. Fleck would approve," Gus said. "What if the winch is part of the illusion's secret?"

"It's not," Fleck said.

"You could be saying that because you don't want to reveal the truth in front of people who aren't sworn to secrecy," Gus said. "It is my fiduciary duty to you to have nothing to do with that winch, that tank, or anything relating to that incredibly gross dead body."

"Oh, for God's sake," Lassiter said. He climbed onto the stage, pushing Gus aside even though the collision took him out of his way, and went to the winch handle.

On top of the stairs, Shawn leapt back when the body started to emerge and nearly fell the seven feet to the ground. But he caught himself on the handrail and, taking the tiniest edge of the corpse's pants cuff that he could get his fingers on, guided the dead man down the stairs as Lassiter gradually lowered him on the winch.

As soon as the body was lying on the ground, Shawn jumped away from it, waving his hand wildly to shake off the corpse-water. "Wipe! Wipe!" he shouted.

"Wipe what?" Gus said.

"It's not a verb; it's a noun," Shawn said. "You're supposed to hand me one of those little moistened towelettes they give you at barbecue joints."

"Maybe I should give you half a chicken and a brisket sandwich while I'm at it," Gus said.

"I'm the detective; you're the assistant—"

"I am no man's assistant," Gus interrupted. "Especially yours. I'm your associate."

"Fine," Shawn said. "I'm the detective, and you're the associate. And the associate is supposed to carry a supply of sanitary wipes in his purse just in case the detective happens to touch something disgusting."

Gus stared at him. "That's the dumbest thing I've ever heard."

"Really? I thought it showed some real consideration on the associate's part. Also, you're supposed to be a pretty blonde. If you're not going to carry wipes, you could at least work on that."

Shawn dried his hands on his shirt and walked back to where Lassiter was kneeling over the body. The man's jacket lay open, revealing a vest bulging at the buttons, barely holding in his gut. Lassiter touched one of the buttons, and the vest exploded open, the liberated stomach sloshing around inside a now-translucent white shirt.

Ignoring the dancing flesh, Lassiter reached a gloved hand into the corpse's jacket pocket and fished around before pulling it out with a scowl.

"No wallet."

"You wouldn't carry your wallet to go swimming," Shawn said. "Of course, you probably wouldn't wear that hat, either."

Lassiter ignored him, turning to Fleck, who'd barely wasted a glance on the dead man. "You sure you don't know him?"

"Positive."

"He wasn't a rival magician? A stalker? Someone your guy owed money to?"

"I already told you—"

"I know what you told me," Lassiter said. "I'm just giving you every opportunity to improve your memory, so that if there's any chance of a connection between this man and you, you'll remember it now, when it can still make you look better rather than worse."

O'Hara moved up beside Lassiter. "What my partner means is that in the heat of the moment, memories sometimes get clouded in ways that make subsequent realizations look less reliable than they are."

"What they both mean is that they hope you're lying and you'll tell them who the dead guy is, because they don't have a clue," Shawn said.

"Thank you for translating," Fleck said, then turned his icy gaze up at Lassiter and O'Hara. "I am a duly sworn officer of the court, and fully aware of my legal and deontological obligations to provide a truthful statement to the police in any matter civil or criminal. If you have reason to believe that I have violated this duty, then you must report me to the bar, or arrest me. Absent such belief, I urge you to cease from making such assertions, or I will see you in court."

Shawn turned back to the police. "What he means is go f—"

"Shawn!" Gus warned.

"Go find out who the dead guy is for yourself," Shawn finished.

"I think we can handle that," Lassiter said.

"Good," Shawn said. "We're going to go look for a Martian."

Chapter Nine

"Let's face it, if you're a Martian who's come to Earth to study human culture, this is where you want to be." Shawn waved out the taxi window as they cruised past the Great Pyramid at Giza, a medieval castle, and the skyline of New York City. "I mean, you could get in your flying saucer and buzz the stratosphere, but think of all the gas you'd use up trying to see as much as you can in four blocks of the Las Vegas Strip."

Gus looked out at the people clogging the sidewalks and wondered what a Martian would think of them. Blinking in the sudden sun after hours in the artificial twilight of the casinos, clutching fat plastic buckets of quarters or thinner plastic buckets filled with fifty-cent margaritas, barely fitting into their XXXL sweatpants, they looked like a population whose spirit had long since been crushed by alien invasion. The Martian might easily be fooled into thinking that his forebears had already taken over.

Or maybe Gus was just feeling uncomfortable about

the meeting they were about to have. When they got back to the Psych office after Lassiter banished them from the Fortress of Magic, Gus flipped on the computer and discovered that Fleck's assistant had already e-mailed them tickets for tomorrow's first Allegiant Air flight direct from Santa Barbara Airport to Las Vegas, as well as an address for an office on East Frontage Street. There were no other instructions, not even a greeting. They were being commanded to appear by a man they'd barely met.

That didn't bother Shawn at all. He'd talked Fleck into hiring them; he couldn't complain if the man actually wanted them to do some work for their money. And they were getting a free trip to Vegas. Normally you had to sit through a three-hour sales pitch for time-shares to get that. They'd jet into town, do a little background, and expense a dinner buffet at one of the casinos. Or if Fleck wouldn't agree to an expense account, they'd just win a few bucks on the slots and use that to buy dinner.

Gus had to admit the plan sounded appealing. But after finding the plane tickets, he did some basic research on Benny Fleck, and he wasn't comforted by a lot of what he found. Fleck was one of the biggest promoters in family entertainment, and his touch seemed to be golden. He hadn't had a flop in a decade, and with every success his shows had become bigger, grander, and more spectacular. He'd spent one hundred million dollars building a special theater for P'tol P'kah in Outer Space, the science fiction–themed hotel and casino, charged two hundred bucks for each of the five thousand intimately arrayed seats, and sold out every show since the gala opening eight months ago.

But Fleck's golden touch didn't seem to give him a thick skin. The Internet was filled with stories about the mogul's revenge on people he felt had crossed him. He'd been sued several times for hiring private investigators to dig up dirt on reporters who got too close to him.

"Where's the downside?" Shawn had asked when Gus told him what the research had dug up.

"Let's see," Gus said. "We're getting into business with a man who is famous for targeting people who let him down."

"And who does he hire for his targeting?" Shawn beamed, clearly feeling he'd bested Gus' logic on this one. "Private investigators. Which means us. So either we find the green guy and we're heroes to the boss, or we don't and we're searching for dirt. Either way, we're looking at a long-term business prospect."

"You think he's going to hire us to dig up dirt on ourselves?"

"That would be silly," Shawn said. "I figure we can do each other. And believe me, I can give him lots of hot stuff about you."

Gus might have continued arguing against the Vegas trip if the door to the offices hadn't banged open just then. Henry Spencer stood in the doorway, red faced and breathing hard. He looked like a cartoon bull who was about to turn into a steam engine in order to flatten the matador.

"What have you done?" he demanded. "Are you so thoughtless, so selfish, that you casually ruin other men's lives just for fun?"

"You used to be a cop," Shawn said without even blinking. "You ruined people's lives for money. Doing it for fun is much less selfish than that."

Henry's hands twitched as if he wanted to put them around Shawn's throat. Then he dropped them to his sides. "All I asked was for you to deliver a present to my friend Bud's bachelor party. You didn't even have to say a word. Waltz in, waltz out; night's over."

"I've never been much of a dancer," Shawn said.

"Why did you have to tell Bud that Savonia was cheating on him?"

"Savonia?" Shawn asked. "An entire country was cheating on him?"

"That's Slovakia," Gus said. "Or Slovenia. I can't keep the two of them straight."

"Apparently a problem you have in common with the bride," Shawn said.

Henry turned an angry eye on Gus. "Don't think I don't blame you for this, too. You could have stopped him."

Gus knew he couldn't have, and he knew Henry knew it, too. But all that knowledge couldn't spare him from the creeping feelings of guilt.

Shawn stepped between Gus and Henry. "I don't know what you want from me. I just saved your buddy from ruining his life with a woman who was cheating on him with his best friend."

"And tore his heart out," Henry said. "He's been lonely forever, he finally meets this lovely woman from Eastern Europe who turns his life around, and you smash it into pieces. Now he won't even return my calls. Worse, I think he's so angry, he turned his fiancée in to the feds—when I went down there to look for Bud, there were ICE agents parked outside. And Lyle, poor Lyle . . . I tried to talk to him and he just drove away. When I followed him, he went straight to a mental hospital. I think you gave him a nervous breakdown. And all I wanted you to do was deliver one lousy gag gift."

"If it means anything, we didn't do that, either," Shawn said. "If you want it back, you'll have to retrieve it from evidence. Now, if you'll excuse us, we have a flight to catch. Be sure to lock the office when you go."

Shawn marched out the door and Gus followed quickly. But even knowing the trouble he was leaving behind, Gus had gotten onto the Allegiant Air flight with a large set of reservations, which could have been a problem because it was nearly more weight than the thirty-four-seat MD-80 could carry.

He grew warier still when he noticed the cab driver was having a lengthy, quiet conversation on his cell phone, and that every time he listened to the person on the other end, he was staring back at them in his rearview mirror.

"Is something wrong?" Gus asked the driver, trying to keep the quiver of fear out of his voice. Ever since he saw *Casino*, he'd had an irrational fear of being vised to death and buried in a hole in the Nevada desert. Now he was beginning to worry that the fear wasn't irrational after all.

"No wrong," the driver sang out as he accelerated through a red light and across eight lanes of cross traffic. "Very, very right."

"But you were supposed to turn left back there," Gus said.

The driver said nothing, just stomped on the gas and wove through the cars ambling up the strip.

"Shawn, do something," Gus whispered urgently.

Shawn pressed the button on his door, rolling his

window down a couple of inches. "I am," he said. "I'm enjoying the ride."

"But he's not taking us to the right place," Gus hissed.

"That depends on whose definition of right you're using," Shawn said. "By the way, you might want to hold on."

"Hold on?" Gus asked. "Why?"

The driver had drifted all the way into the far-right lane, his tires almost scraping the curb. The pedestrians who had spilled off the overloaded sidewalk were leaping back into the crowd. The driver took a quick glance at the road in front of him and yanked the wheel hard to the left. Cars slammed on the brakes as the cab screamed across four lanes of traffic, flew up over a divided median, and zoomed through the four opposing traffic lanes.

When the cab had come to a stop and Gus dared open his eyes, he found they had pulled into a porte cochere built to resemble the entrance to Klaatu's flying saucer. A handsome blond man in a silver space suit was opening his door.

"Welcome to Outer Space," the cabbie said.

"But we were supposed to go to Frontage Road," Gus objected.

"Change of plans, Mr. Guster," the driver said.

Gus stared at him. "How do you know my name?"

Shawn shoved Gus toward the door. "Come on, we're going to be late."

Gus wanted to stay in the cab and demand to be taken to their destination, but the seat was so worn and polished by the thousands of butts that had sat on it, he slid out under the slightest pressure of Shawn's hand. If the space doorman hadn't caught him, he would have landed on his butt.

"What's this all about, Shawn?" Gus demanded.

"I'm guessing a hundred-dollar tip," Shawn said.

Before Gus could demand clarification, Shawn nodded at a large man in an indistinct suit, black sunglasses, and white earpiece. The casino security agent walked quickly to the cabbie's window, exchanged a word or two of pleasantries, and slipped a small sheaf of bills to him.

"What's going on?" Gus said.

"The driver's phone call was from the dispatcher," Shawn said. "I couldn't hear the whole thing, but he was apparently calling the entire fleet looking for the cab with us in it. He'd gotten orders to redirect us to Outer Space."

"But who?" Gus said. "But how?"

"You forgot 'but why,'" Shawn said.

"I didn't forget. I was working my way up to it."

"'But who' has to be Benny Fleck. No one else knew we were coming into town. Or even that we exist. 'But how' most likely involves some new technology such as the telephone."

"Okay, now: But why?" Gus said.

"He didn't feel like waiting in his office for us."

"He couldn't call your cell phone?" Gus said.

"He couldn't," Shawn said. "I'm sure Fleck hasn't dialed his own phone in years. But he certainly could have had one of his assistants do it if the venue change was the only message he wanted to send."

"What other message is there?"

"That this is his town, baby," Shawn said. "And we'd better know who we're working for."

The security guard waved at the cabbie, and the car peeled off in a cloud of exhaust. Before it settled, an Asian spacegirl in a silver minidress materialized in the smoke.

"Mr. Spencer? Mr. Guster?" the spacegirl asked, although there didn't seem to be any doubt in her voice. "Welcome to Outer Space. Mr. Fleck would like you to meet him in the Dark Side of the Moon."

"Is that the space-facing side of Earth's only natural satellite or the multiplatinum album by Pink Floyd?" Shawn said. "I only ask because I don't know if we need to board a spaceship, or just inhale heavily."

The spacegirl flashed them the same smile she would give to a nickel-slots player who spilled his free rum-and–Diet Coke on her while trying to cop a feel. "The Dark Side of the Moon is Outer Space's premier dining establishment, offering fresh fare prepared by Izgon Zubich, one of America's hottest new chefs. I'll be happy to lead you there."

"Lead on," Shawn said.

The spacegirl took off at a pace a racehorse might have envied, negotiating her way around the throngs of tourists and gamblers like a pinball zipping around the bumpers.

Gus was torn between wondering how anyone could move that fast on heels that high and wishing she'd slow down so he could see a little more of the casino. What he did see was everything he would have dreamed of when he was thirteen. The ceiling was an intense field of brightly burning stars, planets, and asteroids. At first he thought it was a static light display, but he quickly realized that it was all moving slowly, as if he were on a spaceship cruising through the galaxy. Every once in a while, the universe would freeze, then start to spin, and then the stars would expand into streaks of light before settling down to reveal a different quadrant of space. Gus recognized the effect as a knock-off of the hyperspace jump from the first *Star Wars*, but it was thrilling to look at nonetheless.

The ceiling only set the tone for the rest of the décor. Like the best casinos in Vegas, Outer Space carried its theme down to the tiniest details, and here everything was designed to look like the inside of a spaceship. The cocktail waitresses were all spacegirls like the one they were following, and the drinks they served came in lidded "zero-gravity" glasses. The dealers were made up as aliens with giant eyeballs bouncing from stalks attached to their foreheads. Gaming tables looked like the control panels for the various incarnations of the starship *Enterprise*—ten-dollar minimum tables mirrored the now-cheesy bridge from the original show, while higher denominations upgraded the look through the subsequent series and movies. And the cashier's cage was set up as an airlock, which not only added visual verisimilitude to the place but forced anyone who felt like cashing in their "plasma credits"—which in any other casino would have been called chips—to stand in a long line and wait to be cycled through the multiple doors. Even the carpet was woven to look like a metal grid, under which was a terrifying plunge to the hundreds of lower decks.

Wherever Gus turned, there was something he wanted to explore in greater depth, but the spacegirl kept marching relentlessly ahead, and he knew that if he took his eyes off her for more than a brief moment, she'd become indistinguishable from her hundreds of hardworking space sisters.

Finally their space guide came to a stop outside a solid slab of polished steel. A giant triangular crystal stood beside it, but aside from that, there was no sign suggesting there was a restaurant here, no menu, not even a door.

"'And if the dam breaks open many years too soon, and if there is no room upon the hill, and if your head explodes with dark forebodings, too,'" the spacegirl said with all the passion and enthusiasm of a near-retirement Disneyland Jungle Cruise operator warning of the dangers of a hippo attack.

Before Gus could ask how they were supposed to get in, the spacegirl took a small flashlight from a metallic stand by the steel slab, clicked it on, and shone it through the crystal. As it passed through the prism, the light fragmented into a rainbow, and when it fell on the steel, the slab rolled silently into the wall. "'I'll meet you on the dark side of the moon,'" she said, then turned and walked away.

"That's a catchy jingle," Shawn said. "Much better than 'Have it your way.'"

Shawn and Gus stepped into the restaurant, which had been designed to look like the surface of the moon, and to feel like it, too, apparently; Gus' oxfords crunched on gray lunar pebbles as they made their way to the one occupied table.

Benny Fleck sat by himself at a four-top in the center of the deserted restaurant. He stood as Shawn and Gus approached, which Gus could tell only because his head was suddenly a little lower than it had been.

"Gentlemen, I hope you don't mind the small detour," Fleck said. "While I was waiting for you at my office, I realized we could all use a good meal. And there are things here you will want to see eventually."

Fleck gestured for Shawn and Gus to take their seats, then climbed back into his own. Gus resisted the sudden impulse to peek under the tablecloth and see if he was sitting on a booster.

"We appreciate the faith you've put in us, Mr. Fleck, and we want to assure you we will find your Martian," Gus said. "And if by any chance we don't, we want to assure you right now it's not through any lack of desire or willingness on our part."

Fleck waved off Gus' preapology. "I have full confidence in the two of you," he said. "I've had a chance to look into your careers, and I'm convinced you're the right men for this job."

"So you had us checked out," Shawn said. "I have to say I'm a little disappointed."

"I do my research on anyone I hire," Fleck said. "It's one reason I'm a success."

"I have no doubt of that," Shawn said. "I just wish you had come to us to do the checking. We could have offered extremely competitive rates."

Fleck studied Shawn closely and decided he was joking. He let out a short laugh, then slapped his hands together sharply. The resulting clap had all the force of a pair of wet tissues colliding, but before the speed of sound would have allowed the sodden thud to travel all the way to the kitchen, three spacegirls appeared at their table, each one lifting a silver platter holding an enormous lobster surrounded by a colorful array of deep-fried vegetables. The spacegirls deposited the platters in front of the three of them, then disappeared back wherever they'd come from.

"I hope you don't mind I took the privilege of ordering for us," Fleck said.

"Not as long as you take the privilege of paying," Shawn said. Gus kicked him under the table.

"If I didn't, it would just appear on your expense report," Fleck said with a smile. "I'm cutting out the middle step."

"Expenses, yes," Shawn said. There was a hint of a self-satisfied smirk tickling the corners of his mouth. Gus gave him another swift kick, and it disappeared before it could do any harm with their new employer. "We will of course try to keep them to a minimum. Although if we have to personally visit your client's home planet, that might run into some dollars."

Shawn picked up a nutcracker shaped like a ray gun and snapped one gigantic lobster claw in half, then noisily sucked out the meat. Gus took advantage of the moment to shift the conversation to actual business.

"It might save us time and effort in our investigation if you could share with us whatever you know about P'tol P'kah," Gus said.

"Mmmph," Shawn agreed, gesturing with the piece of shell whose previous occupant was crammed into his mouth and preventing him from forming syllables.

"I'm sure you're familiar with his recent career," Fleck said, then waited for a response.

Fortunately, Gus didn't spend all of last night Googling Fleck. He'd spent some time looking up the magician as well.

"I guess we know as much as any layperson," Gus

said. "Which is to say not much at all. We know that eight months ago you opened the Starlight Theater for him here in the casino, and that he's played to packed houses ever since. Aside from that, it's mostly what we—and the rest of the world—don't know that's so interesting. P'tol P'kah has never given a single interview. He's never been photographed without his makeup. No one even knows his real name."

"Unless, of course, P'tol P'kah is his real name," Fleck said.

"In which case I know where he is," Shawn said. "Tracking down his mother and father so he can kill them."

This time Fleck didn't spare the effort to convert his faint smile into a laugh. "You say he's never been photographed without his makeup," he said. "And that's how his story is generally reported. Right now, I'm not convinced that's the absolute truth."

"You mean you think there are photographs of him without makeup?" Gus could feel the excitement rising in him, but he tried to tamp it down. He still remembered the bitter disappointment he'd felt when, after years of desperately wanting to see what the members of Kiss looked like without the face paint, he finally did.

"I mean I'm not sure anymore that he's wearing makeup," Fleck said.

"If he's on the run, that's probably a safe bet," Shawn said, dragging a piece of bread through a deep dish of melted butter. "Pretty hard to stay inconspicuous with a complexion like that."

"I mean when he's on stage," Fleck said.

Shawn and Gus allowed themselves to exchange a

quick glance to see how the other was taking this state-ment. It seemed like a bad idea to laugh in the face of a paying client, especially one with a history of ruthlessly destroying anyone he felt had disrespected him. But neither of them was sure what their option was.

"Are you suggesting that P'tol P'kah is actually a Mar-tian?" Gus finally managed to get out without giggling.

"I know how absurd it sounds," Fleck said. "If any-one had said the same thing to me eight months ago, I would have laughed in his face. But I've studied my client for a long time, and I've never seen a hint of any-thing that would contradict his story."

"How about his Social Security number?" Shawn said. "He must have given it to you at some point, un-less Martians don't care about money."

"Oh, they care," Fleck said. "But my deal is with P'tol P'kah's loan-out corporation, so all I have is his company's ID number."

"How about the first time you met him?" Shawn asked. "You didn't just bump into a seven-foot Mar-tian walking down the Strip."

"Not at all," Fleck said. "Our first introduction was as mysterious as everything else about our relationship. One night I was home alone, and he just appeared."

"What do you mean?" Gus said. "He beamed into your living room like Captain Kirk?"

"No, although I don't think that would have surprised me any more than what did happen," Fleck said. "I was watching Jim Cramer on CNBC, the image flickered, and then this seven-foot-tall green man was talking to me directly through the screen."

"How could you tell the difference?" Shawn said. "Oh wait—was he right about something?"

"At first I thought I was dreaming," Fleck said. "Then I got a little scared. I tried changing the channel, but he was on every one. I turned off the TV, but it kept coming back on. So finally I decided I had to listen to him."

"I hope he didn't try to sell you a panini press," Shawn said.

"He invited me to come to an abandoned warehouse in Henderson to see a show that was going to change my life."

"An abandoned warehouse?" Shawn said. "What, he couldn't find a deserted amusement park?"

"I went with some trepidation. I had no idea what I was walking into, but the green monster on my TV screen had been quite explicit that I had to come alone, and it never even crossed my mind to disobey," Fleck said. "When I arrived, a young woman met me and led me into the warehouse."

"Was this Mrs. P'kah?" Shawn asked. "Because maybe we could ask her where her husband went."

"I never learned her name," Fleck said. "I never even heard her voice. And her face and head were completely covered with a hood. She led me to a single chair in the darkened warehouse and gestured for me to sit down. Then she left. I never saw her again. Or maybe I've seen her every day since. I have no way of knowing."

"There's nothing else you can remember about this woman?" Gus asked. "Something about the way she moved, the perfume she wore?"

"Even if there was anything, it would have been knocked out of my consciousness by what happened next," Fleck said. "The few lights that had been on in the warehouse went out and I was in total darkness.

Then a spotlight fell on a glass tank at the other end. And P'tol P'kah stepped into it. He climbed up a set of stairs into the tank, and, well, you saw the Dissolving Man."

"Most of it," Shawn said. "I gather that this time he actually did rematerialize?"

"Right in front of me," Fleck said. "Then he reached out into the darkness and dragged a table over to my chair. On that table were a contract and a fountain pen. He said one word to me: 'Read.' Then the lights blinked out for a second, and he had disappeared."

"Hey, that's how we were going to present our contract," Shawn said. "I can't believe that green giant stole our idea."

Gus didn't even bother kicking Shawn under the table. Fleck was so lost in his memory that he didn't seem to hear him.

"What I read in that contract was outrageous," Fleck said. "I was to build a special theater to P'tol P'kah's exact specifications. It would hold no fewer than five thousand people, the seats were to be arranged so that every member of the audience had a clear view of the stage, and—"

"And that they'd all pay two hundred bucks to attend?" Shawn guessed.

"No, that was my call," Fleck said. "Once I ran the numbers on just how much this was all going to cost me. Because the stage was just the beginning. I needed to provide him with a place to live."

"Houses aren't exactly rare around here," Gus said, remembering the colorful mosaic of real estate signs so closely packed together that they could be seen from the plane on the descent into McCarran Airport.

"P'tol P'kah didn't want a house," Fleck said. "He wanted a floor."

"Well, that's got to be cheaper than a whole house," Shawn said. "Because with a house, you not only have the floor, you've got all those walls. And ceilings, too."

"He wanted a floor of this casino for his private residence," Fleck said. "Or if not an entire floor, then an enormous luxury suite that would be completely walled off from the rest of the hotel. The only entrance would be a private elevator that ran down directly into his dressing room in the theater. There were certain demands about the way the suite had to be furnished, about the level of room service he demanded be provided, the housekeeping that needed to be performed only while he was on stage. There was a long section detailing how much he was to be paid, and how it was to be wired directly into an untraceable offshore bank account. And, of course, there were his key demands—he would grant no interviews, make no public appearances besides his own shows, and meet no people other than me."

"And when you were done laughing?" Shawn said.

"I signed."

Gus thought back on all the articles he had read about Fleck's incredible business acumen, the punishing deals he extracted out of everyone who ever dealt with him, and tried to reconcile that with what he was hearing now. "Just like that?"

"You saw the Dissolving Man," Fleck said. "In all my years as a promoter, I'd never come across anything so breathtaking. It reminded me of the first time I saw Cirque du Soleil—only with a fraction of the payroll expenses. If the green guy's schtick seemed a little heavy-handed at the time, I figured that just meant he knew how to work his image."

"I'll say," Shawn said.

"Usually with these guys, they put up a good front at first," Fleck says. "They're trying to sell you like you're one of the rubes. And then once the contracts are signed and the drinks are poured, they let the mask slip a little. But that never happened with P'tol P'kah. He showed up for every one of his shows. Occasionally we exchanged a couple of syllables, but aside from that he was completely inaccessible."

"You seemed like you were pretty good buddies last night," Shawn said. "You didn't both show up at the Fortress of Magic by accident."

"I received a phone call that afternoon," Fleck said. "A woman's voice told me that he had wearied of the sniping from his fellow magicians, and wanted to put it to a rest for good. That was the way she talked, by the way."

"Do you think it was the same woman you met in the warehouse?" Gus asked.

"No way to know," Fleck said. "Whoever she was, she called from a blocked number. I had my internal security people try to track it down via phone records this morning, but they couldn't do it. And my internal security people are very good. Anyway, as I was walking up the hill to the Fortress, I saw P'tol P'kah standing outside, waiting for me. We entered, and you know the rest."

"Some of the rest," Shawn said. "We don't know what happened to . . ."

"P'tol P'kah," Gus prompted.

"Yeah, him," Shawn said. "So, if you could just fill in that little piece, we'd have everything we need to complete our investigation."

Fleck's eyes narrowed as he stared at Shawn, trying to decide if what he was hearing was some kind of joke, or a sign of total incompetence. "If I knew what happened to P'tol P'kah," he said in a growl that made the Fortress of Magic's electronic hounds sound like kittens, "I wouldn't have hired you to find out what happened to P'tol P'kah."

"Of course you wouldn't," Gus said quickly. "That was, um . . . That was . . ."

As Gus floundered helplessly, Shawn stepped in. "An investigative technique. Sometimes people know more than they're aware they know. That knowledge is locked away deep in the subbasement—"

"Subconscious," Gus corrected.

"But sometimes it can be brought to the surface if we use the elevator of the unexpected question," Shawn finished.

Fleck considered this for a moment; then the scowl left his face. "I understand that you two are unconventional investigators, and you will employ the occasional unconventional technique. That is one reason I hired you."

"And the fact that we were there," Shawn volunteered. This time Gus kicked with all his strength, and despite the short distance between their feet, clearly managed to inflict some pain. "There to assist you in your hour of great need, that is."

Fleck ignored the interruption. "But if you ever try to trick me again, if you even idly speculate that I am in any way responsible for the disappearance of someone who is not only a brilliant performer, but who has become personally very close to me, I will be displeased. Do I make myself clear?"

"Yes, sir," Gus said quickly. He could see that Shawn was running through a list of possible responses, but a gentle nudge with his foot in the exact spot where his last kick landed persuaded him to supply a simple nod.

"Good," Fleck said. He thudded his hands together, and the spacegirls returned to whisk the platters away. "This meal is now concluded."

"What, no dessert?" Shawn said.

Fleck reached into his breast pocket and took out a plastic card. "I do not intend to guide your investigation, but I assume you will want to begin with the suite P'tol P'kah calls home. This key will operate the elevator from his dressing room. My only request is that you leave everything exactly as you found it. If you are able to find my client and he is healthy and able to return, I don't want him to feel that his privacy has been violated. Is there anything else?"

"Just one question," Shawn said, moving his leg out of the way in case Gus was planning another assault on his ankle. "What if we find P'nut P'brittle and he doesn't want to come back?"

Benny Fleck didn't move. His facial expression didn't change; his body language wasn't altered in any way. But Gus somehow got the impression that their lunch host had become much taller than the missing Martian.

"P'tol P'kah has a contract with me," Fleck said calmly. "I'm sure his only desire in this or any other world is to live up to it. But if you find him and he suggests in any way that he'd prefer not to return, you must do as he wishes. Leave him be and let me know."

"Yes, sir," Gus said, a wave of relief washing over him.

"Let me know exactly where he is," Fleck continued. "My internal security people will do the rest."

Chapter Ten

"Shawn, he's going to kill him."

Gus stood in the middle of P'tol P'kah's penthouse suite, still nauseated from the thirty-nine-story ascent in the private elevator from the dressing room. He took a step across the brilliant white carpet to where Shawn stood looking out the floor-to-ceiling windows, but as soon as he did, the room started spinning again. He might not have minded this so much, except that the suite was large enough to house the entire Goodyear blimp fleet with room left over for most of the Macy's Thanksgiving Parade balloons, and that was a mighty big space to have twirling around his head.

"You're right," Shawn said.

At least that was progress. As they had followed yet another silver-suited spacegirl through the employee tunnels that ran from the restaurant's kitchen to the backstage area of the Starlight Theater, Shawn had refused to acknowledge there was anything ominous in the last part of their meeting with Fleck.

"We've got to do something."

"Absolutely," Shawn said. "I'm putting twenty bucks on the champ."

"What champ? What are you talking about?"

"That." Shawn pointed out the window. Fighting off his wooziness, Gus managed to cross the room and join him, only to see that Shawn was looking out at an enormous sign in front of Caesar's Palace, advertising tonight's heavyweight championship. "I know a lot of people have been saying the champ's past his prime, but Montoya won't last three rounds."

Down below, the cars looked no bigger than the Hot Wheels Gus and Shawn used to play with, and Gus turned away quickly before his nausea teamed up with incipient vertigo to make him pass out.

"I don't care about a fight, Shawn," Gus said in between deep, heavy, regular breaths. "I care about what's going to happen if we find P'tol P'kah and he doesn't want to come back here."

"Are you kidding?" Shawn waved his arm around the suite. One wall was covered by a flat-screen TV the size of a freeway exit sign. A door on the opposite side led to a closet that seemed to run the entire length of the hotel tower, and it was filled with endless iterations of a custom-made outfit perfect for the stylish Martian—slacks in black and khaki, blazers in blue and black, white shirts, and leather loafers, all in sizes Yao Ming could swim in. And if Yao were a guest and he felt like some actual nonsartorial swimming, another door opened onto an Olympic-sized indoor pool. The steel-and-marble gourmet kitchen was stocked with every kind of snack food Shawn and Gus had ever heard of and many they hadn't. "Who wouldn't want to come back here?"

"I don't know," Gus said. "Maybe someone who gets nauseated in fast elevators. Someone who's afraid of heights. Or maybe a guy who dissolves in a tank of water, never rematerializes, and leaves a dead guy floating in his place."

Shawn took a moment to think through what Gus was saying. "You have a theory?"

"Yes," Gus said. "And it's the same one you have, because it's the only one that makes sense."

"The only theory that makes sense is the one that starts with a Martian dissolving in water?"

"That's his trick," Gus said impatiently. "We both know he didn't really dissolve."

"You were the one who thought it was so impressive."

"Shawn!"

"Okay, fine," Shawn said, plopping himself on a plush, down-filled leather sofa. "Let's assume that P'tato P'tahto isn't really a Martian. He's just another stage magician. What do we know?"

"That the Dissolving Man is a trick."

"And?"

"And the reason we can't figure it out is because the solution is too obvious," Gus said, settling down in an overstuffed armchair.

"So if we take away all the razzle-dazzle, the basic illusion is that the magician is locked into some kind of cabinet, the lights go out, and he slips out through some secret exit. Meanwhile, he's got a device that instantly clones him and delivers the clone wherever the beam is pointed."

"That's the solution that's so obvious, no one would ever figure it out?" Gus said.

"It is to anyone who saw that Hugh Jackman movie,"

Shawn said. "Although it's also possible he has a twin brother who hides out in the audience. But do Martians even come in twins? There's a lot of basic research that hasn't been done on that issue."

"Yes, I'm sure it's the cloning machine," Gus said. "You've nailed this one. Except for one thing—the lights never went out."

"Sure they did," Shawn said. "Remember that blast of light at the very end? It blinded us all for a few seconds—plenty of time."

Gus thought back and realized that anything could have happened in that time and he never would have known—he was not only blind, but the roaring sound could easily have covered just about any noise.

"So P'tol P'kah did his trick as usual. Then instead of appearing in the audience, he ran," Gus said. "That's what I was saying. He wanted to get away from this gilded cage, and he set up the entire Fortress of Magic show as a ruse to allow him out. But where did he go? And more to the point, who's the dead guy in the tank and how did he get there?"

"I have an idea on that," Shawn said. "But let's hold off on the dead guy for a minute. Instead we should—"

"Let's not," Gus interrupted.

"What do you mean, 'Let's not'?" Shawn said. "This is my theory, and I get to lay it out however I want to."

"Sure, when you're talking to Lassiter or to Chief Vick or to a client," Gus said. "Then you can lay out your explanation step by step, making sure every piece is in the perfect place to build audience expectation. Then you hit them with the big finale, and everyone's left thinking you're a genius. But you don't need to sell me, so why don't you just say who the dead guy is now?"

"In the time it took you to lay out that objection, I could have explained everything."

"No, you couldn't," Gus said. "You couldn't explain a cheese sandwich in less than five minutes." Gus pressed his fingertips to his forehead and scrunched up his eyes as if he'd been hit with a migraine. "I'm sensing something. It's a condominium. No, wait, it's a comic book. No, close to a comic book. It's—it's a condiment! Yes, I'm sensing mayonnaise. It's saying, 'Put me next to the lettuce.'"

"Those explanations are what brings in the lettuce for both of us," Shawn said. "And why are you getting so irritable, anyway?"

Gus got up from the couch and stalked to the refrigerator. He opened the freezer and put his head next to the ice tray, trying to cool down.

"I don't know," Gus said. "Maybe it's that we've promised a dangerous man we'd find his client, and now we realize that the client was actually trying to get away from him, and our client only wants us to find him because he wants to kill him."

"And you think that puts us in an awkward position morally?" Shawn managed to excavate himself from the sofa cushion he'd sunk into and walked over to the refrigerator. Gently he pulled Gus back from the freezer and closed the door.

"I think it could make us accessories to murder," Gus said.

Shawn opened the freezer again, then reached in and pulled out an unopened box of grape Popsicles. He tore open the box and offered it to Gus, who accepted one. Shawn unwrapped a Popsicle for himself, then put the box back in the freezer.

"You can relax," Shawn said. "P'tontius P'kilate isn't running away from Benny Fleck."

"P'tol P'kah," Gus said, more out of reflex than any hope that Shawn would ever get the name right.

"Yeah, right, that guy," Shawn said.

Gus waited for an explanation. Shawn sucked on the Popsicle, his lips turning purple.

"How do you know that P'tol P'kah isn't running away from Fleck?" Gus said finally.

"Because," Shawn said, "he doesn't exist."

Chapter Eleven

"Yes," Gus said. "I think we've already determined that he's not a real Martian."

"It's not that he's not a real Martian," Shawn said between sucks on the Popsicle. "It's that he's not a real person."

"We're standing in his apartment."

"Are we?"

Although Gus was pretty sure he knew the answer, he took one long look around the luxury suite just to confirm that the walls hadn't melted away to reveal that he was actually in his own bed, having an insanely elaborate dream. "I can't speak for you," he said, "but my feet are definitely on the thirty-ninth floor of the Outer Space Hotel and Casino in an area that's been turned into an apartment for the exclusive use of P'tol P'kah."

"Then why hasn't he used it?" Shawn said. "Look how clean this place is."

"So Martians are better housekeepers than you," Gus

said. "Besides, the hotel has an entire staff of chamber-maids."

"Okay," Shawn said. "So when he wants to watch *Wheel of Fortune*, do the chambermaids come up and act it out for him?"

Gus stared at him blankly. Shawn gestured with his Popsicle at the enormous flat panel on the wall. "That TV isn't hooked up to anything," he said.

"Maybe it's wired into the wall," Gus said.

Shawn went over to the TV and fished around in the space between its bottom edge and the top of a long credenza. He came up with a sheaf of loose cables. "It's not wired into anything."

Gus tried to apply part of his mind to the idea that this had some significance. But mostly he was staring at the bright purple Popsicle that Shawn was holding over the white, white carpet.

Shawn walked over to the closet and pulled one of the mammoth sport coats off its hanger. "He's got all these clothes, and he hasn't worn any of them," Shawn said. "The pockets are all sewn shut; the shirts are all folded and still pinned." He pulled a shirt off the shelf and tossed it to Gus. When he caught it, Gus could feel the crackle of the manufacturer's tissue between the layers of cotton.

"So maybe he's decided the codpiece look works for him," Gus said, remembering how the Martian was dressed—or, rather, not dressed—at the Fortress of Magic.

But Shawn wasn't listening. He'd found a small door set into the back wall of the closet. "Cool," he said.

"What's cool?" Gus chided himself for letting Shawn

change the subject, but he couldn't help responding to the interest in his friend's voice.

"Laundry chute," Shawn said. "Looks like it goes all the way down. Want to see?"

Gus felt a new wave of vertigo just thinking about peering down a thirty-nine-story shaft. "You can describe it to me."

"Well, it's a chute," Shawn said. "And it looks like they've thought of everything. They've even got rungs built into the sides so you can retrieve your shirt if you decide it's not really dirty."

"That's not a laundry chute. It's an emergency exit," Gus said.

"Well, that explains why no one ever sees him leaving the hotel. But still, once he's out, you've got a seven-foot-tall green man walking down the Strip essentially naked, and no one has ever noticed?" Shawn said, pounding his point home by waving the Popsicle. "There's never been a single photo of him out in public."

Gus tried to imagine a reason for that, but his mind was mostly occupied by the sight of Shawn's Popsicle. And particularly by a small corner at the top, where the tip of the stick was showing through. There was a small crack in the purple ice, and it was growing every time Shawn employed the frozen treat as a pointing device.

"All this can only mean one thing," Shawn said, using the Popsicle the way an orchestra conductor wields his baton. "And that's—"

"No!" Gus cried out, but it was too late. The top corner of the Popsicle had broken off and a one-inch chunk of frozen water, high fructose corn syrup, artificial Concord grape flavoring, and—most crucially—indelible purple food coloring was hurtling through the air on a trajectory that, no matter its initial velocity, would result in a collision with the brilliant white carpet within seconds.

Gus didn't hesitate. He ran the length of the room after the artificially sweetened projectile. But he wasn't fast enough; the frozen treat was already breaking up as it spun through the air, sending drops of purple to land in a Pollock-worthy pattern on the carpet. And the main piece was only inches from the ground. Gus launched himself at the missile, flying through the air, twisting his body around, and stretching out his arm to snag the ice chunk before it could land.

But Gus' hand closed on air as his face skidded across the carpet. Out of the eye that wasn't embedded in the short shag, he saw the purple ice explode as it made contact with the floor, turning several square feet of white into a brightly colored Rorschach blotch. A shift of the eyeball revealed Shawn staring at him quizzically.

"Okay, maybe it can mean more than one thing," Shawn said. "But that seems like a pretty dramatic way to make an objection."

Gus climbed back up to his feet and immediately wished he hadn't. From above, the stain was even uglier.

"Look at that," Gus said, pointing down at the purple blotch. "We've got to find a way to clean it up."

"I believe it was you who mentioned just moments ago that the hotel has an entire staff of housekeepers," Shawn said.

"And if P'tol P'kah comes back before the maid does?"

"Then we're the greatest detectives in the history of the world, and who cares that we made a little mess?" Shawn said, sucking on what was left of the Popsicle.

"Benny Fleck doesn't want his client to know we were in his apartment," Gus said. He picked the folded shirt up from the ground where he'd dropped it and marched it back to the closet, sliding it onto its correct shelf. "That means not pulling his clothes out of the closet, not leaving the TV cables hanging in the air, and definitely not leaving giant purple stains on the white carpet."

"Maybe that's how they like their carpets back on Mars," Shawn said. "He'll think Fleck was so concerned about his well-being that he had the rug painted."

Gus closed the closet and went back to the kitchen area. Ducking behind the island, he started opening cabinets in search of cleaning supplies.

"And besides—" Shawn broke off as Gus slammed a cabinet loudly.

"There's nothing here," Gus said. "No rug cleaner, no bleach, not even any dish soap."

"If you'd let me finish my 'besides,' you would have known that," Shawn said, "because my 'besides' went to exactly that point."

"Okay, fine," Gus said, standing up. "Besides what?"

"Besides," Shawn said, "he doesn't live here. Because he doesn't exist."

"He insisted Fleck build him this place," Gus said. "Why did he do that—just for fun?"

"I don't know much about the ways Martians have fun, but that seems like a long shot," Shawn said. "No, I think he did it to throw people off his trail."

"What trail?" Gus said. "Until last night, he was doing eight shows a week in a theater built specifically for him. No one would have needed a trail to find him. They just needed a ticket."

"That would only have led them to P'nut P'butter," Shawn said.

Gus waited for Shawn to finish his thought, then realized he was waiting for the correction. "P'tol P'kah," Gus said.

"Right, that guy," Shawn said. "They'd need the trail to find Tucker Mellish."

"Who is Tucker Mellish?" Gus said. "Is that the dead guy? Are you finally talking about the dead guy? Because it's only been about seven minutes since you started to explain, and I'd hate to hurry you."

"The dead guy is not Tucker Mellish," Shawn said, "unless I'm much more impressive than I think, because Tucker Mellish is a name I just made up."

"Well, that's certainly helpful," Gus said. "So glad we had this conversation." Now he knew Shawn was going out of his way to annoy him. And it was working. But Gus refused to give Shawn the satisfaction of seeing it on his face, so he turned his back and started opening cabinets as if he hadn't given up on finding cleaning supplies.

"Tucker Mellish is a made-up name, but he's not a made-up person," Shawn said. "He's a stage magician, and a pretty good one. An inventive guy, he's particularly good at coming up with new wrinkles on old illusions. For example, he could take the old gag where the magician disappears out of a box and reappears in the crowd, and flash it up by using a tank of water instead of a cabinet."

Gus could feel himself becoming interested in Shawn's story. But he wasn't ready to give his friend that satisfaction yet, either. He kept banging open doors, finding stacks of untouched dishes and unopened boxes of food, but nothing that actually suggested someone had ever lived here.

"I think it's safe to say that Tucker Mellish was rising in his field," Shawn continued. "I'd guess he was building a reputation at least with other magicians, if he didn't have a mass audience yet. And when I say he was building a reputation, I mean that they all hated him, since that seems to be how they convey professional respect for each other."

Gus pulled open a cabinet next to the sink and found a trash compactor. It was the cleanest trash compactor he'd ever seen, and he doubted that a piece of trash had ever come near it. Maybe there was something to what Shawn was saying.

"So put yourself in Tucker's position," Shawn said. He moved around the kitchen, trying to catch a glimpse of Gus' face, just to see if he was listening. But Gus kept moving in the other direction and keeping the back of his head aimed toward Shawn wherever he went. "You've been practicing all your life to be a great stage magician and you've finally developed the skills to make it happen. You're rising up in your field, probably just beginning to talk to promoters about national exposure, and then it happens."

Gus could feel his muscles tightening as his body tried to turn him around to look at Shawn for the explanation. But he used all his willpower to force himself to stay in place. "What would that be?"

"You go to see one of the most powerful promoters in the business," Shawn said. "He tells you he loves your work and he's going to make you a superstar. But before he launches your tour, he needs to know a little more about your act. He needs to see the designs for your illusions. You're nervous about sharing your secrets, of course, but this man is a legend, so you leave them behind. Days go by and you keep waiting for the great man's call, but it never comes."

This was too much for the muscles in Gus' back to fight. They forced his body around. "How do you know all this?"

"And then you see the news item in *Conman Weekly*, or whatever the magicians' trade paper is called. One of the promoter's biggest clients has just announced a huge national tour—and the tricks he's promising are the same ones you left your plans for in the promoter's office. Now you call and call, but no one ever returns. Your rage is building. This is your life's work, and it's been stolen from you. Late one night, you break into the promoter's office, and when he laughs at you, it's too much. You snap. In fact, you snap his neck. You're gathering up your materials, when his assistant comes into the office. Terrified, she picks up a beaker of acid and hurls it into your face—"

"Wait a minute," Gus said. "Why is there a beaker of acid in a tour promoter's office?"

"You expect the assistant to fight off an enraged magician with her bare hands?" Shawn said. "Anyway, now you're horribly deformed and you're wanted for murder. If you ever want to be seen in public—which is really all you've ever wanted—you need to come up with some kind of disguise."

"If only to hide from the copyright lawyers." Gus felt

a wave of disappointment crashing through him. For a moment there he really thought Shawn had figured out something significant. "Because you've lifted your entire life story from *The Phantom of the Opera*."

"First of all," Shawn said as Gus turned back to exploring the cabinetry, "*The Phantom of the Opera* was written more than a thousand years ago, so it's long out of copyright—"

"Gaston Leroux published his original novel in 1910," Gus said as he slammed shut a cabinet holding an unused espresso machine, a blender still in its original packaging, and a George Foreman grill that had clearly never met a piece of meat. "So yes, that is in the public domain. But in that book, as in several film adaptations and the longest running show in Broadway history, the phantom was deformed at birth. The story you just stole was invented for the 1943 Claude Rains movie, and if you want to tangle with the powerful and brilliant intellectual property lawyers at NBC/Universal, you can do it without me."

"You're getting bogged down in details," Shawn said. "You have to listen to the broader point."

"A point can't be broad," Gus said. "That's what makes it a point."

"Whatever," Shawn said. "This guy Tucker Mellish—"

"This guy that you invented."

"This guy I didn't invent with a name I did," Shawn continued. "Forget about the acid. Forget about the stolen plans. He's on the run."

"From what?"

"Could be anything," Shawn said. "Maybe he owes money to the mob. Maybe he owes a fortune in child support. Maybe he's wanted by the police."

"Sure, for drowning chubby men in his disappearing tank." Gus opened and slammed a couple more cabinets, finding nothing of interest inside.

"It could be," Shawn said. "Maybe he's a serial killer. But whatever he is, he couldn't stand the thought of not performing in public anymore, so he concocted this entire Martian persona to allow himself to be seen in public without being identified."

"So why make Fleck build him this apartment?" Gus said.

"Misdirection," Shawn said. "The magician's best tool. Everyone who's the slightest bit interested in P'stuffed P'imento—"

"P'tol P'kah," Gus repeated by rote.

"Right, that guy," Shawn said. "Anyone who's interested in him is never going to take his eyes off the one place they're certain he'll be. And that lets Tucker Mellish run around without anyone watching him."

Gus had to admit the theory made sense. At least he had to admit it to himself. He wasn't convinced he felt like admitting it to Shawn, whose behavior had been so appalling, it didn't deserve the reward. Besides, that still left one big question unanswered.

"So who's the dead guy? Gus asked, bending down to check the last few cabinets.

"I have no idea."

"You told me you did," Gus said.

"I thought if I kind of ramped up to it, the solution would come to me," Shawn said. "And it might have, if you hadn't distracted me with all that endless blather about mayonnaise."

Gus was about to respond with a retort so perfect it would have sealed Shawn's mouth through the next leap year. But before he could utter the words, he opened one last cabinet and what he saw there froze his tongue to the roof of his mouth.

"I mean, really," Shawn said. "I'm trying to solve the most baffling murder of this or any other generation, and you keep going on about condiments. And I get thrown off my point, I lose track of my thought, and bang zoom, a killer walks free. So I hope that you and Miracle Whip are happy."

Gus stared into the cabinet, trying to make sense of what he was seeing. He recognized the shapes, of course. They were tall, thin tubes, flat on the bottom and rounded on top, with a smaller tube extending from the apogee. They were gray metal, flecked with nicks and scratches. He had seen these things a million times before. He knew exactly what they were. But they shouldn't be here. There was no earthly reason for them to be here.

"Are you sure about your theory?" Gus finally asked.

"Why, you have a better one?"

"Yes, but it's not mine. It's Fleck's," Gus said.

"Fleck didn't have a theory," Shawn said. "Unless you mean when he said that his client was a real Martian. You're not suggesting you believe that?"

"I'm not suggesting anything," Gus said. He hoisted one of the scuba tanks out of the cabinet. "I'm just wondering why anyone who was born on this planet would need to bring his own air with him."

Chapter Twelve

As a physical barricade, the seal was completely useless. It was just a piece of paper—slick green paper backed with some kind of sticky stuff. A box cutter would go through it like a spoon through whipped cream. Even a butter knife would be enough to tear it open.

But as a moral barrier, the seal was inviolable. It wasn't a piece of paper; it was the entire American system of justice. It was the triumph of order over chaos, of civilization over savagery. It was proof that mankind was capable of understanding that there are societal obligations more important than any one man's desires. It was everything Detective Carlton Lassiter believed in.

That was why his hand shook so badly as he lifted his Swiss army knife to cut through it.

Lassiter didn't want to break the seal. He was the one who ordered it slapped on the door to the show-room at the Fortress of Magic, and he was the one who vowed to track down and incarcerate anyone who even thought about tampering with it. Because as much as he wanted access to the magician's machinery inside, he knew a judge had sent down an order prohibiting anyone from examining it. And even though Lassiter had strong reason to believe the judge was motivated by his own personal issues and not by the rational pursuit of justice, the detective could not use that suspicion as an excuse to ignore the order. To do so would be to invite anarchy.

Instead, Lassiter put all his years of experience to work for him. If he couldn't study the scene, he'd find another way to solve the crime.

Only there wasn't another way.

It had been thirty-six hours since Lassiter had finished interviewing the last of the magicians, and as he stared at the black print on the electric green seal, his head was still pounding from the experience. It wasn't the fact that none of them knew how the green giant had disappeared that bothered him. He expected that. It wasn't even that none of them would admit knowing anything about the dead man. It was possible that they really had never met him, or that if they had, they weren't used to seeing him floating dead in a tank of water, and the new circumstances made recognition impossible.

What was making his head continue to throb was the way that each of the self-styled magicians insisted that P'tol P'kah was a talentless hack who wasn't capable of shuffling a deck of cards, and whose disappearance was the most obvious kind of trickery. And yet every time he asked one of them to give him a clue how the missing man had accomplished his disappearance, they all suddenly swore an oath of allegiance to something they called the Magician's Code. Apparently that was a sacred oath that forbade them to reveal the secrets of a fellow prestidigitator's tricks.

Right.

Carlton Lassiter hadn't become head detective of the Santa Barbara Police Department because he was stupid or gullible. He had clawed his way to that position by virtue of his superior intellect and keen instincts, along with a city budget crisis that resulted in a hiring freeze shortly after his employment, eliminating many potential competitors. He knew when he was being lied to, and he didn't like it. He didn't like it at all.

The magicians were all lying about this "code." There was one simple reason they wouldn't tell Lassiter how the green guy had achieved his escape: They didn't have a clue. It didn't take a detective as good as him to hear the jealousy in their voices when they described their rival as a fraud and a hack. If any one of them had a hint how the Martian Magician had pulled off his stunt, it would have been all over the Internet before Lassiter had a chance to ask his first question.

If the secret behind the miraculous disappearance was the greatest mystery Lassiter had to deal with, his headache probably would have subsided to a dull throb. But right now everything about this case was conspiring to constrict the blood vessels in his scalp. Even questions that should have been easy were turning out to be unanswerable.

To start with, there was the dead guy's identity. Lassiter had personally supervised Detective O'Hara as she ran his fingerprints last night. He would swear in court that she had done everything right. But the system had been silent ever since. He sent the prints through every database he had ever used, and it kept coming up blank. Apparently the victim had never been arrested, which while frustrating, wasn't necessarily surprising. But as far as the computer systems could discover, he'd never applied for a passport, requested a driver's license, or opened a bank account anywhere in the country. He put the dead man's image through a facial recognition program and didn't come up with a single match.

Lassiter was a strong enough detective that he had long since learned how to fall back on his own skills when the computers failed, as they so often did. He studied every piece of the dead man's clothing, searching for any clues to his identity. But there were no personal possessions in any of the pockets, and the clothes themselves were all national brands in stock sizes. They could have come from any store in any city in any state.

Lassiter had hoped the hat would provide a significant lead. After all, you don't see that many people wearing bowlers in the United States. But the reason for that turned out to be not that no one bought them, but that they rarely took them out of their closet. The hat in question, technically a wool felt derby with a sixteen-ligne grosgrain band and grosgrain-bound brim edges, could have been manufactured by any of a dozen companies and purchased on any of a hundred Web sites, not to mention uncounted retail establishments, and purchased by any of tens of thousands of customers. If its late owner hadn't removed the label, they might have been able to narrow down its provenance, but without the tag, it was hopeless.

The body didn't offer any more clues to its identity. Its former occupant was a forty-year-old white male, five foot six inches tall, 195 pounds. He was in good health, and there were no drugs or alcohol in his system. Cause of death was drowning. Analysis of the contents of his lungs confirmed that it was the same water that filled the tank, matched to a sample that had soaked into Lassiter's slacks when he had knelt by the corpse.

And that was making Lassiter's head hurt, too, because he couldn't figure out how the death had happened. This guy was young and relatively fit. He wasn't drunk or drugged. So how did he end up drowning in a water-filled telephone booth? How did he get in there, and why couldn't he get out? And how did he drown so quickly?

Lassiter knew there was only one cure for his headache. He needed to see that tank. If he could only figure out how it worked, he was certain the rest of the answers would fall into place. Unfortunately, it was in a locked room in his least favorite place on Earth, sequestered behind crime scene tape and protected by a court order.

He'd spent most of the morning on the phone, searching for a judge willing to overturn the order forbidding him to examine the tank. Many of them sounded sympathetic at first, but when they heard it was Albert Moore they were being asked to reverse, they backed off. Apparently Moore had a reputation as a street fighter, and few were willing to risk his anger. A couple of jurists didn't seem to mind that challenge, but when Lassiter mentioned that it was Benny Fleck who'd requested the sanction, they all suddenly found new reasons to refuse his request.

Lassiter had learned many valuable lessons during his years on the force. He had studied the Reid Technique to master the three components of interrogation. He had taught himself how to maneuver his way through an uncooperative bureaucracy. He had even figured out how to get the mechanics at the SBPD to make sure the air conditioner in his unmarked sedan would keep working through the worst of the Santa Barbara summer. But the most important thing he'd learned was that if a murder isn't solved within the first forty-eight hours, the odds of the case ever being closed plummeted to almost nothing.

The man in the tank had been dead for thirty-six of those forty-eight hours and Lassiter was no closer to finding his killer. The clock was ticking and its hands were dripping blood.

When Lassiter left the station in his unmarked sedan—the air conditioner blowing a stream of cool into his face—he told himself he was just going for a drive to clear his head. When he pulled up in the parking lot down the hill from the Fortress of Magic, he pretended there were some rooms he might not have checked out thoroughly the night of the drowning.

But now that he was standing outside the closed showroom, the blade trembling over the paper seal, there was no way he could hide from what he had really intended all along. He was going to violate the principles that had driven him his entire life. He was going to flout that court order, slash through the seal, and find out what trick the missing magician had used to make his escape.

Lassiter pressed the tip of the blade into the crack between door and jamb, just above the top edge of the seal. One swift move and it would be done—the same motion as shaking someone's hand, that was all. And if the hand he was shaking belonged to chaos, anarchy, and the destruction of the rule of law, he was willing to do it as long as that would keep a killer from walking free.

Lassiter's mind sent an order through his neural pathways down to his arm. Time to move. *If it were done when 'tis done, then 'twere well it were done quickly*, he quoted to himself. Lassiter couldn't remember where that phrase came from, but he was pretty sure that whoever said it had some unpleasant job to complete and felt much better when he'd gotten it all over with. His mind repeated its order. But his unconscious seemed to be blocking it. His hand trembled, but no more. Irritated at himself, the detective placed his other hand on top of the one holding the knife and pressed down.

The knife hand pressed back up.

This was unacceptable. Lassiter had made the decision to break the commandments he lived by for the greater good. How dare one of his body parts rebel like this? Did his hand really believe it was better than the rest of him? He pressed down harder on the knife hand. The paper at the top of the seal began to crinkle down. Another second and it would be done.

"Carlton, stop!"

Lassiter cursed under his breath. It was bad enough his arm was trying to reverse his decision. Now his conscience was speaking to him like Jiminy Cricket. Well, he'd spent his entire life following the orders of his extremely controlling conscience, and this time it could get out of his way—even if it did speak in a melodious, oddly familiar female voice.

"Yo, Lassie, give it up!"

Lassiter froze. He was willing to accept the concept that his conscience would actually speak to him in words. But there was no way his own personal conscience, a resident of his own personal brain, would ever speak in *that* voice. He turned to see that Detective Juliet O'Hara had come up behind him, and she was followed by Shawn and Gus. For some reason Gus was carrying a dinged-up scuba tank.

"You have to leave this area, Detective," Lassiter said with all the sternness he could muster. "For the sake of your career, you must not be a part of this."

"That's very generous, Carlton—"

"Generous?" Lassiter interrupted. "I am about to violate every precept to which we swore loyalty when we donned the proud blue of the Santa Barbara Police Department. When this case is over, I will have to turn myself over to Internal Affairs. They will strip me of my badge, my gun, and my honor, and I will spend the rest of my unhappy life working as a security guard at malls and multiplexes."

"That could be pretty sweet," Shawn said. "Just think, if we bought a ticket to one movie, you could let us sneak in to all the others."

"Only on weekdays, though," Gus said. "We don't want to get you in trouble if there are sell-outs."

Lassiter was so used to Shawn's and Gus' callous disregard for anyone but themselves that their obvious pleasure at the tragic consequences of his noble self-sacrifice didn't surprise him. But he was shocked to his core when he noticed his partner stifling a smile.

"Is this funny to you?" Lassiter said. "I am one knife stroke away from ending my career to further justice."

"It's okay, Carlton," O'Hara said. "We've come to help you."

"You can't. This is my task alone. Like the poor Hobbit carrying that ring through Mordor to the Crack of Doom, I must bear my burden and do—"

Shawn reached past Lassiter, and the detective saw a quick glint of metal. Shawn stepped back. Lassiter looked at the door. To his horror, there was a deep slash all the way through the seal.

"Oops," Shawn said.

"If you think that's going to make any difference, it won't," Lassiter said. "If I use this act of vandalism to further my investigation, I am still guilty. In fact, unless I arrest these two and see them prosecuted for their crime, I'm as guilty as they are."

As he said the words, Lassiter had to admit he felt a slight temptation to do just that—to say to hell with the murder and use this defacement of the entire judicial system to put these two delinquents in jail once and for all. But he knew that just as he was willing to sacrifice his own career to catch a killer, he'd have to be willing to sacrifice this pleasure.

"No one's guilty of anything, Carlton," O'Hara said soothingly.

"There was a court order—"

"Which we have followed to the letter," O'Hara said.

"And not just any letter," Shawn added. "This letter."

Shawn turned to Gus, who reached into his shirt pocket, pulled out a much-folded piece of paper, and slapped it into Shawn's outstretched hand like an OR nurse handing the surgeon a scalpel. Shawn unfolded the paper and held it up for Lassiter to see.

"The letter states that we have been employed by Benny Fleck to find his missing client," Shawn said. "That makes us his duly authorized agents."

"And the court order written by the Honorable Albert Moore of the California Superior Court for Santa Barbara County prohibits you from examining the device without the express permission of P'tol P'kah or his duly authorized agents," Gus said.

"And we're even better than that, because we're duly authorized agents of a duly authorized agent," Shawn said. "That makes us dually duly authorized. You don't get more authorized than that. Or more duly."

Lassiter stared at them suspiciously, then turned to O'Hara. "Is this true?"

"All the papers seem to be in order," O'Hara said. "And we witnessed Fleck hiring these two ourselves."

She was right. They did. It all seemed to make sense. Even if there was a court challenge later, Lassiter knew he'd be on firm ground. He could see justice done without sentencing himself to a life of inhaling popcorn fumes. It was everything he'd hoped for.

"So let's go," Shawn said. "That tank isn't going to investigate itself."

Shawn reached past Lassiter and pushed the door open. Lassiter took one step toward the threshold, then stopped. This was too good to be true.

"Wait one minute," Lassiter said. "Why are you doing this? What's the catch?"

"Don't be so suspicious, Lassie," Shawn said. "All we want is a little interagency cooperation. And Jules said it was okay."

"We're pooling our resources," O'Hara said quickly before Lassiter could object. "They needed a little help with their investigation; we needed a little help with ours. So we made a deal."

"What kind of deal?"

Gus lifted the scuba tank and tossed it to Lassiter, who staggered back as he caught it. "You need our authorization. We need your lab to analyze the contents of this tank."

"What is it?" Lassiter said suspiciously.

"If we knew, we wouldn't need to have it analyzed," Shawn said.

"But we think it's Martian air," Gus said. "Or not. Either way, it would be really useful to know."

Lassiter thought it through carefully. On the one hand, he hated the idea of donating precious police resources to these two frauds. On the other hand, if he agreed, he'd have a good chance to solve a murder, find a missing person, and salvage his career.

"On one condition," Lassiter said after due consideration.

"What's that?" Shawn said.

Lassiter heaved the scuba tank back at Gus, who managed to snatch it out of the air before it crashed on the floor. "You carry it."

Lassiter didn't wait for a response. He turned and marched into the showroom.

The tank was just as they had left it. The lid stood open, and there were small pools of water on the ground where the body had lain. The enormous boots still sat under the weight of the column of water.

Lassiter moved slowly toward the tank. Deep down he wanted to run to it like a child after a departing ice cream truck, but his training told him to use the approach to assess the situation carefully.

Shawn and Gus clearly had no such training. They blasted past him, and Gus was pushing the airplane stairs back against the side of the tank before Lassiter was halfway across the room.

"This is an official police investigation," Lassiter commanded. "Stand back from the tank."

"Or at least you make sure you share everything you find with us," O'Hara said. Lassiter glared at her. She shrugged. "They got us in here, Carlton. It's their investigation, too."

Lassiter sighed. He hated having anyone else interfere in his work, but he knew she was right. There was nothing he could do to stop them. But at least he could keep them from despoiling his crime scene before he could see exactly what they were doing. He quickened his pace to a half run and got to the tank just as Shawn was beginning to climb the stairs.

"What are you planning to do?" Lassiter said as O'Hara caught up with him.

"I figured I'd jump in the water, dissolve into a zillion tiny pieces, and see where I end up reintegrating," Shawn said. "Then I'll come back and tell you where I went."

"Do you know how to do that?" O'Hara asked.

"How hard can it be?" Shawn reached the top of the stairs and stuck a toe of his running shoe into the water. "I just need one favor."

"What's that?" Lassiter said.

"If any of my molecules don't reintegrate with me, I need you to fish them out so I can stick them back on later."

"Are you sure you know what you're doing?" Gus hissed up at him.

"Do I ever?"

Shawn reached down and touched the water with his hand, then shivered. It hadn't gotten any warmer in the hours since the Martian vanished. He stood up and was about to step in when the doors to the showroom crashed open.

"Step away from that tank!"

The speaker was a tall woman in a dark suit. Even from across the room, she exuded authority. She carried her black purse as if it contained a small arsenal, and her posture suggested she wouldn't hesitate to use it.

"It's okay," Gus said. "We're duly authorized agents of Benny Fleck, and we've authorized these two fine police detectives to be here."

"I don't know who this Fleck is," the woman said. "But I am ordering you away from that tank as a duly authorized agent of the United States government."

Chapter Thirteen

In general, Shawn Spencer did not respond well to authority. When directly ordered to do anything, his first, instinctive response was to do precisely the opposite—which might explain why his career as a waiter didn't last any longer than its first night.

But there was something in this woman's voice that made Shawn's feet move back from the edge of the tank before he had a chance to refuse her command. Looking down, he saw that it had had a similar effect on Gus, who had moved several feet away from the stairs. And the two detectives, who were trained to follow orders, were all but standing at attention.

Shawn took a deep breath and strolled casually down the steps, fighting off his own desire to salute. "United States government, eh?" he said with as much jauntiness as he could muster. "Think I've heard of them. Big outfit, works out of a swamp near Virginia?"

The woman stalked toward them, her black eyes never leaving Shawn's face as she came. As she approached, she seemed to be constructed entirely out of angles and edges. Her body was thin, sharp, and hard; her face a caricaturist's delight of cheekbones and eyebrows, high and fierce.

"Step away from the stairs, sir," the woman ordered Shawn, and again he felt his body obeying before his instincts could object.

"This is an official Santa Barbara police investigation," O'Hara said.

"Not anymore," the woman snapped. "Now it's a federal matter."

Gus noticed an odd look on Lassiter's face. At first he thought the detective might be about to throw up. But he quickly figured out what it really meant, and the realization made *him* briefly consider throwing up. Lassiter was attracted to her.

O'Hara clearly didn't share her partner's feelings. "Federal government's a mighty big thing," she said. "You want to narrow it down a little for us?"

"It's pretty obvious," Lassiter whispered to her. "Look at this woman. Everything about her screams Homeland Security."

"If you mean she's pushy, arrogant, and probably incompetent, I'm tempted to agree with you," O'Hara said without lowering her voice. "But I'd still like to know who she is before I walk away from a murder case."

"Major Holly Voges, U.S. Army, retired," the woman said.

"You see?" Lassiter said. "She's military."

"She's retired," O'Hara said.

"Then why is she here?" Lassiter said.

"I know," Shawn said, jumping lightly down the last

few steps. "This place looks just like a Veteran's Center. She's looking for a cup of coffee and a game of checkers."

Major Voges turned the depthless black eyes back in his direction. "I am retired from the military," she said. "I am here at the explicit direction of the federal department for which I now work."

"And what division would that be?" O'Hara said. "Or is it so classified it doesn't even have a name?"

"I bet that's it," Lassiter said. "This is one of those off-the-books, black-funding operations, isn't it?"

"If it were, I certainly could neither confirm nor deny it."

Lassiter turned excitedly to his partner. "Did you hear that?" he said. "She just neither confirmed nor denied what I said. What does that tell you?"

"That I still haven't seen any identification," O'Hara said. "And until I do, she could be one of the stage magicians with a fake name and a clever schtick."

"It's not all that clever," Shawn said.

"I don't know," Gus said. "Seems pretty clever to me. Claim you're from the Federal Bureau of Magic, you're here to search them, and then you keep pulling rabbits out from everywhere."

"That's just a Harry Potter knockoff," Shawn said. "J. K. Rowling clearly delineated an entire modern government ministry devoted to the dark arts, complete with an investigative division. So what could possibly be new about this gag?"

Two men in dark suits and white earpieces stepped into the room and took positions on either side of the double doors. After a moment, a forklift rumbled in behind them and steered for the stage.

"Well that, for one thing," Gus said.

"What is that doing in here?" O'Hara said.

"This tank and everything in and around it are being seized under federal statute 99-245-876, section forty-eight, subparagraph nine," Voges said coolly. "If you attempt to stop my men, you will be subject to prosecution."

O'Hara positioned herself between the tank and the forklift. "Not until I see some identification."

Major Voges reached into her purse. Gus half expected her to come out with a bazooka. Instead, she produced a slim black wallet. She flipped it open and handed it over.

O'Hara stared at the ID in disbelief. "Federal Communications Commission?"

"That's what the badge says," Voges said calmly. "Specifically the Office of Engineering and Technology, Equipment Authorization Branch."

"What possible jurisdiction does the FCC have in a murder case?" O'Hara demanded.

"Absolutely none at all." Voges' eyes never strayed from O'Hara's face.

"Let me rephrase that," O'Hara said with a calm that Gus knew cloaked anger rising toward rage. "What authority does the FCC have to preempt any local law enforcement activity that does not directly relate to issues of communications?"

"Again," Voges said, "absolutely none at all."

"Then maybe you could give me one good reason why I shouldn't impound your forklift and throw all four of you in jail for obstructing justice."

"No," Voges said. "I can't do that."

O'Hara glanced back at her partner to see if he was

going to step in. But Lassiter was staring at the major in unabashed awe. "Detective Lassiter," she hissed, "we have a situation here."

"We do," Lassiter said. "And that's why we should back off and let the major do what she needs."

O'Hara pulled her partner off to one side and whispered furiously at him. "This woman has no jurisdiction here. She's some low-level functionary in a bureaucratic division that has nothing to do with any crime more serious than stealing cable signals. How can you possibly suggest that we back off?"

"For exactly that reason," Lassiter said.

"For exactly *what* reason?"

Lassiter held up one finger to suggest she watch and learn, then stepped back to the major. "Explain one thing to my partner, please," he said. "Why exactly would a bureaucrat from the Federal Communications Commission be involved in a murder investigation?"

"There is absolutely no reason," Voges snapped.

O'Hara let out a sigh that could be heard in Bakersfield. Lassiter shot her a look, then continued. "So if an operative from the FCC were to appear at a crime scene in California with three agents at her side and order the local police to stand down, would it be a logical assumption that her job title is actually cover for a different government position? Something that could not be discussed in the open without jeopardizing national security?"

"You might suggest that," Voges said. "I couldn't possibly comment."

Lassiter cast a quick look back to make sure O'Hara was following him. She seemed to be, but she clearly wasn't happy about it.

"We won't ask you to," Lassiter said. "But I hope you understand that without some clarification of the issues involved here, we can't simply walk away from our own investigation. You need to meet us halfway."

Voges looked him over with all the enthusiasm of someone who'd just discovered that the stray cat she was petting had a wide white stripe down its back. Then she snapped her finger and waved at the agent driving the forklift. It lurched into gear and headed straight for the tank.

Before the prongs could touch steel, O'Hara leapt across the room and positioned herself directly in front of the tank. There was no way to pick it up without crushing her.

"I advise you to move, Detective," Major Voges hissed.

"I advise you not to tamper with my crime scene."

"I don't think you're going to like Guantanamo Bay," Voges said. "Especially with multiple broken bones. The medical care there really doesn't live up to its reputation."

O'Hara didn't move. The forklift crawled closer.

"Detective O'Hara, stand down!" Lassiter said.

She didn't move. The forklift was inches away, the prongs already surrounding her. The yellow steel of the lift touched her chest and pushed her back against the tank. O'Hara reached into her purse and pulled out her gun, leveling it at the forklift driver's forehead.

Lassiter cursed under his breath. The situation was going to hell. But his partner had made a move, and he had to back her up. He yanked out his gun, but by the time he had it aimed at the major, she was already leveling an automatic pistol at him.

"Let's stay calm here," Lassiter commanded. His gun shifted between the major and her two agents.

"Drop the weapon, Detective," Major Voges said, a dangerous edge in her voice.

"You first," Lassiter said.

"And back this thing away from me," O'Hara said to the driver, "or you'll be driving a forklift in hell."

"I said stand down, Detective!" Lassiter shouted.

"When they do," O'Hara said calmly, or as calmly as she could with all the air pressed out of her lungs.

Across the stage, Gus and Shawn watched in horror. Well, Gus watched in horror. Shawn was mostly just watching.

"We've got to do something," Gus said.

"Before we find out who's going to win?" Shawn said.

"Between Detective O'Hara and eight thousand pounds of solid steel?"

"The major can't weigh that much, even if she is made of metal," Shawn said. "And even if she does, I put ten bucks on Jules."

"They're not going to start mud wrestling, Shawn," Gus said. "This army woman is crazy."

"That's where you're wrong," Shawn said. "This *re-tired* army woman is crazy."

"You have to do something."

Detective O'Hara's breath was coming in short gasps as the forklift compressed her ribs into her lungs. Her finger tightened on the trigger.

Shawn shrugged. Then he looked over at the major. And he *saw*. Saw the American Airlines ticket peeking up out of her bag, the letter *d* at the top. Saw a small stripe of blue ink protruding from the sleeve of one of her agents. Saw the bright white lip on the tan face of the forklift operator.

Shawn pressed his fingertips to his temples and let out a howl. "My molecules!" he moaned. "Bring them back! Bring back my molecules!"

Startled, the forklift driver took his foot off the pedal, and the machine stopped moving forward. O'Hara released the pressure on the trigger. Major Voges wheeled toward Shawn, aiming her gun at him. "What the hell is that?" she snapped.

"My guess is it's a call from beyond," Gus said. "It's a psychic signal direct from P'tol P'kah."

"He's a local crank, and that's the junior crank," Lassiter said. "Ignore them."

"Yes," O'Hara wheezed. "Ignore them—at your peril. Shawn Spencer is Santa Barbara's premier psychic detective."

"And after you're done with him, I'll take you to meet Santa Barbara's premier homeless guy," Lassiter said, keeping his gun trained on Voges' agents. "I think we can resolve our differences here between law enforcement professionals."

"Is that before or after you're all dead?" Gus said.

"My molecules are flying across the country," Shawn said. "We need to stop them. We need to catch them. I need my molecules back."

"I'm ordering you to remain silent," Voges said to Shawn.

"And so am I," Lassiter said.

"Can't stay silent," Shawn howled. "Must tell the entire country to look out for my molecules. Alert the entire population to watch for them. Got to tell the press the entire story . . . every bit of it."

Major Voges glared at Shawn. "This is an issue of national security. It must not be reported."

"No one is going to interfere with national security," Lassiter said.

"Must tell the whole country," Shawn moaned. "Starting in Washington DC. I think a lot of my molecules are there right now."

"If you want him to shut up you'd better get a court order fast," O'Hara gasped. "But you'd better choose the right judge, because there aren't a lot who will grant an order of prior restraint."

"Or maybe we can all just work something out right here," Gus said quickly. "Releasing Detective O'Hara would be a good first step."

Voges turned her glare on Gus for a moment, then signaled the forklift driver, who backed off. O'Hara took a deep breath of air into her lungs, held it for a long moment, then exhaled slowly.

"This must not go public," Voges said. "I can't explain the reasons, but this must remain secret."

The major slipped her gun back into her purse. After a moment, Lassiter reholstered his.

"All we want to do is solve a murder," O'Hara said, still breathing heavily. "You stand out of our way; we'll stand out of yours."

"I cannot let you examine this device," Voges said.

"And we can't let you take it back to Washington until we do," O'Hara said.

"Kids, kids." Shawn strolled over to the two women and put his face between theirs. "Didn't Mommy and Daddy ever teach you anything about sharing? If you can't play nicely together with your toys, then Mommy and Daddy have to take them away until you can."

"Get back, Shawn," O'Hara said.

"He's right," Lassiter said, although the look on his face suggested that it was painful for him to do so.

"Detective Lassiter!" O'Hara warned from between clenched teeth.

"We have a standoff here, Detective," Lassiter said. "And it's not going to be settled at our pay grade. We need to back off and let our superiors work this out."

"And until then?" O'Hara said.

"We put the seal back in place," Lassiter said. "And we'll put a guard on the place."

"Like I'm going to trust some Santa Barbara police officer to keep you out," Voges said.

"About as much as I'm going to trust one of your goons," O'Hara said.

"We'll each put a guard outside the door," Lassiter said. "They can watch each other."

O'Hara and Voges considered it, and then both took a step back. Shawn clapped Lassiter on the back.

"Nice job, Lassie," Shawn said. "We make a pretty good team. If that multiplex gig doesn't work out, you've always got a place at Psych."

"Get away from me, Spencer," Lassiter said.

"I will," Shawn said. "But don't you think you ought to mention the morgue?"

"The morgue?"

"You know, the place where they keep the bodies?" Shawn said. "The ones you might want to investigate later?"

Lassiter thought this over, then turned back to Voges. "Do we need to post guards at the morgue as well?"

"Only if you plan to keep me from taking the body back to DC," she said.

"Then it's done," Lassiter said.

Major Voges snapped her fingers and her three agents retreated to the doors, slipping through without ever turning their backs to the tank.

"I can't believe you're letting her get away with this," O'Hara hissed to Lassiter. "You were willing to throw away your career for a look at that tank."

"My career, yes," Lassiter said. "But not my nation's safety."

"She works for the FCC," O'Hara said. "She's in the equipment authorization department. She probably spends her days testing TV remotes to see if they cause carpal tunnel syndrome."

"James Bond officially worked for Universal Exports Ltd.," Lassiter said. "That doesn't mean he didn't have a license to kill."

"You told me there was no such thing," Shawn said.

"He was right," O'Hara said. "It's fiction. All of it was fiction."

"I understand your frustration," Lassiter said. "I share it. But I look at a situation from every angle, I eliminate everything that's impossible, and then I know that what's left over, no matter how improbable, must be true."

"Sherlock Holmes is fiction, too, Carlton," O'Hara said.

Shawn clapped his hands over Gus' ears. "Don't say that," Shawn said. "I haven't told him yet."

Gus shook Shawn off his head in time to hear Lassiter say, "We'll look into this woman. We'll check her out in every way. But for right now, there's only one explanation that makes sense, and that's that her FCC ID is a cover for some secret position. If that turns out not to be the case, we'll take turns dunking her into that tank until she talks. Until then, let's err on the side of national security."

Detective O'Hara thought it through, then jammed her gun into her purse unhappily. "I'm not getting chased off this case."

"I'm not, either," Lassiter said.

"Us, neither," Shawn said.

"Oh, joy," Lassiter said.

Shawn and Gus left the detectives standing outside the showroom, facing off silently against Major Voges and her agents until a uniformed officer could be found to take guard duty. As they walked down the steep hill to the parking lot, this time unmolested by electronic guard dogs, Gus tried to figure out what had just happened.

"Do you really think that scary woman is from the government?" Gus said.

"Definitely," Shawn said. "Did you see her shoes? Plain, dull, comfortable, and moderately priced. The hallmark of the government worker."

"But is she with the FCC or Homeland Security?"

"That depends on who P'Torky P'kig really is."

"P'tol P'kah," Gus sighed, knowing that Shawn wouldn't explain any further without the obligatory correction.

"Right, that guy," Shawn said. "If he's a holographic projection from a new kind of projector, she's probably with the FCC."

"We felt the floor tremble when he walked."

"So probably not a holograph," Shawn said. "Which means she could be who she doesn't say she is."

"Why would Homeland Security be chasing a missing magician?"

"Maybe he really is a Martian," Shawn said. "Or maybe he's a spy. He uses the magic act as a cover to travel from town to town, stealing secrets and passing them to his undercover contacts wherever he goes."

"A brilliant idea," Gus said. "Except that he didn't travel from city to city. He never left Las Vegas. What kind of secrets can he steal there?"

"Which casino has the best buffet?"

"Couldn't the undercover contacts just try all the buffets and find out for themselves?"

"Not if they had a small budget," Shawn said. "Despite what you might think, some of those places are really expensive. And then they put a lot of cheap items up front so you'll fill up on bread before you can get to the good stuff, like the crab legs and lobster tails."

"Let's come back to this later," Gus said.

"Good. Because I'm suddenly hungry."

They reached the car and Gus fished in his pocket for his keys. "But if she really is from Homeland Security, how did you get her to back off?"

"She didn't want publicity," Shawn said. "You saw that."

"So why didn't she just arrest us all?"

"Because whatever she's doing here, it's not an official DHS operation," Shawn said.

"And you know that how?"

"The little *d* on top of her plane ticket," Shawn said. "It's a fare code. She flew DC to LAX in a full-price business-class seat," Shawn said.

"Last I heard the government had lots of money," Gus said. "At least they act like they do."

"Right," Shawn said. "So if this really was a crisis involving national security, she would have taken a DHS jet."

"How do you know they have one?"

"Their budget is like fifty billion dollars," Shawn said. "Can you imagine having fifty billion dollars and not buying at least one jet? And even if they didn't, they would have sent her on a military transport."

"Maybe it's not an emergency."

"In which case she would have flown coach," Shawn said. "Federal officials aren't allowed to fly business class."

Gus hit the remote on his key fob and the car doors popped open, but he didn't want to get in until he was sure he understood what Shawn was saying. "They'll spend millions buying a jet, but they wouldn't spring for a business-class ticket? That doesn't make any sense."

"Then I must be wrong," Shawn said. "Oh, wait, this is the federal government. I'm right. Can we get out of here now?"

Before Gus could answer, Shawn opened his door and got in. If Gus wanted any more answers, he'd have to get in, too. He buckled himself into his seat, but he didn't start the car.

"Okay, fine," Gus said. "What else?"

"There's more?"

Gus waited until Shawn gave in.

"Did you see the upper lip on that agent?" Shawn said. "It was bright white, while the rest of his face was tanned. Which means he had a mustache until a day or so ago."

"And?"

"And another one of the agents had a dragon tattoo

running down his arm," Shawn said. "At least, I assume it ran down his arm. The tip of the tail was sticking out of his sleeve, and it's hard to imagine anyone having just the tip of a dragon's tail tattooed on his wrist."

"Which means what?"

"Homeland Security agents can't have tattoos or facial hair," Shawn said. "These are rental guys she picked up in LA."

"So she's a phony."

"Not necessarily," Shawn said. "It's quite possible that Major Voges had some vacation time coming and she decided to spend it interfering with an ongoing criminal investigation."

"That one doesn't work for me."

"Then how about this?" Shawn said. "There's something terribly, terribly wrong, and whatever it is, it's something that Major Voges was supposed to take care of. She probably even told her superiors that she had. But she screwed up, and now it's worse than either of us could ever possibly imagine."

"Like what?"

"Did you miss the part about it being worse than either of us could ever possibly imagine?" Shawn said. "That means I can't imagine what it is. But think of everything that Homeland Security has screwed up that no one got fired for. And now imagine that Major Voges is afraid she will be if anyone finds out what she's done."

Gus thought about it and shuddered. "We're doomed."

"I think that's probably right," Shawn said.

"What are we going to do?"

"I'm thinking about a nice game of pin the tail on the donkey."

Chapter Fourteen

It was about the art. About the precision of his movements, the subtlety of his misdirection, the speed of
his fingers, and the stealth of his hands. It didn't matter whom he was performing for. He had astonished
the crowned heads of Europe and amazed the jaded
jet-setters of Monte Carlo, but their reaction was no
more important to him than that of any other group
who sought release in the presence of miracles.

There were those who claimed to pity Barnaby
Rudge. He could hear them whispering in the Fortress
of Magic. He, the great Rudge, who had traveled to India to meet the guru, if not quite with the Beatles, then
at least with Herman's Hermits. Rudge, who had been
painted by Warhol and filmed by Jodorowsky, who had
exchanged phone numbers with Anita Pallenberg and
Bianca Pérez-Mora Macias before losing both beau-
ties to Keith and Mick. Rudge, who would have electri-
fied an entire nation when he performed his greatest
illusion, the Groovy Gap, on the Smothers Brothers

Comedy Hour on April 11, 1969, if only those idiots had shut up about the Vietnam War for one more week instead of getting themselves cancelled.

Now, he had heard the whisperers say, Rudge was so forgotten, people assumed he stole the idea of using a Dickens title for his stage name from David Copperfield, when it was so obviously the reverse. He was reduced to playing to tiny crowds for peanuts. He had lost everything.

But Rudge knew he had lost nothing. As long as his fingers could still move, his art was still alive. And his art was all that mattered.

Barnaby Rudge bowed to his audience as he transitioned between illusions. The show had been going superbly. The scarves had flowed out of his sleeves like water down a mountain streambed. The Chinese linking rings had clashed together like armies in the night. There was a small hitch when he reached into the false bottom of his top hat and discovered that he'd left his pint of Cutty inside with the cap partially unscrewed and the dove he'd meant to produce had suffocated on the whiskey fumes. But he had improvised a clever bit of patter to distract the crowd as he disposed of both *chapeau* and *oiseau*, and no one seemed to notice the lacuna in the performance. And the rabbit, that irresistible pink-nosed climax to his act, the one that never failed to rouse the audience to a standing cheer, was nestled safely beneath the false bottom of his dove cage. This would be a show for the ages.

With a grand flourish, Rudge produced the cane that in moments he would transform into a bouquet of lovely flowers. The sight of so much color exploding from a simple black stick would elicit awed sighs from his audience, and while they were marveling, he'd use their stunned focus on the blooms to set the switch on the dove cage. It was all going perfectly.

Rudge felt a sticky blob slap against his cheek—avian revenge for the dove's demise, perhaps. No matter. He would allow no bird to disturb his act when it was nearing its climax. He reached up to wipe it off and his hand came back slimed with green and pink. There was a brown circle in the middle of the blotch, which he realized was most of one of the icing *a*'s in "Happy Birthday."

Rudge glared out into the crowd to see who had flung the frosting at him. The culprit wasn't hard to find. It was little Jimmy Eisenstein, whose tenth birthday the magician had been hired to help celebrate. Rudge could tell it was Jimmy who had iced him. He still held the frosting catapult—in this case a white plastic spork—aloft, now reloaded for a second assault. But even without the weapon, Rudge would have known who had committed this assault, because while Rudge had been consumed with the details of his performance, the entire audience of second graders had slipped out of their folding chairs and drifted away from the living room, leaving only the birthday boy to appreciate the act.

"Stay that missile, you fine young man," Rudge boomed out cheerfully. "And I will show you the wonders of the Orient."

"If you mean the rabbit, it peed in the birdcage and it's dripping through the bottom," the lovable young scamp retorted. "And I saw you flip that switch on the back of the cage. What does that do—unhook some door so you can reach through the fake floor?"

Rudge let out a hearty laugh, fighting off the urge to throttle the dear lad. Every magician worth his gold lamé suit had encountered hecklers, and the worst were the ones who had dabbled in the art themselves. Clearly this boy was planning a career on the stage. Maybe he even hoped to model his act after Rudge's.

Normally, the magician would have stifled the interloper with one of his special zingers. But there was a keen intelligence in the youngster's eye, and since there were no other spectators to disillusion, perhaps he could use this as a moment to share his precious secrets.

"If you'd care to approach, young man, I might be persuaded to show you how to make the rabbit appear," Rudge said.

"I'll wait until the cage stops dripping pee," Jimmy said.

"I have other miracles I could teach you," Rudge said, glancing over to see a stream of rabbit urine dripping out of his dove house and bleaching the blue carpet beneath it a dingy yellow.

"My dad said you could probably make our entire liquor cabinet disappear if someone didn't keep an eye on you," Jimmy said.

Rudge glowed at the compliment. It had been many years since he'd practiced the illusion of the vanishing furniture, but it was good to know he was still remembered for it. "That is a particularly advanced glamour," Rudge said. "Perhaps we should start with a smaller miracle and work our way up."

"Whatever," Jimmy said. "Can you tell me what my dad did on his last business trip to Omaha that made my mom so mad?"

"What kind of magic is that?" Rudge said.

"The kind the other guy is doing."

Jimmy pointed out through the glass sliding door to the far end of the backyard, where the entire troop of ten-year-olds had clustered around a skinny, badly dressed man, who barely looked older than them, and his slightly better-dressed sidekick. As the interloper pressed his fingers deep into his forehead as if in communication with the Great Beyond, Rudge realized where he had seen him before—in the crowd at the Fortress of Magic.

With a shiver of disgust, Rudge realized what he must be dealing with—a pair of those self-styled "bad boys of magic." Sure they were bad boys, in the same sense that basal cell carcinomas could be considered the "bad boys" of the metabolism. They had no respect for the Art. Their only interest was self-promotion. They froze themselves in ice cubes or buried themselves in glass coffins or hung by their toes for a month over Niagara Falls, and they had the temerity to call those stunts magic. They were acts of endurance, of self-immolation, of stupidity—but there was absolutely nothing magical about them.

These impostors had taken over almost every corner of the business. They sucked up all the increasingly rare TV time dedicated to professional magic. They got the best showroom bookings. They got the covers of all the trade papers. But there was one corner they would not steal from the true artists of the profession. They could not steal away the wonder in the eyes of children. Rudge would not allow it.

Barnaby Rudge marched out of the house and across the yard to where the interlopers stood surrounded by second graders. He pushed through the throng of children and glared at the bad boy with a stare that had paralyzed tigers in Bombay.

It took the bad boy a moment to acknowledge his presence, no doubt trying to figure out how to save face now that he'd been confronted by his superior. Instead, he bent down to one of the kids. "Your teacher thinks you're a genius and your parents want to send you to a special school for advanced students," he said. "And now you're terrified because the only reason you've done so well on tests is that you found copies of the teachers' editions of all your books in a thrift store and you've been cheating all year."

The kid gaped up at him. He looked as if he wanted to deny the charges; then he broke down. "What do I do?" he whispered.

"I read auras; I don't tell futures," the bad boy said. "But I'm pretty sure the advanced school textbooks have teachers' editions, too."

The kid brightened again, and the bad boy searched the crowd for his next victim. Rudge stepped forward.

"Out, fraud," Rudge boomed, an accusing finger in the bad boy's face.

The interloper shrank back under the force of Rudge's disapprobation. "Do not evict me, oh great wizard," the interloper begged. "I seek only to learn at the feet of the master."

At least that's what he meant to say, Rudge could tell from the quaver in his voice. The actual words were closer to "Say, how do you get rabbit pee out of gold lamé anyway?" but Rudge knew that one question would lead to another, and soon he would be begging for all the secrets of the magician's art. Rudge's will began to weaken. The Eisenstein boy was pretty young to take on as an apprentice; this new one was old enough to drive to the liquor store to do Rudge's shopping when it was necessary. And he came with a sidekick, whom he could turn into a valuable ally if the student ever turned on the master. Best of all, the newcomer was doing a pretty good job of entertaining the children, which meant that Jimmy's father would have no grounds for cutting Rudge's negotiated fee for the appearance.

"Your act has promise, young wizard," Rudge said, and waited for the glow of joy to spread across his incipient assistant's face. "If you choose, you may study with me. I can teach you to take it to the next level—and all the way to the highest level."

"Like you did with the Martian Magician?" the young man said, an awestruck tone cleverly hidden under a veneer of stylish cynicism.

Perhaps that was meant as praise. After all, that green thug was the highest-grossing act on the Vegas Strip. But the very thought that he would have anything to do with the villain who was destroying stage magic forever was enough to undo an entire week's worth of blood pressure medication.

Still, if this young pup was impressed by Marvin the Martian, Rudge could use that to teach him some of the higher skills. Let the kid think he was going to follow the fake's lead, and meanwhile teach him the real art. By the time class was over, his pupil would understand why the momentarily popular act was such a catastrophe.

"Well, yes," Rudge said. "Everything he knows, he learned from me."

The bad boy leaned close to Rudge, his face glowing with admiration. His eyes seemed to take in every inch of the magician's face, then his body. And then there was some kind of shift that Rudge couldn't understand, but he seemed to be appraising Rudge's very soul.

"I knew it," the youth said. "There was no way that someone could perform a miracle like the Dissolving Man without learning it all at the feet of a master."

"That is very perspicacious," Rudge said. "Your mind is strong and clear."

"And then he rode that illusion he stole from you to the top of the entertainment industry without giving you the credit you so richly deserve," he continued. "How justifiably enraged you were, how righteous in your fury. Not because you wanted that kind of money and fame for yourself, of course, but because he was damaging the art form."

"Yes," Rudge said.

"But you saw one way to stop him before he destroyed the entire world of stage magic," the youth said. "You would use the very trick he stole from you against him. You would expose him on stage as a fraud and a charlatan, and he would slink off, back into anonymity forever."

"I, um, what?" Rudge said. This was sounding less and less like an eager acolyte heaping praise on his new master.

"Because only you, Barnaby Rudge, knew the secret of the green man's water tank. Only you were wizard enough to sabotage it," he said.

"And what a brilliant way to ruin your rival." It was the sidekick talking now. "Up on stage in front of every important magician working today. With one little flick of your wrist, you would kill his act forever."

"Too bad you accidentally killed that chubby guy, too," the youth said. "That's even worse than when your pigeon died inside the top hat."

"The pigeon was just resting," Rudge said quickly, looking around to see if the goons from the SPCA had started following him again. "I chose not to disturb her sleep, so I moved on to the next illusion."

"So you didn't kill your bird, but you admit you killed the chubby man," the youth said.

"No," Rudge said. "I didn't. I couldn't. I don't even know who he was. I never saw him before."

"You didn't have to see him, because it was murder by remote control," the sidekick said. "While everyone was partying at the Fortress, you slipped into the showroom and sabotaged the tank. Probably just had to fiddle with that latch."

Rudge felt an odd glow of pride. All he had to do was admit to this charge and he would go down in history as the greatest practitioner of stage magic since Houdini—the man who gave P'tol P'kah his greatest illusion, and then, when he misused it, took it away from him again. But as the glow faded, Rudge remembered that all of Houdini's great talent couldn't save him from a ruptured appendix. In fact, it was his immortal reputation that sent him to an early grave, as some drunken college lout felt compelled to test the magician's claim of a stomach impervious to any blow. If Rudge were sent to prison, there was no doubt what his fate would be. He would be besieged by fellow felons pleading with him to teach them the art of escape. And when they realized that this was not something that could be picked up in an afternoon, but that needed to be studied over decades, their frustration would turn to rage, and that rage would turn against him.

"I couldn't have," Rudge said. "I was in the bar all night until P'tol P'kah stomped in."

"Or you made it appear that you were in the bar."

Rudge reached into his jacket pockets and pulled out receipt after receipt. He threw them in the youth's face. "Look at them," he demanded. "Did I conjure up these bar bills?"

"If you can make a rabbit appear out of thin air, it shouldn't be hard to conjure up a receipt."

"You saw me confront him in the main parlor. How could I have been rigging his device if I was right there?"

"Did we see you?" the faux acolyte said. "Or did you perform some particularly cunning illusion to make us think we saw you?"

"Maybe he has a secret twin brother who stood in for him," the sidekick said. "Or a machine that manufactures clones."

"I don't know any cunning illusions!" The words forced their way out of Rudge's throat before he could stop them. "I do tricks; that's all. Tricks I buy out of some mail-order catalog! I haven't come up with a new gag in two decades!"

Rudge was aware that an entire birthday party's worth of children was staring up at him. He didn't care. Let them stare. It felt astonishingly good to tell the truth.

But the sidekick didn't seem to want to accept it. "You taught P'tol P'kah the Vanishing Man."

"I taught him nothing!" Rudge shouted. "I have no idea how he did that illusion."

"I find that hard to believe," the youth said. "A man of your great talent."

"It's true," Rudge said. "I was desperate to know how he did it. I spent a fortune going to his show, studying it from every angle, searching for the tell. You can ask any of the other magicians."

"How would they know?"

"Because they all did the same thing," Rudge said. "I used to see them at the performances whenever they could scrape together the two-hundred-dollar ticket price. Except for Phlegm, of course."

"What, you wouldn't see the show if you were congested?"

"Phlegm is a person," Rudge said. "At least she claims to be a person. You saw her—that tattooed freak show who sticks knives in her eyeballs."

"You know," the sidekick said, "some people might think it odd for a guy in a gold suit stained with rabbit pee to call anyone else a freak show."

"It's not an insult; it's a fact," Rudge said. "Back in the nineties, she was part of one of those New Vaudeville tours. Her act was Phlegm, the One-Woman Freak Show."

"So she didn't go to see the show to figure out how he did it?"

"Are you kidding?" Rudge said. "She was the only one who didn't buy tickets. She got a job as a cocktail waitress so she could see it twice a night. Still didn't do her any good."

The two bad boys exchanged a glance, as if they were trying to decide if he was telling the truth. Rudge decided to nudge them along.

"P'tol P'kah was the best of us," Rudge pleaded.

"I think before he disappeared for good, some of his peers—so-called peers—were beginning to think he actually did have magical powers. Or was really from Mars. Or anything that would explain how he could actually dissolve in a tank of water. Because no one ever saw through the trick."

"I want to believe you," the youth said. "I really do. But your talent is so great, I can't imagine an act you couldn't duplicate, or even improve on, with just a little effort."

"No, please, you have to believe me," Rudge said. "The last time I actually earned my fee was during the Reagan administration."

The youth and his sidekick seemed to think it over; then they both shrugged. "Nah," the sidekick said, "we can't see that. Not after the brilliant show you put on this afternoon."

"It wasn't brilliant," Rudge pleaded. "It couldn't even keep the attention of a bunch of second graders. My dove died of alcohol poisoning. My rabbit ruined the carpet."

"We all know misdirection is the secret of any great magician's art."

"I've got proof!" Rudge said, suddenly remembering. "I videotaped every one of P'tol P'kah's performances that I saw."

Now both the youth and the sidekick looked interested. Rudge pressed his point. "I can give them to you. I can take you to them right after the party."

For a moment, the youth looked like he was going to give in. Then his face hardened. "I think we should go now."

"Why?"

The youth pointed back at the house, where Jimmy Eisenstein's father was storming out through the glass door, carrying the still-dripping rabbit cage. Behind him, there was a path of bleached drops on the carpet.

"You drive," Rudge said.

Chapter Fifteen

"VHS?" Gus looked down at the huge pile of videocassettes on the desk in front of them. "Who uses VHS tapes anymore?"

"Probably someone who earned his last three-digit paycheck right after they stopped making the Betamax." Shawn was on his back, reaching up behind the credenza on which the TV sat, searching with his hands for a free set of inputs to which he could attach the rented video player. With a grunt, he managed to force the jacks into their sockets, then stood up and pushed the credenza back against the wall.

"Ready for the magic," Shawn said. "And by 'magic,' I mean a crummy video of some cheap stage trick."

"Are you back to that?" Gus said, walking over to the machine and slipping in a tape. "Because I saw your face after the Dissolving Man. You were as amazed as anyone else."

Gus pressed PLAY, but all the TV showed was a screen full of snow. Shawn was about to dive back behind the credenza when there was a clunk as the tape reached its end and started to rewind.

"First of all," Shawn said, "I thought I was quite clear that any amazement I might have been registering was dedicated almost entirely to the sight of the chubby dead guy floating in the tank."

"Almost entirely?"

"I'm being honest," Shawn said. "I was also amazed that people pay two hundred bucks to sit through that act."

"So now you're going to tell me you know how he disappeared?" Gus said.

"I haven't figured it out yet, but I will," Shawn said. "And when I do, everyone who was impressed is going to feel pretty stupid."

"What is it with you and stage magic?" Gus said.

"It's a fake."

Gus stifled the desire to say "and so are you"—first, because Shawn was completely aware of that, and second, because he was interested in the answer to his question and didn't want to see the conversation spin out in another direction.

"Luke Skywalker's a fake," Gus said. "Batman's a fake. Bugs Bunny's a fake. He doesn't even look like a real rabbit, but that doesn't stop you from laughing every time he dresses up as a woman and kisses Elmer Fudd."

"Because there's no one standing outside the theater saying, 'Come in here and see a real rabbit dressed as a human seducing a bald guy,'" Shawn said. "Which is just as well, because if they did, everyone involved would end up in prison."

"So your entire problem with stage magic is that people pretend it's real magic?"

Before Shawn could answer, there was a thunk from the VCR as the tape finished rewinding. Shawn grabbed the rental remote and hit PLAY. The machine whirred into life, a sideways green triangle appeared in the upper-right corner of the frame, but the rest of the screen stayed black.

"That's great," Gus said. "He's probably been storing his tapes next to his magnet collection."

"Worse," Shawn said. "Look."

Gus peered at the screen and saw a tiny pinhole of light in the center. The hole was moving, bobbing up and down in a jerky motion. "What is that?"

"I'm guessing it's the buttonhole in a raincoat," Shawn said. "You can sort of see the stitching around the edges."

Gus went to the TV and brought his eyes a couple of inches away from the screen. There were stitches around the sides of the image.

"He recorded the entire act through his buttonhole?" Gus said.

"That would explain why he taped it so many times," Shawn said. "Maybe he got a different inch of the tank every time and he was planning on stitching them together later."

Gus was reaching for the EJECT button when the lighted hole stopped moving around on the screen, and then went out altogether. After a moment of blackness, the TV was filled with the image of P'tol P'kah's stage set, the water-filled tank at the back.

"That's a little better," Shawn said. "As long as he doesn't need to hide the camera from security again."

The edges of the screen went dark as the houselights went down, and a roar of applause came through the

TV speakers. After a moment, the green giant stomped out onto the stage. He was every bit as compelling on the small screen as he had been in person, Gus was surprised to discover, and his presence just as strong.

P'tol P'kah lifted his mammoth green arms for silence, and then started rushing around the stage faster than any human could do. It wasn't magical; it wasn't scary. If anything, the Martian's movements seemed comical. It seemed like a strange strategy for someone who understood stagecraft as well as he did. And then Gus realized that the speed wasn't P'tol P'kah's doing.

"Stop fast-forwarding," Gus said, reaching to snatch the remote out of Shawn's hands. "I want to see this."

"What we need to see is the Dissolving Man," Shawn said. "That's the end of the act. And while I'm sure our client would be happy if P'erry P'mason could get people to fork over two hundred bucks for a three-minute show, I'm going to bet we've got a long way to go until we get there."

"Maybe I'd like to see his other tricks," Gus said.

"Maybe you'd like your name on the building," Shawn said. "Then you could say how we run our investigations. But since it's my name on the building, I get to decide."

"Your name is not on this building," Gus said.

"I didn't say which building my name is on," Shawn said.

"Sorry, I must have forgotten about the Shawn Spencer Towers downtown," Gus said.

"It so happens that my name graces one of the finest examples of Spanish Revival architecture in Santa Barbara," Shawn said.

"Which one?"

"The police station," Shawn said.

"The police station is now named for you?"

"I didn't say it was named for me. I said my name was on it," Shawn said. "And it is. Prominently in blue marker."

"Because you put it there," Gus said. "You wrote 'Jules Hearts Shawn' on the back wall by the Dumpster and then spent the next day trying to scrub it off before anyone could see it. And when you finally realized what indelible really meant, you took the 'Reserved for Head Detective' sign off Lassiter's parking space and covered it up."

"Only until such time as the statement can be determined to be completely accurate," Shawn said. "I'm a stickler for facts when I deface public property. Anyway, that's not why we're not going to stop fast-forwarding before we get to the Dissolving Man."

"So what is?"

"The fact that we're already there." Shawn pressed PLAY just as P'tol P'kah wheeled a more ornate version of the airplane steps up to his tank. "At two hundred bucks a head, you'd think he could afford an assistant to help with the manual labor."

Gus stared at the screen, transfixed, as P'tol P'kah performed his signature illusion. He tried to make himself study the act for flaws, for the momentary bit of distraction that would reveal the real secret of the trick, but he kept getting lost in the spectacle. It was almost as astonishing to see the Martian dissolve on video as it was live. As it had in the Fortress, the performance ended with a great explosion of light and sound. The video image flamed into white as the sudden brightness overwhelmed the camera's sensors. But this time when the image came back, just as the house-lights were rising, there was an audible gasp from the audience, and then a burst of applause.

"What's happening?" Gus asked. "I can't see anything."

That wasn't entirely true. He could still see the stage. But the tank was empty—no chubby corpses this time—and the stage itself was deserted. What was it the crowd was seeing?

Even Shawn looked frustrated. "Come on, you moron," he muttered to the cameraman. "Show us something."

As if responding to Shawn's irritation, the camera jerked around the showroom, giving them a good view of the audience, all of whom were staring up at the ceiling. Some were pointing. Finally the camera lens followed their gaze and tilted straight up.

P'tol P'kah hung by his palms from the ceiling, his hands apparently adhering to the slick surface. To the gasps of the crowd, he pulled one hand free and reached out to grab one of the free-hanging lights. It gently lowered him to the floor, where he stood perfectly still while the audience went wild around him.

"Wow," Gus said. "It's even better when he finishes it."

"You really think so?" Shawn said. "I kind of like the dead guy. You don't see that in a lot of acts."

"And you do see this?"

Shawn stared at the screen. "What's that?"

"Umm, a giant green man dissolving in a tank of water and reappearing on the ceiling, thirty feet in the air?" Gus said.

"No, that." Shawn froze the image, then walked over

to the TV. He pointed at the bottom-right corner, which was filled by an out-of-focus black blob.

"Somebody's head?" Gus guessed. The fact was, it could have been almost anything.

"Give me another tape," Shawn commanded, and when Gus was too slow to move, he grabbed the entire stack off the desk and brought them over to the TV. He ejected the tape they'd been watching and slapped in another one. This one, too, hadn't been rewound. Shawn hit PLAY, and before it could begin to rewind automatically, he began searching manually.

After a moment of static, the image resolved into a scene almost identical to what they'd just seen, only this time a reversed P'tol P'kah was riding the light fixture back up to the ceiling. Shawn studied the image closely, and then froze it.

"There," he said, rapping a spot near the bottom of the screen. "What does that look like to you?"

Gus squinted at the TV. There was something black and rounded blocking part of the camera's view. "It looks like the top part of an igloo," Gus said after careful and serious study.

"Yes, Gus, that's exactly what it is," Shawn said. "Someone came to see a magic show with an igloo on his head. You've really cracked this case wide open."

"On his head?" Gus peered at the TV again. From the angle of Rudge's camera, of course this thing had to be on the head of another spectator, which meant that it couldn't be an igloo. It had to be . . . "A hat?"

"A bowler hat," Shawn said, hitting the EJECT button and slapping in another tape. "I'd be willing to bet that it's *the* bowler hat."

Shawn claimed to see the bowler in the crowd on the

next two tapes as well, although Gus wasn't completely sure. But on the third, as P'tol P'kah took his bows in the crowd, a cocktail waitress dressed as a spacegirl passed close enough to Rudge to jostle the camera, and in the fleeting instant that the lens was pointed away from the Martian, they got a clean shot.

"That's him," Gus said, staring at the living image of the man they'd last seen being hauled out of the water tank. He was wearing the same three-piece suit along with the bowler and he was every bit as chubby in life as he was in death.

"Yes, it is," Shawn said. "Just like it was on the last five tapes."

"So whoever this guy was, he showed up at every performance," Gus said. "Just like the other magicians. Do you think he was one of them, and he drowned trying to figure out the secret of the trick?"

"None of the others recognized him," Shawn said.

"None of the others admitted they recognized him," Gus corrected. "Maybe they were covering up for him."

"Covering up for what?" Shawn said. "Whether or not they said anything, he was still going to be dead. No, I believe they never saw him before."

"But he was at this show all the time, just like the rest of them," Gus said. "They would have seen him in the audience."

"Not if they were focusing all their attention on trying to figure out how P'laster of P'aris was doing his trick," Shawn said. "Or at least whichever part of their attention they weren't focusing on themselves."

"So who is he and what's he doing there?" Gus said, studying the man.

"Looking for Tucker Mellish."

Gus tried to remember where he had heard that name before, but for some reason when he tried, his mind was filled with the image of an exploding purple ink blot. "Who?"

"Tucker Mellish, the guy I made up," Shawn said. "Remember the acid in the face?"

Gus did remember now, although he almost hated to admit it. He would have liked to be able to banish Shawn's most ludicrous flights of fantasy from his head forever, instead of carting them around with all the other bits of trivia that had stuck there.

"He was the fugitive from justice who was cannily hiding out from the law by painting himself green and appearing in front of a thousand people every night, right?" Gus said.

"And twice on Sunday."

"And Chubby Dead Guy's been looking for him," Gus said.

"Exactly," Shawn said. "He's been searching the country with no luck. But just when he's about to give up the hunt, he happens to read about the hot new act on the Strip. It sounds like something Mellish used to do, or to talk about, back before he did whatever terrible thing he did. So he plays a hunch, buys a ticket to Vegas, and comes to the show every night, looking for some bit of evidence that will be enough to get a judge to issue a warrant to let him look under the green paint."

"Somebody must have wanted this Mellish pretty bad, because Chubby Dead Guy has already racked up a thousand bucks on show tickets just in the first five tapes we pulled," Gus said.

"That's the trouble with law enforcement today," Shawn said. "All this obsession with money. Did anyone ever ask Inspector Gerard for receipts when he was tracking Dr. Richard Kimble? Did Jack McGee need to submit expense reports when he was closing in on the Incredible Hulk?"

"Jack McGee was a reporter," Gus said.

"That's it!" Shawn said suddenly.

"What's it?"

"The dead guy," Shawn said. "He's Jack McGee. And the green guy isn't a Martian at all. He's the Incredible Hulk."

"The Hulk. P'tol P'kah is the Incredible Hulk."

"You said yourself the act was incredible," Shawn said.

"I also said it was amazing, but that doesn't make him Spiderman," Gus said. "In fact, I'm going to state categorically that simply because I use an adjective to describe something, that doesn't mean it shares all the properties of every other thing anyone has ever used that adjective about."

"Really?" Shawn said. "I'm giving you a chance to track down a killer superhero and you want to quibble about grammar?"

"What I want is to figure out what happened to P'tol P'kah," Gus said. "And how Chubby Dead Guy ended up that way."

"I suspect half of that comes from too many between-meal snacks."

Shawn ejected the videotape and slapped a new one into the player. He searched backward through the entire tape, but neither of them could see a hint of a bowler anywhere.

"Maybe it's before the chubby guy tracked him down," Gus said.

"No way to tell," Shawn said, "because Rudge's unique system of dating his tapes seems to consist of measuring the decay of any radioactive particles that might have wandered into the plastic."

Gus flipped through the pile of tapes on the floor. None of them was dated, or labeled in any way. He grabbed one at random and handed it to Shawn.

"Maybe we'll have better luck with this one."

Shawn ejected the Chubby Dead Guy–free tape and tossed it back on the desk, then inserted a new one into the player. Unlike the rest of them, this one wasn't wound quite to the end, as if Rudge had finally gotten sick of torturing himself by watching the trick he could never hope to master. Shawn pressed PLAY and then FAST-FORWARD so they could zip through most of the act. Even at top speed, Gus was astonished by the Dissolving Man, although he was quick to point out to himself that this in no way was meant to suggest that P'tol P'kah was one of the X-Men. As he had seen happen in each of the previous five tapes, the Martian Magician dissolved in a final burst of light and sound, and then reappeared on the ceiling. This must have been recorded during one of Rudge's later visits, because he knew exactly where to point the camera to catch the entire descent. Constant practice gave the image a smooth flow as it tracked P'tol P'kah down to the ground.

But when the Martian Magician reached the floor, something was very different. This time the green man didn't lift his arms to encourage a new wave of applause. Instead, he landed heavily on his enormous black boots and, staring at a spot across the showroom floor, bared his sharpened teeth in a terrifying growl.

"What's that about?" Shawn said.

Gus' first instinct was to turn the TV so that they could see whatever had made P'tol P'kah so angry. Fortunately, Rudge apparently shared that instinct. The camera swiveled so fast, the entire audience was reduced to a blur of color, then swung back to find its target—and the Martian's.

Chubby Dead Guy, in all his Chubby Aliveness, stood rooted to his spot on the floor, staring across the room with a look of fear on his face. No doubt this was the result of being confronted by P'tol P'kah's fierce grimace. It looked like he was so scared he was actually crying. Tears dripped down his face. But as Gus leaned closer to the TV, he realized there was too much liquid for it to be tears, especially since it seemed to be running down from his hairline.

"Is it raining in there?" Gus said.

"If it is, it's only because the hailstorm has stopped," Shawn said, pointing at the top of Chubby Dead Guy's head, where two small cubes of ice were zipping around the brim of his bowler.

"Then either he's been bobbing for apples with his hat on, or someone threw a drink in his face," Gus said.

"And I can guess who that might have been." Shawn froze the image and then framed it back until Gus could see a flash of spacegirl silver right where Chubby Dead Guy's hand was disappearing out of the frame.

"Jack McGee is a lech?" Gus said.

"Let's find out."

Shawn pressed the FRAME ADVANCE button and let

the tape jerk forward. Chubby Dead Guy blinked water out of his eyes, but he couldn't stop staring across the showroom at the spot where Shawn and Gus knew P'tol P'kah was brandishing fangs at him. He was so shocked, he seemed not to notice his hand, which, as the camera jiggled, was revealed to still be planted on the silver derriere of his space waitress. And then the camera swiveled back to the Martian Magician, who stomped his enormous black boots as he snarled.

"I don't understand what we're seeing," Gus said.

"If I had to make a stab at it, I'd say that Chubby Dead Guy was taking advantage of the green guy's surprise appearance to cop a feel from the cocktail waitress," Shawn said.

"And she threw a drink at him, right," Gus said. "But why is P'tol P'kah so angry?"

"This goes back to my original theory," Shawn said.

"He's the Phantom of the Opera and Chubby Dead Guy stole his music so he could make the cocktail waitress a star?"

"Okay, not exactly my original theory," Shawn conceded. "But a refinement of it. The green guy is running from the police because he committed a crime, but it was a crime for the greater good. He stole a meat loaf to feed his starving child. But he was caught and sentenced to prison, where he suffered for many long years. Then, when he was released, he went back to his life of crime, pursued by an obsessed detective. At the end of his rope, he was given shelter by a kindly priest, but he repaid this generosity by stealing all his silver. But when he was caught, the priest told the police—"

"This is not a refinement of any theory you've had so far," Gus said. "It's a brand-new theory. Except it's not really new because you're stealing it from *Les Misérables*."

"What country was *Les Miz* published in?" Shawn said.

"France."

"And *Phantom of the Opera*?"

"Also France," Gus said. "So what?"

"So it's the same theory. I just grabbed the wrong book off the French literature shelf," Shawn said. "Like that's never happened to you."

"Maybe you could theorize that P'tol P'kah is actually a red balloon or Babar, King of the Elephants," Gus said. "They're from French books, too. And they've got about as much to do with this case as anything you've said."

"Only because you're not paying attention," Shawn said. "Here's what I'm saying: The green guy is a fugitive from justice, but he's actually a good guy. And the one thing that makes him angry is seeing the poor and weak being preyed on by the rich and powerful."

"Then he's got to be in a bad mood pretty much all the time, living in Las Vegas," Gus said.

"Anyway, he's out there, doing his act, lowering himself into the audience on his lamp cord, and what does he see? Some creep in a three-piece suit and a bowler hat, the very essence of upper-class snobbery, grabbing the ass of a poor cocktail waitress, using sexuality as a weapon to assert his socioeconomic status over hers."

Gus stared at him. "Where did you get that from?"

"One of the beat cops always leaves his copy of *The Nation* in the police station men's room," Shawn said.

"And you read it?"

"Sure. And I learned a lot from the experience," Shawn said.

"Like what?"

"That it actually is possible for a magazine to be so boring you can't even read it on the toilet," Shawn said. "Anyway, the green guy sees this terrible atrocity happening across the showroom and he flies into a rage."

Gus thought that one over for a moment, then shook his head. "A cocktail waitress in one of those outfits is going to get her ass grabbed every thirty seconds in a casino showroom," Gus said. "If P'tol P'kah flew into a rage every time he witnessed it, he'd never have a moment free to dissolve."

"Good point," Shawn said. "And it's hard for me to imagine this entire case revolving around gender politics, anyway, no matter what Katrina vanden Heuvel might think. So maybe I got it backward. Chubby Dead Guy grabs the waitress; she throws her drink in his face; a big chunk of the crowd turns to see what's going on—"

Gus tried to visualize the scene and immediately understood what Shawn was suggesting. "P'tol P'kah sees that half his audience isn't paying attention to him the way they should, so he turns to find out what's taking their eyes off him—" Gus broke off, feeling excitement flooding through his body. This case was actually beginning to make sense for the first time.

"And he sees the man who's been chasing him for all these months," Shawn said. "He's caught. So now he's got a choice. He's built up this new life for himself, he's making ridiculous amounts of money, he's got the biggest act on the Strip, and now it's all going to come to an end. He's got to flee, or be exposed."

"But he's got to know if Chubby Dead Guy was able to track him down here, there's nowhere he'll ever be able to hide completely," Gus said. "He'll be giving everything up, and he'll get nothing in return."

"Which is when he hatches the plan," Shawn said. "He arranges the performance at the Fortress of Magic, knowing that Chubby Dead Guy is going to follow him there. He sets a trap for his victim and kills him, leaving the body in his tank as his final salute to the world of stage magic. And then he takes off his makeup and slips away into the night."

It felt good. It felt right. It felt like victory. Shawn and Gus enjoyed the glow.

"I think we've solved this puppy," Shawn said. "Chalk up another win for the home team."

Gus felt his glow start to slip away. "You do realize we haven't actually solved anything yet."

"I'm willing to concede there are still a few loose ends."

"Like who P'tol P'kah really is and what he was running from," Gus said.

"Details."

"And who Chubby Dead Guy worked for and why he was searching for him."

"Technicalities," Shawn said.

"How he managed to kill Chubby Dead Guy and disappear in front of a hundred witnesses with no one witnessing anything."

"Trifles."

"Why the federal government is involved in this case."

"I'm running out of different ways to minimize your

point," Shawn said. "Could you just lump the rest of your objections into one?"

Gus could. "How about the one thing we were specifically hired to find out," he said. "Where P'tol P'kah is."

"Okay, so there are a few loose middles to go along with the loose ends," Shawn said. "But we have a working theory, and that's half the battle."

"We've already had about ten working theories," Gus said. "So that means we've won five battles. And we're still no closer to figuring this out than we were before."

"Not true at all," Shawn said. "For the first time we can question someone who's actually talked to Chubby Dead Guy and can tell us who he was."

"We can?"

Shawn nodded. "The cocktail waitress."

"They must have a million cocktail waitresses at Outer Space," Gus said. "And they're all dressed exactly alike. So how are we going to figure out which one this is?"

"We already know," Shawn said.

Before Gus could object, Shawn framed the tape forward. At first Gus couldn't understand what Shawn was trying to show him. And then, after a half dozen frames, Gus saw it. As the camera started to whir back over to P'tol P'kah, it caught a brief flash of the spacegirl's arm.

The spacegirl's arm and the tattooed reptiles running up and down it.

Chapter Sixteen

"Who knew there was so much money in the human freak show business?" Shawn said. "How many eyeballs do you have to poke out to buy a three-million-dollar castle?"

They were parked in Gus' Echo, outside a grand Spanish mansion high on a hill overlooking the sparkling Pacific.

"Maybe we've got the wrong house," Gus said, checking the paper in his hand against the tiled address sign set into the long white wall. They matched, but that didn't mean there wasn't a mistake earlier in the information chain.

"Impossible," Shawn said.

"Why?"

"Because it was too hard to get this one," Shawn said. "If it's wrong, we have to start all over again and I refuse to do that."

It had been hard—much harder than either of them would have guessed. It seemed like a safe bet that a woman who was covered in tattoos, called herself Phlegm, the Human Freak Show, and made her living by plunging knives into her eyes would be fairly easy to track down. At least there wouldn't be too much trouble confusing her with any of the other Phlegm, the Human Freak Shows in the phone book. And odds were she'd probably have a pretty good Web presence so that America's legion of knife-in-the-eyeball fans would know where to look for her next performance.

But aside from a couple of fleeting mentions in articles lamenting the failure of the New Vaudeville movement back in the mid-1990s—and a couple more celebrating that failure—they couldn't find any trace of her. They tried to get her information from the membership secretary at the Fortress of Magic, but that august executive insisted she was sworn to secrecy. Even after Shawn and Gus had successfully bribed her with a coupon for two dollars off two pizzas that had come in the mail that day—apparently the Fortress of Magic was not generous with its employees' paychecks—she had been unable to find any listing for Phlegm. Gus had insisted she try a long list of alternate spellings of the word, but the closest the records came was someone named Don Flegman, and he'd died around the same time as disco. They even trolled the seedier parts of State Street on the off chance that she was performing next to the buskers, three-card monte dealers, and charcoal artists peddling sketches of Jimi Hendrix, but no one they talked to had ever heard of an act anything like hers.

Finally, Shawn announced that they would have to call their client. After all, he had employed Phlegm as a cocktail waitress. Gus was nervous about the prospect,

figuring that if they didn't bother Fleck, he might forget he'd hired any detectives and not feel compelled to
destroy them if they were unable to solve the case to
his satisfaction. But as Shawn pointed out cheerfully, a
mogul who once sued a contractor into bankruptcy for
using the wrong brand of Navajo White paint on his
maid's room's ceiling was probably not going to forget
about the two private detectives who'd eaten his lobster and purpled his white carpet.

Fortunately for Gus' nerves, when they called the
number Fleck had given them, the line was answered
by one of his many assistants, an efficient-sounding
young woman who introduced herself as Sandy But-
ler, Associate Assistant to the Assistant Associate. And
when they explained what they were looking for, the
AAttAA assured them it would be neither necessary
nor wise to trouble the big man over something this
minor. She could handle it herself. All she needed was
a name.

That, of course, was the sticking point, because
there was little chance that their subject had applied
for—and gotten—a cocktail waitress position under
the name Phlegm, the Human Freak Show. Sandy ran
a check of the personnel files just to make sure, but
there were no listings for Phlegm or any other type of
mucus in the system.

They were stuck. One woman seemed to hold their
first major clue in this case, and they had no way to find
her—or at least no way that wasn't going to require a
huge amount of work.

"I guess we're going to have to do this the hard way,"
Shawn said into the speakerphone. "If we give you a
couple of dates, can you send us a list of all the cocktail

waitresses who were working then? We'll track them all down until we find the right one."

"I can," Sandy said. "But maybe you'd like me to narrow that list down a little first?"

"Narrow it how?" Gus said.

"Hair color, eye color, height, weight, bra size, place of residence, distinguishing physical characteristics, marital status, citizenship status, food allergies, medical history, legal history, educational history, financial history, sexual history, birth date, birth weight, astrological sign, number of parking tickets paid or unpaid, associations, clubs, political party, Netflix queue, fashion sense, common sense, pets by breed, pets by name, siblings, race, religion, church attendance, favorite book, favorite movie—"

"Wait a minute," Gus said. "Fleck keeps that much information on his employees?"

"Our background investigations are extremely thorough," Sandy said, a hint of pride leaking through her businesslike tone. "Speaking of which, you might want to pop down to Santa Barbara City Hall today. And bring cash. The parking ticket you received at 1637 State Street is exactly one month old, and after tomorrow, late fees are going to kick in."

"I don't know what I find more troubling," Gus said, "that you keep all this information in your database, or that it isn't even correct. I haven't gotten any parking tickets in the last month."

"I'm looking at a digital copy of it on my screen right now," Sandy said. "Apparently you told the ticketing officer that you were a doctor and you had stopped for an emergency. When she pointed out that you were parked in front of a BurgerZone franchise and were walking out eating a Triple Triple, you told her you were a doctor of burgerology and that the emergency was a sudden pickle intervention."

"I never—" Gus broke off. He turned to glare at Shawn, who was gazing calmly out the window, as if he hadn't heard a word of the conversation. "Did you borrow the Echo again without asking?"

"That's a good question," Shawn said. "If I don't ask first, can it really be called borrowing? It's actually much closer to theft. But since I always bring it back as soon as I'm done, technically it's joyriding. And how can we object to any activity that brings a little joy into this cold, hard world?"

Gus had plenty of ways to object, and several of them involved clubbing Shawn about the head and neck with blunt instruments. But he was a professional, and he knew that the worst thing they could do was argue in front of the client. Or even the Associate Assistant to the client's Assistant Associate. "Shawn will make sure to pay the ticket today. Thanks for the heads-up."

"No problem," Sandy said. "You can also let him know that his teeth are past due for a cleaning."

"Oh, I'll definitely make sure he knows about that," Gus said.

Shawn ignored Gus' smile and leaned into the speakerphone. "Did you say you can search your database for distinguishing physical characteristics?"

"Moles, freckles, dimples, wrink—"

"How about tattoos?"

"Words or pictures?"

"Pictures," Shawn said. "Snakes."

"Location?"

"Arms. Upper chest. Possibly lower chest, but we don't know for sure."

They could hear a keyboard rattling as Sandy typed in the information.

"Got a pencil?" she said.

According to the database, Phlegm's real name was Jessica Higgenbotham, and she lived on a street Shawn and Gus had never heard of. When they consulted a Google map, they understood why. It was a brand-new street in a brand-new development of brand-new mansions. This seemed odd even at the time, since they couldn't imagine either of Phlegm's careers bringing in enough cash to pay for luxury housing. But maybe the city had demanded that the developer throw in a couple of "affordable" units, the going exchange rate for permission to erect a fleet of multimillion dollar eyesores on the area's rapidly diminishing store of open space.

After a quick stop at city hall to pay the parking ticket, they drove up into the hills above Santa Barbara until they found a hilltop that had been carved off, leveled, and dotted with pink Mediterranean villas. They drove right through the development, assuming that the handful of lower-priced homes or apartments would be as far from the breathtaking ocean views as possible without actually being located underground. But the houses stayed just as grand all the way back, and the only people who looked like they might qualify for subsidized, affordable housing were the occasional gardeners and pool cleaners.

As they were cruising back toward the entrance, Shawn spotted a sign for Phlegm's street, and they followed it until they reached the number AAttAA Sandy had given them. It was a sprawling, three-story Spanish. The sales brochure had probably called it a hacienda, but in style, size, and intent it was much closer to one of the original missions, designed to intimidate as much as impress.

"Boy, are we in the wrong business," Shawn said. "If I'd only stopped using my eyes to see and started parking knives in them, we could be rich by now."

"All we know is that this is the address Phlegm gave the casino," Gus said. "For all we know, she just picked a street name out of the air."

"I don't know about you, but I've never breathed air that had anything like 49523 Mariposa Del Suerte floating around in it," Shawn said. "If you're going to make up an address, you choose something that sounds generic."

"So maybe she used to babysit for the owners," Gus said.

"Because she'd be such a good role model for the young 'uns," Shawn said.

"Or she cleaned their house or delivered pizza to them or robbed the joint once," Gus said. "Or she works for a real estate agency. There are a million ways she could have come up with this address."

"A million and one," Shawn said. "It could still be that she actually lives here."

Before Gus could answer, Shawn was out of the car and halfway up the long flight of stairs that led to a heavy door, black iron studs planted firmly in old oak. Shawn lifted a ring dangling from a metal lion's mouth and let it fall on an iron strike plate just as Gus stepped up next to him. Gus couldn't imagine how the clank of metal on metal could even penetrate the wood, let alone be heard throughout the dozens of rooms this house must contain. But even as Shawn was reaching to clank the ring again, they heard the unmistakable sound of high heels on tile clacking toward them.

The door swung open silently and Shawn and Gus found themselves facing an elegant blond woman in her early thirties. She was dressed in St. John's finest midrange casual business suit, her hair cascaded down over her shoulders, and the diamonds in her ears, on her ring finger, and around her neck could have purchased the Psych agency's services well into the next millennium.

The woman stared at them, surprised. Gus realized she hadn't come to answer their knock on her door; she was on her way out.

"Can I help you?" the woman said, but it was clear from her tone of voice that even if she had the power to assist them, she was quite certain that she would choose not to exercise it.

"Yes," Shawn said, positioning himself directly in front of her to block her way. "I'm Shawn Spencer, manager of Santa Barbara's finest steak house, the Dead Cow. And this is Rattus Norvegicus, my head dishwasher."

"I don't eat meat and I've never heard of your restaurant," the woman said. "If this is some kind of promotion, I'm not interested. Now, if you'll excuse me, I'm late for a very important meeting."

She stepped out through the door, right where Shawn had been standing. But if he thought he was blocking her, he found himself backing away as she came toward him, as if she were projecting some kind of force field. She pulled the door closed behind her, jiggled the handle to make sure it was locked, then started toward the stairs.

"You could help save this poor man's job," Shawn said, pushing Gus toward her.

"I doubt it," she said, but she hesitated. "What can he possibly have to do with me?"

"Well, you see, in the steak house trade, the chief dishwasher's most important task is to keep track of the steak knives," Shawn said.

"They're very expensive," Gus said. "You'd be surprised how many customers walk out the door with them."

"And in last night's count, we turned up one short," Shawn said. "This is the third one Rattus has lost, and if he can't account for it, that's his job."

The woman stared at them in disbelief. "You're accusing me of stealing a utensil designed for food I never eat from a restaurant where I've never been?"

"Not exactly," Shawn said. "We just think you might have accidentally misplaced it. You know, you meant to put it back on your plate, but instead you jammed it into your eyeball."

Gus studied the woman's face closely for any sign that she knew what Shawn was talking about. He might as well have been studying the iron lion holding the door knocker, for all the change he saw.

"There should be a security patrol coming through the neighborhood any minute," she said. "Please feel free to continue trespassing on my property until they haul you away."

She walked down two steps, then took a sharp left down a path leading to the garage. She reached into her purse and must have hit the button on a remote, because the garage door glided open silently, revealing a sparkling blue Porsche convertible and an empty space where another car would park.

"So much for that lead," Gus said. "Now what do we do?"

"Follow her," Shawn said. "And when we catch up to her, find out about her conversation with Chubby Dead Guy."

"It's not the right woman, Shawn. She gave Fleck a phony address."

"And you say that why?"

"First of all, look at her."

Jessica Higgenbotham was making that easy to do. She'd popped the trunk on the Porsche and was leaning in to get something.

"So she cleans up well," Shawn said.

"And she didn't react at all when you hit her with the knife-in-the-eyeball thing."

"Oh, but she did," Shawn said.

"She didn't even blink."

"Exactly," Shawn said. "You mention something about eyeball injury, and that's exactly what people do. They blink. It's like a guy crossing his legs when you mention the concept of castration. Or fidelity."

"That's ridiculous," Gus said.

"You're probably right," Shawn said with a sigh. "Say, did I ever tell you about the time I went fishing with my dad and this old guy down the pier from us got a hook stuck in his eyeball?"

"What does that have to do with—" Gus broke off, feeling his eyelid fluttering angrily. He slapped a hand over his eye until the blinking reflex passed. "Okay, fine. She's immune to the eyeball thing. And there is a very slight physical resemblance in the features of her face. But the hair's completely different, the voice is completely different, and—"

"And what?" Shawn said.

"And that." The woman dropped her purse in the trunk, then peeled off her suit jacket, revealing a silk tank top underneath—a silk tank top and two long, bare, tanned arms.

"Quick, Gus," Shawn snapped. "To the Psych-mobile!"

Shawn flew down the stairs and was buckled into the passenger seat before Gus got to the car door. Climbing in, Gus started up the car and slapped it into drive.

"Where to?"

Shawn pointed through the windshield at the Porsche zipping down the street. "Follow that overpriced car!"

"She's not the same person."

"Then you've got two choices," Shawn said. "You can follow her and let me make a fool of myself, or you can call Benny Fleck and tell him his database is wrong."

Gus didn't take a second to think over the choices. He slammed his foot down on the gas and the Echo spurted away from the curb.

Chapter Seventeen

They followed the sports car down the steep road past downtown. As it reached the entrance to the 101 South, its blinkers flipped on and the car accelerated onto the freeway.

• "Faster," Shawn commanded. "You're going to lose her."

"Yes, there is that danger," Gus said as he steered the Echo up the on-ramp. "Because it's much harder to spot a bright blue Porsche on four lanes of open freeway than in a maze of twisting streets."

As the ramp leveled off onto the 101, Gus pointed out the windshield. The Porsche was a handful of car lengths ahead of them and three lanes to the left.

"Do you want to tell me now why we're following this woman, or do you want to wait until we're actually in Los Angeles?" Gus said, eyeing the freeway sign that said they were eighty-eight miles away from the city.

"Better yet, why don't you tell me?" Shawn said.

"Because this is your theory, not mine," Gus said. "So you know the reason and I don't."

"Which is why it will be good for me to hear it coming from you," Shawn said. "When I tell myself something, it always sounds like a good idea. When you talk I'm much more objective."

"I think the word you're looking for is 'objectionable,'" Gus said. But he knew that Shawn wouldn't tell him anything until he'd taken at least one solid guess. "Okay, Ms. Phlegm claimed she lived at a house she couldn't possibly afford, so it's definitely a fake address. But it's not the kind of fake address you make up, so it's got to be a house she knows. All right so far?"

"More or less," Shawn conceded.

"And when we got to the fake address, we met a woman who couldn't possibly be described as a human freak show, but who does bear some similarity to the one who sticks knives in her eyeballs."

"So far so good."

"So you have deduced that when she was filling out the cocktail waitress job application, Ms. Phlegm put down her sister's address," Gus said, feeling a small thrill of triumph as he put the pieces together. "And the woman we're following, the one who looks slightly like her, is actually her sister."

"Which means . . ."

"That we're following the sister either in hopes that she'll lead us to our real target, or we're going to confront her again and make her tell us where Phlegm is hiding."

"That's very impressive," Shawn said. "There's only one little piece that's wrong."

"Which one?"

"Remember this morning when we stopped for coffee and you told me to go ahead and get the jelly doughnut because my hips weren't getting fat?"

"Yes."

"Everything after that."

Gus glared at Shawn, but before he could say anything, Shawn shouted in his ear, "Get over."

"If she's going to Los Angeles, isn't it better if we aren't right on her tail?" Gus said, sticking happily in the right lane. "This way she doesn't see us in her rearview, and if she wants to get off, she's got to come over to our lane."

"That's if she's going to Los Angeles," Shawn said. "Or Ventura, or San Diego or Oxnard—or even anywhere else in Santa Barbara. But it's not the case if she's going—" Shawn broke off as he peered up at the car ahead.

"Going where?" Gus said.

"There!"

Shawn grabbed the wheel and shoved it to the left. The Echo flew across three lanes of traffic, barely missing an Escalade and squeezing past a school bus. When the sounds of horns blaring proved to Gus that he was still alive, he cracked open his eyelids to see the Porsche slowing down to take the one left-hand exit remaining on the entire 101 freeway, Hot Springs Road in Montecito. The Echo was close behind.

"How did you know she was going to do that?" Gus asked, working to get his breathing back under control.

"It's amazing what you can figure out if you keep your eyes open while you're driving," Shawn said. "She's turning left up ahead, by the way."

"Yes, I saw the signal."

"And then she's going to make an immediate right," Shawn said.

"And you know that how?"

"The same way a Martian dissolves in a tank of water," Shawn said.

The Porsche turned left half a block ahead of them. By the time the Echo followed, the sports car had disappeared. All they could see were the high stone walls that hid the local multibillionaires on one side of the street from the mere single-billionaires on the other. But when Gus found a side street leading up to the right, he took it and saw their target right in front of them.

"If you even pretend for one second you did that with magic . . . ," Gus warned.

"But it is magic," Shawn said. "The magic of social climbing."

The road jaunted to the left, and Gus saw the Porsche driving through a set of massive wrought-iron gates. A sign over the gates read LITTLE HILLS COUNTRY CLUB.

"Little Hills?" Gus marveled. "Isn't this the most exclusive country club in the country?"

"They like to think they're just particular," Shawn said. "For instance, they completely repealed their 'No Irish need apply' when Ronald Reagan came back to the area to live at the ranch after his presidency."

"Ronald Reagan wasn't Irish," Gus said.

"No, but his great-grandparents were," Shawn said. "And that was a matter of great concern for the membership committee."

The Porsche stopped briefly—almost wistfully, Gus thought—at a sign that directed members toward a parking lot on the left and guests to one on the right, then slid right into the lot.

"Now what?" Gus said as the Porsche pulled into a spot.

Shawn pointed to a narrow road paralleling the guest entrance and a small sign at its mouth reading SERVICE ONLY.

"That way."

Gus steered the Echo down the narrow gravel road. "What are we looking for?"

"We'll know when I see it," Shawn said.

After a couple hundred feet, the road opened up to a plaza ringed by small, Spanish-style buildings.

"Just wait here," Shawn said, and leapt out of the car. He ran into the open bay of what looked like the service station at the never-built Spanish Conquest Land at Disneyworld, grabbed something off a shelf above a couple of partially disassembled golf carts, then threw himself back into the Echo's passenger seat. "Now go, go, go!"

"What was that all about?" Gus said, throwing the car into reverse and backing down the narrow road to the junction.

"Something for snakes," Shawn said, gesturing for Gus to drive into the guest parking lot.

As the Echo made the turn into the lot, the majesty of the Little Hills Country Club spread out in front of them. The golf course ambled over acres of real estate more valuable than anything outside Midtown Manhattan. And rising out of the emerald sward was the clubhouse, a Spanish castle that looked like Papa Bear to the ursine Baby that was the Higgenbotham house. Gus pulled into a space a couple of rows behind the Porsche. "Now what?"

"That."

Jessica Higgenbotham stood by her car, waiting as a tall, handsome man in a polo shirt and khaki shorts walked up to her. She looked up as he clasped his hands on her bare shoulders and leaned down for a quick kiss.

"Is that what this is all about?" Gus said. "Are they having an affair?"

"Is who having an affair?" Shawn said.

"I don't know." Gus realized he had absolutely no idea whom they had been following or whom she was meeting.

"And even if who is having an affair, who is who having an affair with?"

"What?"

"Exactly," Shawn said. "So let's stop spreading those terrible rumors. You should be ashamed of yourself."

Shawn jumped out of the car and walked over to Jessica Higgenbotham and the tall man. Gus locked his car door, then ran to catch up to him.

"We didn't have a chance to finish our conversation," Shawn said. "And I wanted to give you a chance to put things right before your all-important interview."

When Gus was in second grade, one of the other children had gotten overexcited toward the climax of a particularly intense match of tag and had peed in his pants. That was the last time he could remember seeing a look of disgust as intense as the one on Jessica Higgenbotham's face.

"Who's this, honey?" the tall man said, clearly making an effort to stay pleasant until all the facts were in.

"He says he's the chef at some restaurant I've never heard of," Jessica said. "And this other guy is his dishwasher. They showed up at our house and started making ridiculous charges about missing silverware or something."

"And they followed you here?"

"Apparently," she said.

The tall man ran his gaze over Shawn and Gus slowly. "I don't understand why you're harassing my wife," he said in an amiable tone that still managed to convey an undercurrent of menace. "But if your camera crew doesn't appear in two minutes to prove that this is some kind of reality-prank-show gag, I'm going to have to ask club security to hold you until the police arrive."

The tall man took his wife by the elbow and steered her toward the clubhouse.

"I don't have a camera crew," Shawn said. "But I will admit I'm not really a chef."

Shawn and Gus waited for an anxious second. If she kept walking, which everybody in the parking lot knew she should, they would lose their chance to question her. But Shawn's behavior was too outrageous for her to let it go. She pulled her elbow away from her husband's grip and wheeled around on them.

"Then who the hell are you?" she snapped.

"My name, as I told you, is Shawn Spencer," Shawn said calmly. "I run a little private detective agency in town. But I am also the official background investigator for the Little Hills Country Club."

"And who's this guy?" Jessica said with a glance toward Gus. "Your henchman?"

"No, actually he really is my chief dishwasher," Shawn said. "You'd be amazed at how much china gets dirty in this job."

"My name is David Higgenbotham, and I don't see you as being the official anything for the Little Hills Country Club," the tall man said, "because then you would know that denim is not allowed anywhere on club grounds."

"My position forces me to work undercover, Mr. Higgenbotham," Shawn said. "As distasteful as it is to me, sometimes that even means wearing denim on the grounds. Now, I have a few questions for your wife."

"It's a little late," the tall man said. "Jessica's final interview starts in five minutes."

"And that interview can last half an hour or half a day," Shawn said. "It's really up to you at this point. I suppose if it's not important to you that you two are admitted, we have nothing left to say to each other."

The Higgenbothams exchanged a look that told Shawn everything he needed to know. Well, almost everything. The rest he learned when he took a closer look at David and *saw*. Saw the shield in place of a rearing pony on the polo shirt, with a knit fish between two books across its top. Saw the tiny white scars on his hands.

"You've got two minutes," David Higgenbotham said.

"Then I'll skip the boring stuff you know about," Shawn said. "Like the years the two of you spent touring with a vaudeville revival troupe, her as a one-woman freak show and you as the knife thrower."

This was the moment Gus was waiting for—when they laughed in Shawn's face. Because there was simply no way Jessica Higgenbotham was the same tattooed woman they'd seen the other night. And David? He looked as if he'd been bred in a special pen somewhere in a compound on Kennebunkport or Martha's Vineyard. His anticipation of seeing Shawn acknowledge that he was wrong and Gus was right would almost be worth all the time they'd wasted on these two.

But David Higgenbotham didn't laugh in Shawn's face. He didn't turn up his nose in disgust or wrinkle his brow in confusion.

"The admissions committee knows all about our past," David said. "We were completely up-front about it. And they don't have a problem with it. As they explained, they're all past fifty, which means their late-teen and early-adult years were in the 1960s. They know all about youthful indiscretion."

Gus couldn't believe what he was hearing. Or, more accurately, what he was seeing. Or even more accurately, what he wasn't seeing. He was staring at Jessica's arms and seeing nothing but smooth, tanned, beautiful skin.

"And when you gave up performing, you got your MBA at Wharton, and you've been a respectable member of society ever since," Shawn said.

"If you consider CFO of the Central Coast's largest telecommunications start-up to be respectable," David said. "Now, what's this all about?"

"We just need to confirm that neither of you has been performing lately," Shawn said. "There have been rumors of a New Vaudeville revival, and if you're thinking of being part of it, you can't be part of us."

"Absolutely not," David said. "We made a pact when we moved into the straight world that this is where we would live forever. And to prove that, we both went through endless hours of incredible pain having our tattoos removed. Isn't that right, honey?"

Jessica's face had gone pale. Oddly, the rest of her was the same golden tan it always had been. "Yes," she said. "Incredible."

"So if that's all you have for us, it's time for my wife's interview," David said.

"Absolutely," Shawn said. "Sorry to waste your time."

Gus couldn't believe it. First Shawn had uncovered her identity, and now he was letting her walk away without even questioning her. He couldn't let that stand.

"But we saw you at the Fortress of Magic the other night," Gus said. "You remember, the night P'tol P'kah disappeared."

"That's ridiculous," Jessica said.

"Outrageous," David said.

"I knew I should never have taken you off plate duty," Shawn said. "Apologize to these good people."

Gus glared at Shawn, but Shawn glared back even harder—and then topped it off with a full frontal tsk-tsk. He turned back to the Higgenbothams.

"Please allow me to apologize for my dishwasher," Shawn said. "On behalf of the entire Little Hills Country Club, on whose hallowed ground he will never be allowed to tread again."

Shawn held out a hand to David, who took it and gave it a hearty shake. Then he turned to Jessica. She reluctantly extended a hand to him, and he took it in both of his. As he did, Gus heard a squooshing sound and saw Jessica staring at Shawn with a look of pure bafflement.

"I am so sorry," Shawn said as he pulled back his hands, revealing the squort of orange goo he'd squished onto the back of her hand. "I forgot I was holding that. Please, let me help get it off."

Before she could pull her hand away, Shawn was rubbing at the spot with the tail of his untucked flannel shirt. Wherever he rubbed, Gus could see brightly colored snakes emerging like chicks out of their eggs. With a jolt, Gus realized that what Shawn had oozed onto her hand was not orange goo but Orange Goo, the grease remover used in mechanics' shops. Apparently it was just as efficient in removing spray-on tan as it was on motor oil. That's why he'd made Gus drive him down to the cart repair bay.

Jessica realized it at the same time Gus did. She snatched her hand away and buried it deep inside her purse. Her face, which had gone white just moments before, flared red with rage. And yet her arms were still the same golden shade of tan.

"I'm sorry, did I hurt you?" Shawn said. "Let me see that."

He reached for her hand, but she shoved it deeper into her purse.

"Is everything okay, honey?" David's voice quavered with concern. It was hard for Gus to imagine this soft, sweet soul hurling knives in a traveling carnival.

"I'm fine," she said firmly. "Why don't you go ahead and let the committee know I'll be right in. I'll just clear up any loose ends with these gentlemen."

David gave her a questioning look, then turned and trotted toward the clubhouse.

"Who the hell are you and what do you want?" she hissed at Shawn as soon as David was out of earshot.

"Just who we said we are," Shawn said.

"Except for me being a dishwasher," Gus added. "I also work for Psych Investigations."

"Oh, and that thing about working for the country club," Shawn said. "We don't do that."

"What a shock," Jessica said. "So what is your main line of work? Blackmail? Extortion? Or just ruining innocent people who've never hurt you?"

"We saw you at the Fortress of Magic," Gus said. "And we have you on tape working as a cocktail waitress so you could get close to P'tol P'kah. So I'm not sure how innocent that makes you."

"Me?" She spit out the word like a curse. "I'm not innocent. I'm a born carny. But David. He's the real thing. All he wants is for us to be members here. And you've come along to ruin it."

Shawn stared off into the distance, then pressed his fingertips to his forehead. "I see a young woman, touring the country, performing acts that fascinate and repel. And in the crowd, a sweet young man who comes to every performance. One day he—"

"Knock off the psychic crap, will you?" she snapped. "I'm sure I'm an open book to all your really special magical powers. So yes, David came from a good family. They were shocked when he told them he was dropping out of college because he'd fallen in love with, well, me. I even tried to talk him out of it, but he insisted on joining the troupe. He started off as a knife thrower, but when the full extent of his talent became known, we started calling him the Amazing Bleeding Man."

"And then you fell in love with him," Shawn said. "So much so that you agreed to give up performing so that his family would accept you. You even had your tattoos removed."

"They seem to have grown back, though," Gus said.

"I couldn't do it," Jessica said. "As much as I loved him—love him—the stage was in my blood. So I told a couple of little white lies."

"And a lot of big tan ones," Shawn said.

"And everybody's happy," Jessica said. "We've got the life David's always dreamed of, complete with a set of anecdotes that will conquer any cocktail party, and I've got a couple of hobbies he doesn't have to know about."

"He didn't notice you were in Vegas three or four nights a week?" Gus said.

"He travels a lot for his job," Jessica said. "No one knew."

"Except for one chubby guy in a three-piece suit and a bowler hat," Shawn said. "And a drink in his face."

"I don't know what you're talking about," Jessica said.

"It's on tape, too," Gus said. "And I'm sure the police would like to know why you denied having ever seen him before he showed up floating in a tank of water."

"I doubt they'd be able to charge you with his murder, though," Shawn said. "They'd probably even have to drop the obstruction of justice charges after a thorough investigation. And I'm sure the membership committee here would be proud to know that at least one of their new members had been completely cleared of any felonious actions."

Jessica looked like one of her knives had slipped clear through the eyeball and penetrated her frontal lobe. "I didn't kill him," she said.

"We know you didn't," Shawn said, "because whoever did must have known the secret of the Dissolving

Man. And since you're joining a country club instead
of booking a Vegas showroom, you don't."

"We just need to know what he said to you that
night," Gus said.

"If I tell you, will you promise to leave David out of
it?"

"We'll do our best," Shawn said.

She sighed heavily. "I used to see him there on nights
when I waitressed. There was always something creepy
about him—and I'm used to people who pay money to
watch me stick knives in my eyeballs. That night as I
was passing by, he grabbed my arm and started telling
me how sexy I was, and how he wanted to see if my tattoos covered my entire body."

"Bet you'd never heard that one before," Shawn
said.

"Only from every man I'd ever met before I discovered the wonders of spray-on tan," she said. "I tried to
pull away, but he squeezed harder. So I threw the drink
in his face, which I hated to do, because they charge us
for that. And then he threatened me—and David."

"He knew you were married?" Gus said.

"He knew who I was married to," she said. "He knew
everything about me. My real name, David's family,
David's business."

"How?" Shawn said.

"He said he worked for the government." Jessica was
near tears remembering it. "He worked for the government, and if I didn't do exactly what he wanted me to,
he'd make sure the next cocktail I served would be a
Mojito at Guantanamo Bay."

Chapter Eighteen

Gus' mind reeled. The dead man floating in the magician's tank was a federal agent. No wonder the police hadn't been able to identify him in any database. He was probably deep undercover, his identity carefully hidden. And no wonder Major Holly Voges had been so eager to shut down the SBPD's investigation.

But like every other revelation they'd come across in the investigation, this one seemed to raise far more questions than it answered. At least when Major Voges showed up at the Fortress, there was a murder to solve. Chubby Dead Fed had been following P'tol P'kah for weeks, maybe months. Why? What possible interest could Homeland Security, or some other, even more secret agency, have in a Vegas magician?

"What else did he say?" Shawn asked.

"Nothing," she said bitterly. "He wouldn't even tell me his name, just said to think of him as Uncle Sam. And that if I didn't do exactly what he said, he would have David's telecommunications firm shut down as a threat to national security and us both locked away as enemies of the state."

"Did he say which agency he worked for?" Shawn asked.

"No, but he made it pretty clear it was something big, important, and unquestionable," she said. "And that he had the authority to do whatever he wanted to me."

"What did you do?"

"I was trying to figure that out, when P'tol P'kah descended from the ceiling and started growling," she said. "The creep let go of me and ran out of the place; I don't know why. And I went home, sprayed on an extrathick layer of tan, and hoped he'd never come after me."

"That's why you were so hostile when we knocked on your door," Shawn said. "You thought we were government agents working for him."

"Yeah, right," she said. "You I was scared of. Mr. Dead Cow."

"I'll have you know I put a lot of thought into that story," Shawn said. "I thought the punch line worked exactly as it was supposed to."

"Which is why I broke down right then and there and told you everything you wanted to hear."

Gus could sense that this conversation was slipping away from where they needed it to go. Before Shawn could parry back at her point, he stepped in. "So when you saw the chubby guy floating dead in the tank, why didn't you say anything?"

"I was hoping it was all over. And I couldn't afford for anyone to know who I really am. Because this," she said, gesturing to her clean, bronze arms, "is who I really am these days. I couldn't risk that just because I wanted to hang out at the Fortress for old times' sake. Now please, I've told you everything I know. Let me go on with my interview. Let me go on with my life."

Shawn thought it over, then gave her a nod. She scurried through the parking lot to the clubhouse, spraying her arm with a mist of tan goo as she went.

"That was an awful lot of time to get us exactly nowhere," Gus said.

"Really?" Shawn said. "We get the piece of information that's going to crack this case wide open, and you say we're nowhere?"

"Which piece of information is that?" Gus said as he started back toward the Echo. "The name of the dead guy? Oh, right, we didn't get it. The agency he worked for? The reason he was following P'tol P'kah?"

"We know he worked for the federal government and that he suggested strongly he was in Homeland Security," Shawn said. "Which sounds an awful lot like the thing Major Holly Voges told Jules and Lassie. Maybe whatever they do is what this case is really all about."

Gus froze with his hand on the car door handle. "You think P'tol P'kah really is a terrorist?"

"Whose secret plot is to destroy America by entertaining us all to death?"

"Then what?" Gus said.

"Remember the basic rule to all magic?"

"That the reason you can never figure out the secret to a trick is because it's so obvious," Gus said. "You've only mentioned it about six thousand times."

"We saw P'rupert P'upkin dissolve in a tank of water," Shawn said with a hint of triumph in his voice. "What is the simplest possible explanation of that trick?"

"Obviously, that he didn't really dissolve."

"One of these cases we should really change positions," Shawn said, opening the car door and slipping into his seat. "Then you can have all the really brilliant insights and I can be wrong all the time."

Shawn slammed his door closed before Gus could say anything. Gus pulled his own door open and leaned in. "And then you can be helpful and supportive, and I can be a smug jerk. And I can dress badly, too."

Gus slid behind the wheel, slamming the door behind him.

"You don't have to take it so personally," Shawn said.

"I don't have to, but I choose to," Gus said. "Just like you choose to be annoying."

Gus started the car and headed off the country club's property. He didn't even waste a glance on Shawn. By the time they were approaching the freeway, Shawn was fidgeting in his seat.

"You still haven't asked what the solution is," Shawn said.

"No, I haven't," Gus said.

"It's really good," Shawn said.

"I'm sure it's delightful," Gus said. "I hope you enjoy it."

Gus drifted onto the on-ramp and merged in with the light midday traffic. He flipped on the radio and found a lite-jazz station. Gus hated lite-jazz, but he knew that to Shawn it had the same pleasing aural effect as a thousand dentists' drills, so he cranked up the volume.

Shawn reached over and slammed his fist into the radio button, nearly punching it through the dashboard. "Okay, fine, I'll tell you," he said.

"Not on my account," Gus said. "I'm good."

Gus reached to turn the radio back on, but Shawn batted his hand away.

"Okay, okay," Shawn said. "Gus, I have a theory about the solution to this case, and it would help me greatly if I could discuss it with you."

"In that case, Shawn," Gus said, repressing his grin of triumph, "I would be honored and delighted to hear your theory."

"Yes, you would," Shawn said, then quickly corrected himself. "What I mean is this: I've been saying all along that the solution to a magic trick is the most obvious one. In this case, we've been looking at a magic act and trying to figure out how he made it look like he was dissolving himself in a tank of water when he really wasn't. But what if we were making the very mistake the green guy needs his audience to fall for?"

"Which is what?"

"Thinking that he didn't really dissolve himself," Shawn said.

Gus waited for Shawn to finish, but there didn't seem to be any more words coming.

"So your theory is that the secret behind the illusion that P'tol P'kah could dissolve himself in a tank of water is that he really could dissolve himself in a tank of water?" Gus said finally.

"You have to admit, it has a certain elegant simplicity," Shawn said.

"The original Volkswagen Beetle has a certain elegant simplicity," Gus said. "The Nike Swoosh has a certain elegant simplicity. The ending of the Tim Burton *Planet of the Apes* has a certain elegant simplicity. Your solution is just plain giving up."

"Really?" Shawn said. "The statue of Abraham Lincoln with a monkey face? Do you want to explain what that meant? That while the guy from *Boogie Nights* was escaping from a planet ruled by apes, the simians were busy rebelling on Earth, and they worked so fast they managed to remodel all of Washington DC before he could get home?"

"It makes more sense than your current theory," Gus said. "People can't dissolve themselves. And if they could, they can't reassemble themselves later."

"That's where the government comes in," Shawn said. "What if they could?"

"What, dissolve people?"

"And reassemble them."

Gus decided to let himself follow Shawn's reasoning, despite the screaming from the logic centers of his brain. "It would be one of the greatest technological breakthroughs in the history of human civilization. We could effortlessly transport people and goods anywhere on the globe. For the first time in human history, physical distance would not be a factor in our movements. We could go anywhere instantly."

"As long as we made sure there were no flies going along with us," Shawn said. "What kind of value would such an invention have to the military?"

Gus thought that through. "I guess the first use would be as some kind of death ray. You could simply dissolve away vast swathes of enemy soldiers and their equipment. But it might be even more useful as an espionage tool. At the very least, you could transport one man into the heart of enemy operations. Imagine how much earlier the Second World War would have ended if we could have teleported one soldier with a bunch of hand grenades into Hitler's bunker."

"And in that case, if a fly got mixed in, it would be even better," Shawn said.

"If the device were larger, you might even be able to get an entire company behind enemy lines," Gus said. "An army equipped with this kind of technology would be almost completely unstoppable. But if something like that actually did exist, wouldn't we have heard of it?"

"Not if it was still experimental," Shawn said. "They wouldn't want anyone to know they were working on anything like it."

"So they test it out in a Vegas showroom?"

"Remember what I said about Major Voges being here on her own?" Shawn said. "She had made some kind of terrible mistake and she was trying to fix it before anyone found out?"

"You think she suspected someone had stolen the technology and was using it in a magic act?"

"It would be one way for the thief to give public demonstrations for potential buyers without fear of anyone else realizing what they were seeing," Shawn said.

"And it also meant he'd never have to reveal himself to buyers who might decide it would be cheaper just to kill him and steal the device," Gus said. It all made sense, as long as you didn't dwell too long on the central impossibility of the dissolving ray. "That's why he went to such great lengths to set up that impenetrable identity."

"Chubby Dead Guy and Major Voges must have

suspected that he was using their stolen toy, but they weren't quite certain," Shawn said. "That's why he went to every performance. And then that one time, the green guy saw him in the crowd and knew he'd been figured out. He needed an escape plan."

"So he set up the performance at the Fortress of Magic," Gus said. "And when it was time for the climax, he dissolved himself out of the tank—and dissolved Chubby Dead Guy in. It would have been instantaneous, so he wouldn't even have had time to hold his breath. That explains why he drowned so fast."

They were coming up to their exit, but Gus didn't feel like getting off the freeway. Right now, driving with the sparkling blue ocean outside his window, he could feel the solution to this mystery falling into place. All of it was making sense. But he knew the second he pulled into a parking place and turned off the engine, the part of his brain he needed for driving would rush in to focus on the problem of P'tol P'kah, and it would find all kinds of holes in Shawn's theories.

But even though oil prices had been falling, Gus was still feeling uncomfortable about the idea of wasting gasoline. And he knew that no matter how far they drove, eventually he'd have to put his entire mind to work on the problem. A quick glance over at Shawn showed him that his partner was having some difficulty with the theory, too.

"It does sound good," Gus said. "I mean, the internal logic all works out pretty well. But we can't really go with it until we can reconcile it with reality."

"That's not what's bothering me," Shawn said.

"What, the fact that what we're talking about is physically impossible?" Gus said. "That's not the problem?"

A look at Shawn's grim face convinced Gus that this was no time for a brain-sucking joyride. He clicked on the signal and drifted across the lanes to his exit.

"That would actually be a good thing," Shawn said. "Because if I'm actually right . . ."

Shawn let his sentence trail off.

"What?" Gus said finally.

"If I'm actually right, there's a crazy man wandering around somewhere out there with an unstoppable death ray," Shawn said. "And we got purple Popsicle on his white carpet."

Chapter Nineteen

A ugie Balustrade stepped into his bathroom and locked the door behind him. There was no reason for him to turn the latch, or even to close the door—Augie had lived alone since his last girlfriend moved out two years ago, and he hadn't had a single guest over in at least six months—but this was a habit he'd developed in his early teens, and no matter how hard he tried, he couldn't break it.

Checking the knob to make sure the door was secure, Balustrade steepled his fingers together and turned them inside out until they cracked. Then he waggled each one from every joint until they were as loose as they could be. Only then did he produce the deck of cards from his vest pocket.

How many times had he laid out fifty-two cards on the back of the toilet, effortlessly fanning them across the slick white porcelain, flipping them over, expanding and contracting them like an accordion? He'd practiced the basic moves four hours a day, seven days a week, fifty-two weeks a year for forty-seven years now—sixty-eight thousand four hundred thirty-two hours, two thousand eight hundred fifty-one days. Almost eight full years, nearly a sixth of his life, he had dedicated to this simple set of tasks, and still he knew he could get better.

When Augie was little, his father used to hit him if he caught Augie with a deck of cards. To Martin Balustrade, cards were the tools of hustlers and victims, thieves and suckers, and he hadn't worked his entire life so that his son could grow up to be a low-life. Martin's grandfather had been a peasant in the Old Country, his father had worked with his hands building the rails and bridges that made this country strong, and Martin had made the transition into small business with that most traditional of entry-level entrepreneurships, the mom-and-pop dry cleaning store. (Although in this case it was only the pop dry cleaning store, since Mom had long since run off with a man who operated a traveling pony ride for small children.) It was more than a cliché; it was Augie's destiny that he would take the family name one more rung up society's ladder, finding prominence as a doctor, lawyer, or corporate executive. His future son, in turn, would then climb all the way to the top, so that his own descendants could tumble into decadence. This, Martin would explain nightly in place of a bedtime story, was the American dream, and it was their responsibility to live it out or die trying.

That might have been fine with Augie, had he not sneaked out of his house one Saturday when he was supposed to be doing his chores to see a matinee of some movie all the kids at school were talking about.

He didn't quite get the appeal of watching four singers with weird accents and weirder haircuts be chased around London by a bunch of hysterical girls, but everybody in his class had already seen it, and he was tired of being left out of the conversation. Halfway to the theater, though, he saw something that would change his life forever.

It was only a cardboard box, flipped upside down so that its bottom became a tabletop. And behind that tabletop, an indistinct man in a slick suit was yammering to the passersby as his hands flicked through a small stack of playing cards.

Augie had no idea what the man was saying, and he didn't understand why he was standing on a street corner, or why people walking by would stop, put down a dollar bill, then walk away without it. All he saw were the three cards the man laid out on his makeshift table, the way they moved, changed, flew, the way the man would put down four cards and make them look like three, the last one disappearing into his palm.

The movie began and ended three times while Augie watched the man's hands and the cards, and if a beat cop hadn't ambled by and chased the swindler away, Augie might have stayed there for the week.

From that moment on, his life was set. He began to study up on what his father called "card tricks," but what he quickly learned was called "sleight of hand." And then he began to lock himself in the bathroom. For the first few months, his father would hammer on the bathroom door and scream for him to come out, and for Augie, that was some of the best training he ever received. He learned early how to ignore the loudest heckler. And if he finally had to submit to weekly sessions with a therapist to discuss what his father assumed was the real reason he spent four hours at a time behind a locked bathroom door, that merely taught him more about the art of dissembling.

From that moment on the street corner, Augie never doubted that he would spend his life performing up close magic with playing cards. What didn't occur to him then, or for many years, was that the marketplace for such an act was extremely limited. The thing that Augie loved so much about his art form—the close, personal nature of one man, two hands, and fifty-two cards—also severely limited its commercial possibilities. If you planned to make an elephant disappear, you could do it in a theater that would accommodate thousands. But if all you wanted was to make a certain card appear in the glove compartment of a locked car belonging to a man you'd never met, there was simply no way to sell a lot of tickets. Fortunately, making money was never among Augie's chief concerns. Even when Ricky Jay, the preeminent, up-close magician of the age, did figure out a way to make a healthy living from his work, Augie didn't waste a moment cursing himself for missing the opportunity. His father had willed him the tiny bungalow where he'd grown up. The sale of what had grown to be an empire of three dry cleaning establishments and a half dozen coin-op Laundromats provided a small nest egg, and as long as he could buy a case of Bicycles for less than twenty dollars, he didn't need anything else.

Except an audience—and that had become increasingly difficult over the last few years as stage magic had reentered the mainstream of pop culture. Magic had become show business, and Augie couldn't compete with the expectations of the spectacle-sated crowds. He didn't object to Siegfried and Roy or David Copperfield when they took their illusions to a ludicrously large scale, because he knew they were at heart master craftsmen, and the tricks they performed were based on the same set of skills they all shared.

But then there was P'tol P'kah, whose act, he was certain, was designed to destroy everything Augie loved about his art. Because what Augie did—and what every one of his predecessors had done for generations before him—was based on precise technical skill. Uncountable hours of practice went into the tiniest movement. This was the real secret of the professional magician. The genius of the act lay not in the trick, no matter how clever, but in the huge amount of work it took to master it.

The so-called Martian Magician was something else entirely, Augie was sure. This dissolving man trick really was just that—a trick. He didn't know how the green guy was pulling it off, but he could tell that the secret was technological, not manual. And if all it took to be considered a great magician was access to the most expensive toys, then his art would be reduced to the level of the pop music industry, where computers could turn any moderately talented teenage girl into the next singing sensation.

Augie was not going to let that happen. He'd been studying P'tol P'kah's act for months, and he was almost certain he would have figured it out if he could have seen the Dissolving Man just once or twice more. That, he knew, was why the green giant had vanished after his aborted performance at the Fortress of Magic. He must have known he was going to be exposed. He must have known he was going to be exposed by Augie Balustrade.

But if this fraud thought that simply dropping out of sight was going to protect his secret, Augie was going to make sure he learned just how wrong he was. Let the others chatter on about what a terrific exit they had seen. Let them scramble for the opportunity to take over the enormous showroom. Augie was going to expose him.

It wasn't going to be easy, but nearly drowning in the Martian's tank at the Fortress performance had finally given Augie an idea of what the trick's secret might have been. He hadn't been able to see much when he was upside down and underwater, but as he looked out at the audience, he was pretty sure he could see a tight grid of tiny wires running through the glass walls. The most likely explanation was that these were merely reinforcements to keep the tank from exploding over the audience, but Augie thought they might have another purpose, as well.

It was still just a theory, but he was chasing hard after further evidence and hoping for some real information soon. If he could have had a few uninterrupted minutes with the dissolving tank, he was sure that what he'd find would match up with what he was assuming. But since that wasn't going to happen in this or any lifetime, Augie had begun to make some phone calls. He wasn't asking specific questions yet, just grounding himself in basic theory. But every bit he learned made him more confident that he was on the right track.

Augie scooped the cards up in his left hand and with a graceful wave arced them through the air so they landed facedown in his right palm. He twitched the muscles of his right hand, and the cards flew up again, this time landing in his left, the faces alternating up and down. One more twitch and the deck disappeared from sight. He reached into his jacket pocket—Augie always dressed for business before practice—and pulled out the cards, which were now arranged by suit.

He was about to fan them across the toilet tank again, when he heard a hissing noise. That was nothing new for the bungalow his father had left him; Augie spent almost as much time jiggling the toilet handle to stop it from running as he did working with the cards. His hand was halfway to the lever when he realized that the sound was both higher and louder than any running water he'd ever heard.

And it was coming from outside the bathroom door.

Maybe a pipe broke and there's water spewing all over the kitchen, Augie thought. But before he could visualize the location of the main valve, he heard something else outside the bathroom.

A footstep.

No, more than a footstep. It was a deep, hard thud pounding against his floorboards.

There was another thump and Augie realized what it was: the sound of a heavy boot stomping across his living room.

A huge, heavy, black boot.

There was another stomp, this one much closer to the bathroom door.

Augie's hands shook with fear, and the cards scattered over the floor. The green giant was here. It was coming for him.

Get hold of yourself, he commanded his body. *He's not a real Martian. He's not a real giant. He's probably not even a real magician.* If only he could make his hands stop shaking, he knew he could figure out what he should do.

But for the first time in sixty-eight thousand, four hundred thirty-two hours, Augie Balustrade had no control over his hands. Or his feet, which seemed to have sunk two inches into the tile floor so that lifting them was impossible.

At least his neck still worked, and he swiveled his head around to look for a way to escape. There was a window, but it had been nailed shut years ago when Augie's father thought he was using it to slip out of the house during his mammoth bathroom sessions. He could break the glass and slither out, but it was so small that only his ten-year-old self could have made it through.

Flight was impossible. The only alternative was to fight. But Augie's hands had never been formed into fists. In junior high, he was beat up every day for a month by a bully named Stacy Starkweather, who kept telling him that all he had to do to stop the punishment was fight back. Augie never did, not once, and finally Starkweather—who was related to the serial killer of the same name only in temperament—finally gave up on him. Although Augie liked to tell himself that his tormentor finally came to respect his principled stand, he knew deep down that he really only got bored.

But Augie also knew the only principle behind his stand was the love of his craft. He would sacrifice nose, eyes, stomach, legs, and whichever other part of him the bully chose to pick on, before he'd risk damaging one of his hands on the kid's thick skin.

He needed a weapon. A razor would do. At least, an old-fashioned straight razor would. But Augie shaved with a rechargeable electric, and unless the intruder was insanely ticklish, it wouldn't help him at all. Augie yanked open drawers, tearing through their contents, hurling Q-tips and cotton swabs and Band-Aids and tube after tube of hand cream on the ground. If only he had a proper nail file, the kind with the sharpened point, but Augie's superstitions about damaging his fingers kept him away from those dangerous tools. Instead, he tossed box after box of disposable, blunt-ended emery boards into the bathtub. Somehow he didn't think the threat of mild abrasion would do much to keep the Martian monster away from him.

Augie saw a glint of steel at the back of a drawer. He thrust his hand in and came out with the prize: a set of nail clippers. They weren't Augie's—he'd never trust his fingers to anything so imprecise. They must have belonged to his father and been hidden in this drawer for years.

Hands trembling, Augie peeled the slim layer of metal away from the body of the clippers. It swiveled out smoothly, the semisharp point of the file adding a good three inches to the length of his weapon.

It wasn't much, Augie knew. At best, he'd have one chance. He needed to aim precisely at the most vulnerable spot on the giant's body, and he needed to hit it hard and thrust the blade deep. That might buy him enough time to get through to the kitchen and out the back door.

Augie realized the stomping sounds had stopped. There was silence from the rest of the house. Was it possible that the monster had gone? That he had searched the place, yet somehow missed the bathroom where Augie was hiding? Walked past the locked door, thinking it was solid wall?

It didn't seem possible. That would be like winning the lottery on the same day you hit the superfecta. And Augie had never been a great believer in luck, especially his own. But the sounds had stopped. No stomping, no hissing.

Augie crept quietly to the bathroom door—and waited. He waited for what seemed like hours, like days. He waited until the sun burned out and the moon fell into the sea and the universe died of heat loss. And then, slowly and carefully, he placed his right hand on the doorknob and turned.

Still nothing from the rest of the house.

He turned the knob the rest of the way, catching his breath as the dead latch eased silently out of the strike plate. Keeping the knob twisted all the way to the left to prevent any stray sounds, he gently pulled the door toward himself until there was a tiny crack spilling light from the hallway.

Augie stayed frozen, waiting to see if anyone had noticed the movement. Again, all was still. This might actually be the day for him to buy lottery tickets at the racetrack. He took a deep breath and yanked the door the rest of the way open, clutching the nail clippers tightly in his free hand.

At first, Augie saw only the corridor and a wink of sunlight coming from the kitchen window at its end.

And then he saw the sharpened teeth—and heard the monster's terrible roar as it lunged at him.

Augie closed his eyes and struck out with the nail clippers, knowing that this time, his hands wouldn't be enough to save him.

Chapter Twenty

The neighborhood was one of those quaint parts of the city dating from an ancient time when citizens of Santa Barbara still believed that the population who spent their lives serving their superiors, cleaning their houses, fixing their cars, or serving their dinners, should be allowed to live within a gas tank's drive from them. The houses were designed and built for people who would use them to live in, possibly raise children in, not simply as markers to prove how much more money they had than their neighbors.

That meant there were no Moorish castles on this block, no Spanish palaces, or quasi-Mediterranean supervillas. Instead, there were simple, one-story cottages and ranch houses, few with more than three bedrooms and a good number with only one bath. The small front yards were mostly patches of brown lawn, and there weren't many houses not in need of a fresh coat of paint. A few blocks in either direction, the houses started to get bigger and newer as the older places were being replaced by lot-spanning micromansions, but this area was essentially untouched. Had the real estate boom gone on for another year, this street might have been demolished to make room for a fleet of grander dwellings, but the discovery that the area had been the dumping ground for a local chemical company's effluent before being developed for housing tended to make the land here less attractive to spec builders. Small wonder that you could still buy a house on this street for as little as eight hundred thousand dollars.

If there were any houses still standing after today, that was. Right now, that seemed to be in question.

Both ends of the block had been closed off by fire engines. A squadron of police cars was arrayed up and down the street, and uniformed officers were pounding on doors, grabbing the residents who opened them, and racing them away beyond the fire engine boundaries. A boxy gray truck loomed in front of a particularly shabby Cape Cod, the words BOMB SQUAD emblazoned on all sides to chase away any residents who might have ignored the police pounding on their doors.

Shawn and Gus stood with Detectives Lassiter and O'Hara, staring at the Cape Cod.

"This is fun," Shawn said finally. "Tomorrow you should all come over and stand outside my house."

"No one asked you to come along, Spencer," Lassiter said. "I think we can handle this perfectly well without your help."

"What, standing around and watching while no one does anything?" Shawn said. "Nobody does that better than me."

"He's the champ," Gus said. "He never misses an episode of *Private Practice*."

"This is called staging," Lassiter said. "We're getting all our people into position, evacuating the civilians out of the area, and then we move."

"That's not very interesting," Shawn said. "In the movies, this part is handled in a few quick cuts."

"Or a montage," Gus said.

"Only if the house in question is located in 1987," Shawn said. "And then the audience spends their time wishing all these cops would turn their weapons on Kenny Loggins before he starts another song. The point is, we're supposed to cut in right before the action starts."

"If what you want is a movie, go see one in a theater," Lassiter said.

"That's a good idea," Shawn said. He turned to Detective O'Hara, who was snapping her cell phone shut. "How about it, Jules? We could catch a matinee of all twenty-two Bond movies, and probably still make it back before anything actually happens."

"Shawn, you shouldn't even be here," O'Hara said. "It would probably be best if you and Gus moved back behind the line."

"And miss all the excitement?" Shawn said. "Besides, you brought us here."

Technically, that was true, but it certainly hadn't been on purpose. Shawn and Gus had dropped by the police station to see if there had been any test results back on the air in the canisters from the Vegas penthouse. When they got there, they found Lassiter and O'Hara strapping themselves into Kevlar on their way to the door.

"Jules, Lassie!" Shawn said as the two detectives bustled past him.

"Can't talk, sorry," O'Hara said. "Come back tomorrow."

The front door closed behind them.

"They didn't just do that," Shawn said.

"They so did," Gus said.

"Didn't even stop to apologize," Shawn said.

"Or to let you have the last word," Gus said.

"Exactly," Shawn said. "I have a reputation to protect around here. Whenever anyone leaves the room, I get to make a pithy quip that sums up the essentials of the mise-en-scène in a way that not only adds some much-needed levity to our tragedy-besotted world, but gives a unique perspective that often leads everyone involved to see the situation in the correct light."

"It's amazing that they go anywhere without your services," Gus said.

"It's amazing they think they can get away with it," Shawn said.

They could hear sirens starting up and the squeal of rubber on asphalt as a fleet of police cars tore out of the lot.

"What's more amazing is that they seem to have been right about that," Gus said.

"Not as long as my name is on this building," Shawn said, grabbing Gus by the shoulder and propelling him toward the station's rear exit.

As they made their way back, Gus finally understood what a young salmon must feel when it comes time to spawn. They were definitely swimming against the tide, as a swarm of police officers jostled past them on their way to the front door. Of course, Gus reasoned, a salmon was probably pretty sure that something good was going to happen when he finally reached the end of his upstream voyage, and Gus couldn't imagine what they were going to find in the alley behind the station, besides a couple of Dumpsters and some really bad smells, but Shawn wasn't giving him a choice in the matter.

Finally they reached the exit and Shawn threw open the metal door. Lassiter's car was wedged lengthwise across the alley, an inch of clearance on either side. The detective backed up the sedan until the bumper hit the wall of the courthouse that sat behind the police department, then spun the wheels left, slammed the gearshift into drive, and jerked forward until the front bumper hit the back of the station. He spun the wheels back the other way, jammed into reverse, and made it back three inches before tapping the rear wall again. Through the windshield, Gus could see that Lassiter was talking the whole time. He couldn't hear anything through the car's closed windows, but it wasn't too hard to tell exactly what the detective was saying.

"Come on," Shawn said to Gus, and pushed him toward the passenger's side of the car. Before Gus made it to the rear door, Shawn had already slid in behind Lassiter.

"Need a little help, Lassie?" Shawn said cheerily as Gus got in next to him.

"Get out of the car, Spencer," Lassiter said, putting the stick into drive and inching forward again.

Shawn pulled on the door handle, but the lock didn't open. "Sorry, Detective, I can't make it work," Shawn said. "It's like you use this car for transporting criminals or something."

"Transporting criminals is exactly what I don't want

to do right now," Lassiter said. "Detective O'Hara, please pull these two out of the backseat."

"You're almost free, Carlton," O'Hara said. "Do you really want to take the time? Besides, maybe they can be some help."

Shawn and Gus put on their most helpful expressions and leaned into the rearview mirror. Lassiter yanked the mirror around so he could see past them to the alley and backed up until he bumped into the courthouse wall. He twisted the wheel around and put the car into drive.

"If I ever find out who moved my parking space, I'm going to be filling out officer-involved shooting reports for the rest of my life," Lassiter said, pointing up at the RESERVED FOR HEAD DETECTIVE sign stuck onto the side of the station. Gus could make out traces of blue marker poking out from the right side, a *WN* and a heart's height above it, *ES*.

The front bumper scraped the side of the station, and then the car was free. Lassiter flipped on the siren, slammed his foot down on the gas, and the sedan rocketed forth into traffic.

During the short, fast drive to the Lower Eastside, Shawn tried to strike up a conversation with the detectives, or at least supply them with a pithy quip that would sum up the mise-en-scène. But neither Lassiter nor O'Hara seemed interested in chatting, and Shawn was having difficulty summing up the situation when he didn't have any idea what was going on.

Lassiter's car screamed onto the residential street just as the fire engine was backing across the mouth to block it off, and pulled up outside the dingy Cape Cod.

"You two stay in the car," Lassiter commanded as

he jumped out and crouched behind the open door. O'Hara did the same thing on her side.

"Sorry, Lassie, I can only follow one order at a time and I have to do it in the order I get them," Shawn said. "So I'm still working on getting out of the car."

Shawn slithered over the front seat and slid out past O'Hara, then pulled open the back door for Gus. They crouched down behind her.

"So," Shawn said, "what's going on here, anyway?"

"We're not sure," Detective O'Hara said, tightly surveying the scene. "There were reports of an explosion."

Shawn looked around. All the houses seemed to be intact.

"Not exactly Trinity, is it?" he said. "If it was a bomb, I think it fizzled."

"Or that's what they want you to think."

The voice was female and familiar, and the second Shawn heard it, he felt his arm moving to salute. He grabbed his hand and pulled it down, then stood to see Major Holly Voges coming up to the car.

"It's a standard technique of terrorists these days," Major Voges snapped. "They set off a small explosion and wait until the area is swarming with police, fire fighters, and EMTs. Then they set off a much bigger bomb, taking out the first responders."

"You spend a lot of time researching terrorists at the Federal Communications Commission?" O'Hara said icily.

"Hey, they're all over the TV," Shawn said.

"And the radio," Gus said. "Soon as you turn one on, you're going to learn something about them."

"Major Voges," Lassiter called across the car, "what's the situation here?"

"I'm just an onlooker, Detective," Voges said. "Here to lend whatever assistance I can. But I'm not the one to ask."

"Then who's in charge?" Lassiter said.

A tall man dressed head to toe in Kevlar stepped up to Lassiter. "Captain John Sturges, bomb squad," he said. "We've got the area nearly secured, and we're readying a robot to enter the premises."

"Thank you, Captain," Lassiter said.

"Did anyone ask the robot how it feels about that?" Shawn said. "Because it might not want to sacrifice its life for us puny humans."

"Can you tell us what you know?" O'Hara said, ignoring Shawn.

"At two forty-seven p.m., we got several reports of an explosion from inside this house. The 911 operators who took the calls asked if it might have been a shot, but apparently the people who live in this neighborhood are familiar with the sound of gunfire, and they said it was different. We've tried to contact the homeowner, one August Balustrade, but there's no answer."

Gus was certain he'd heard that name somewhere before, but he couldn't place it. Shawn was faster.

"Balustrade?" Shawn said. "Fat, balding guy with a face like a cherub? Real big with the five of hearts?"

"We'll know when we get in there," Sturges said. "That is, if he's in one piece."

Lassiter inserted himself between Shawn and Sturges. "Is that all?"

"One of the neighbors, a Mrs. Wilma Naugatuck, reported seeing a woman fleeing the house just after the explosion."

"Was she injured?"

"Mrs. Naugatuck said her face was discolored, as if she'd been caught in an explosion," the captain said. "And the explosion seems to have blown her clothes off. She ran out in her underwear."

Down at the end of the street, a uniformed officer waved at them. Sturges nodded back at him, then turned to Lassiter. "We're clear."

"Let's send in the robot," Lassiter said.

"Hold on a second," Shawn said. "Let's talk about this woman in her underwear."

"Let's not," O'Hara said. "Your adolescent fantasies can wait until we've cleaned up this mess."

"I'm not sure there is a mess," Shawn said. "The neighbor said her face was discolored as if from a bomb blast?"

"That's what the lady told us," Sturges said.

"Let's say you're a skilled, bomb professional," Shawn said.

"He is," Lassiter said.

"No, say the words, all together now." Shawn raised his hands as if to conduct a group sing-along, but no one seemed interested in joining him. "Fine, whatever. Anyway, in all your years of skilled, bomb professional experience, have you ever known anyone to emerge from an explosion with their clothes blown off and their face charred black?"

"Only in *Bugs Bunny* cartoons," Sturges said.

"And, judging from all your years of skilled, bomb professional experience, are we now in the middle of anything resembling a *Bugs Bunny* cartoon?" Shawn asked.

"Only one of us is," Lassiter snapped, then cast an accusatory glance at Gus. "Maybe two, if you count Tweety Bird over here."

"Lassie, I'm trying to—"

Lassiter cut Shawn off with a wave of the hand. "Interfere with an ongoing police operation. Now, get out of the way." Lassiter turned back to Sturges. "Go ahead, send in the robot."

Shawn tried to object, but Lassiter walked away. Shawn studied the scene, then nudged Gus hard. "You heard the man."

"I heard the man," Gus said, "but that doesn't mean he was talking to me."

"Of course he was," Shawn said. "When they write the history of Santa Barbara, you'll go down as the city's finest semiprofessional robo-mime."

"They have written the history of Santa Barbara," Gus said. "In fact, they've written many histories of Santa Barbara. And not one of those voluminous texts has included or ever will include a single word about the short-lived trend of robo-miming, or any of its practitioners, myself included."

Shawn glanced at the bomb squad truck and saw a metal box on miniature tank treads rolling down a metal ramp that extended from the open rear doors.

"Fine," Shawn said. "If we fail to solve this case, I only hope that Benny Fleck never learns it was because you were unwilling to do something you once did to impress girls or pick up spare change to feed your comic book addiction. 'Sorry, Benny,' I'll have to explain, 'we thought your case was fairly intriguing, but ultimately not quite as important as *Deathlok the Destroyer*, number fifty-seven.' I'm sure he'll understand."

Gus glared at him. "You wouldn't."

"I'm sworn to tell the truth to my client, especially when it serves my purposes," Shawn said. "And right now, my purposes are to keep Lassie from destroying his own crime scene."

"You mean your crime scene," Gus said.

"I like to think of it as our crime scene," Shawn said. "Now robo."

Gus sighed, then tightened his face into an impassive mask. He straightened his posture, stiffened his joints, and glided through two mechanical steps before freezing in place. He turned his head exactly ninety degrees to survey the area, then eased it back into starting position. He might have allowed himself a moment of self-congratulation at his ability to snap into robot mode after twenty years without a moment's practice, but the discipline of the act required keeping his mind entirely blank.

Gus swiveled on the balls of his feet, then started toward the front door of the Cape Cod, his arms moving mechanically with every step.

"What the hell is he doing?" Lassiter snapped.

"You said you wanted to send in a robot," Shawn said. "Gus does the best robot in Santa Barbara. It's in all the history books."

"I mean a real robot," Lassiter said. "That thing."

The metal box was all the way out of the bomb squad truck now, and a flock of technicians were huddled around it, flipping switches, checking readouts, and tightening the treads.

"What's the point of sending in a robot with no personality at all?" Shawn said. "With no heart and no soul, just a mindless box that beeps and boops and rolls around? Don't you realize that real robots look like Haley Joel Osment and yearn endlessly through the centuries for the adoptive mothers who casually toss them away when they have real children? Would this metal cube be content to sit at the bottom of the ocean, dreaming of Mom while eternity ticks away?"

"Eternity *is* ticking away," Lassiter snapped. "Every time I talk to you. And where is he going now?"

"More importantly," Shawn said, moving to block Lassiter's view of Gus, "what the heck were those alien things doing at the end? I thought I'd fallen asleep and another movie had started while I was napping."

Lassiter shoved Shawn aside. "Guster, stop!"

Gus was robo-walking across the street toward the Cape Cod's door, head swiveling and forearms rising and falling with every shuffling step. He'd always liked robo-miming, but he'd forgotten just how satisfying it could be to transform himself into a mechanical device, to feel the weight of two imagined C batteries nestled in the small of his back, to know only the sensations of the servo motor. He was so caught up in his robotic self that he didn't notice the detective shouting at him. He'd stopped caring that he was walking toward a crime scene, or even that there might be a live bomb inside the house he was approaching.

"Come back, Gus!" Detective O'Hara shouted.

Gus kept shuffling forward.

"Get him back here!" Lassiter commanded Shawn.

"But that's within the crime scene perimeter," Shawn said. "Civilians aren't allowed, not even those who frequently do excellent work in collaboration with the Santa Barbara Police Department."

Robo-Gus hit the first of three low steps with the tip

of his shoe, then shuffled back a couple of inches. He stopped, swiveled his head back and forth, then moved forward again. This time when he reached the stairs, he stopped, lifted his knee until his thigh was parallel with the ground, then placed his foot on the first step.

"Stop him now!" Lassiter yelled.

"Yes, sir," Shawn said, and ran across the sidewalk to join Gus, who was walking in place, his chest pressed against the front door. "It's okay; you can stop aerobosizing."

Gus took a couple of seconds to wind down, shaking the life back into his joints. "What are we doing here, Shawn?"

"Blowing this case wide open," Shawn said. He reached for the door handle.

"Stop!" Gus hissed. "You may be blowing us wide open. Or up."

"Only if there's a bomb inside." Shawn grabbed the doorknob, gave it a sharp twist, and pushed the door open.

Chapter Twenty-One

As they closed the door behind them, Gus and Shawn could hear the shouts from the police outside—and another, more ominous sound.

"Something's ticking," Gus said. "It's the bomb."

"It's a grandfather clock," Shawn said, walking toward the timepiece in question, which was the only thing moving in the dusty living room. "But even if it was a bomb, I wouldn't be too worried."

"Because being blown up is such a lovely way to spend an afternoon?"

Shawn came back to the entry hall and grabbed Gus' arm, pulling him into the living room. "Because the first one didn't seem to have any effect at all."

Gus gazed around the sparsely furnished parlor. The couch was old and beginning to sag in the middle; the upholstery on the arms of the two big chairs was worn down almost to threads. The wallpaper had begun to peel off at the corners. The room was tacky, dated, and unappealing, but the one thing it definitely wasn't was exploded.

"You heard what Major Voges said," Gus said. "They set off a small bomb to lure the first responders in, and then get them with a bigger one. We've been lured."

Shawn sighed heavily and disappeared through a door. After a moment, Gus heard him cry out.

"What is it?" Gus called, dreading the answer.

"Come here, quickly," Shawn said. "We don't have a lot of time."

"You found a timer, didn't you?" Gus froze in place. *What does it feel like to be blown up?* he wondered. *Is it painful? And if it is, do you feel the pain in all the various pieces scattered around the room? Or is there more of a central agony?* "Is it counting down in big red numbers? Do we have less than a minute left? Because I've got a lot of life to flash back on before I die, and I'm not sure a minute will be enough."

"There's no timer," Shawn said. "Now get in here."

Gus didn't want to. He wanted to turn around and tiptoe to the front door. After all, if they were both blown up, who would come to visit Shawn's grave every day for the next eighty years? He owed it to Shawn to leave, to stay alive to pay him the homage he was due.

"Gus!" Shawn called. "Now!"

Fine, Gus thought. *If that's the way he wants it, let his grave go unvisited.* Gus walked slowly to the doorway Shawn had disappeared through, and found himself in a long corridor. Shawn was at the other end of it, waving at him. As Gus followed, Shawn retreated into a room. When Gus reached it, he found himself in what must have been Balustrade's den, a wood-paneled box furnished with a worn leather couch and a television that could almost certainly receive color broadcasts.

Shawn was in the middle of the room, and he was leaning over something that didn't look like any bomb Gus had ever seen.

As he got closer, Gus could see that it was the tuxedo-clad body of the magician who'd slipped the card into his sock at the Fortress of Magic. He was sprawled out on his stomach, the crowbar that had been used to shatter his skull still lying beside his head.

"Is he dead?" Gus asked as he got closer.

Shawn didn't bother to answer, and as Gus moved into the room, he could see that it was a foolish question. Gus gestured down at the crowbar. "How hard would you have to hit someone with that to kill him?"

"Not so hard it would sound like an explosion to anyone except the guy getting hit," Shawn said. He was staring down at the dead man's hands. Even in death, his fingers were immaculate. Except for the ring finger on his right hand. There was something dark underneath the nail.

"Car keys," Shawn said, and Gus handed them over without even thinking. Shawn used one key to pry under the dead man's fingernail and eased out a thick piece of rubber, so dark green it was almost black.

"What's that?" Gus asked.

"More to the point, what's this?" He used the key to pry open the magician's left hand, which was locked into a fist. Inside, he was clutching an old clicker-style TV remote.

"I think that's what they used to change channels back when they had only three of them," Gus said.

"Not much of a weapon, though," Shawn said.

"Good point," Gus said. "That's probably why he's dead and the guy with the crowbar isn't."

"No, think about it," Shawn said. "You're about to die; there's nothing you can do about it. Why would you pick up the TV remote as your last act?"

"So no one would find out you were watching *The Mentalist*?" Gus said. "I mean, really, who could believe a show with such an idiotic concept?"

"To send a message."

Gus stared down at the remote in the dead man's hand. "And that message is what—I'd rather die than go on watching this show?"

"Exactly," Shawn said.

Shawn was about to pick up the control when they heard the front door bang open. "Police!" Lassiter yelled from the entry. "Come out with your hands up!"

"I'm in the shower," Shawn called back. "Can you just slip it under the door?"

Gus probably didn't hear Lassiter's muttered curse, but he knew so precisely what that curse would have been, he might as well have. After a moment, Lassiter and O'Hara burst through the door into the den.

"What kind of twisted game of Russian roulette are you two playing?" Lassiter said. "Don't you realize you could both have been killed?"

"Apparently we missed our chance." Shawn pointed down at the magician on the floor. "He beat us to it."

"Step away from the body, Shawn," O'Hara said. "I'm going to call this in."

"You can do that if you want to," Shawn said. "But there really isn't much point. I've just solved this entire case."

Chapter Twenty-Two

Gus gripped the bars with both hands and bellowed down the prison corridor. "Let us out!"

"Yes, that's certainly going to work." Shawn was stretched out on the hard metal bunk, hands laced behind his head. "You've got to wonder why in the entire history of incarceration, no one ever thought of asking to be let out before."

Gus wheeled on him, furious. "This is all your fault."

Shawn yawned. "I'm not the one who robo-walked right into a crime scene. Therefore, it wasn't me who interfered with said crime scene."

"I only did it because you told me to," Gus sputtered.

"Getting us both into trouble," Shawn said. "Really, if you'd start using a little independent judgment, we'd be better off."

Gus looked around the cell for a weapon, but there was nothing that wasn't bolted to the ground or screwed into the wall.

"We weren't arrested for interfering with a crime scene," Gus said, falling back on the only weapon available to him, his words. "The charge was obstruction of justice."

"What does that mean, anyway?" Shawn said.

"It means that you claimed you knew the identity of Balustrade's killer, but when Lassiter asked who it was, you wouldn't tell him," Gus said.

"I merely said that he needed to supply me with a few basic items and assemble a small group of suspects within the next twenty-four hours and I would explain it all," Shawn said. "That's hardly obstructing justice. More like delaying it."

"Why didn't you just tell him?" Gus demanded. "That way we'd be free, Benny Fleck would pay us, and we could think about something other than the fact that in a couple of hours I'm going to have to go to the bathroom and there are no doors here."

"If it meant that much to you, you could have told Lassiter who did it," Shawn said.

"I would have," Gus said, "only I don't know who that is. Because you wouldn't tell me."

"Damn right," Shawn said. "Not if you're going to blab it all over the place."

At the far end of the corridor, a heavy metal door swung open with a creak. Gus heard sturdy, sensible pumps clacking on the concrete.

"Let me out!" Gus shouted. "Let me out and I promise to testify against Shawn!"

Santa Barbara Police Chief Karen Vick stepped up to the cell and gazed at Gus with the same calm, cool gaze she always had for them. And as always, her calm and her coolness made Gus stop worrying about whatever had been making him nervous and made him start worrying about what she might be thinking.

"I'd be careful about making that offer too loudly," Chief Vick said. "There are some members of this force who would be only too happy to take you up on it."

Shawn hopped off the bunk. "Fortunately, you're not one of them."

"Fortunately, I'm not one of them *yet*," Chief Vick said. "But my patience isn't infinite."

"I don't see why," Shawn said. "It's not like your bathroom doesn't have doors."

Gus had long marveled at the way Chief Vick seemed completely unaffected by even the most non-sequitursiest of Shawn's non sequiturs. This time was no exception.

"I am prepared to release the two of you," she said. "Before I do, I need to ask you a few questions. First, do you know who killed August Balustrade?"

"We do," Shawn said.

Gus was about to object that *they* most certainly did not, but Shawn silenced him with a look.

"Do you know what happened to P'tol P'kah?"

"We do," Shawn said.

"We do?" Gus said. "I mean, of course we do."

"Do you plan to explain this to the Santa Barbara Police Department at any time in the near future?"

"A great magician never reveals his secrets," Shawn said. Gus kicked him in the shin. "But he's happy to reveal someone else's. So yes, all will be explained."

"When?"

"Tonight," Shawn said. "At the Fortress of Magic."

"Of course," Chief Vick sighed. "I suppose you have a list of people you want us to bring there."

"Funny you should mention that," Shawn said, pulling a piece of paper out of his shirt pocket. "By the way, the booking officer should have taken this away from me. I could have used it to pick the lock, dig through the concrete, tunnel five hundred miles, and end up in Mexico."

Chief Vick eyed the list dubiously. "That might have made more sense than what you've got here. And what's this?" she said, flipping the paper over to reveal a second list.

"Just a few things we'll need before the big show," Shawn said.

"A digital video camera, a quart of bourbon, police reports from the night of the disappearance, a twenty-two-ounce steak with onion rings," she read.

"You can forget that last one," Shawn said. "That was only if we were ordering our last meal."

She glanced down the rest of the list. "I'll see what I can do about these. Anything else?"

"I'd asked Lassiter to have some tests run on a tank of air," Shawn said. "Has he had a chance to do that, or has he been too busy arresting people who are trying to solve his case for him?"

"Detective Lassiter is a man of his word," the chief said, a touch of frost in her voice. "If he says he'll do something, he will do it. Especially if it will help bring a criminal to justice."

"So?" Shawn said. "Results?"

"It was air, Mr. Spencer," Chief Vick said. "Just plain old air. Nothing remotely Martian about it."

Gus watched Shawn carefully, looking for any trace

of disappointment. But if Shawn was hoping for proof of interplanetary involvement before tonight's de-nouement, he wasn't displaying the letdown.

"Is that all, Mr. Spencer?" the chief asked.

"One more thing," Shawn said. "Pull your guard off the door at the Fortress of Magic."

"I'm happy to put my man back on the streets," Chief Vick said. "But it's not going to do you much good if the government agents are still there."

"What do you think the bourbon is for?" Shawn said.

It took only a few minutes for Shawn and Gus to be processed out of the jail, and a few more for Gus to cel-ebrate the fact of a toilet stall enclosed by solid metal on four sides. By the time he emerged, informed enough about the inequities of global trade to participate in a symposium, thanks to the most recent issue of *The Na-tion* that some officer had left hanging on the handicap rail, Shawn was hefting a cardboard box full of supplies. Chief Vick had come through, even if, for the bourbon, she'd had to substitute a two-thirds-full bottle of cheap scotch from the desk of one of her detectives.

Since they'd left the Echo in the police parking lot when they'd ridden with Lassiter and O'Hara to Bal-ustrade's house, it was only minutes later that the box was safely stowed in the backseat and Shawn and Gus were on their way to the Fortress of Magic.

They rode in silence, as Gus refused to ask Shawn what he had figured out and Shawn declined to volun-teer. Even as they climbed the long hill up to the For-tress' front door they didn't speak, except for once, when Shawn asked Gus to carry the box and Gus declined on the grounds that since he didn't know how the items inside were to be deployed, he didn't want to leave himself vulnerable to new charges of obstruction.

Only when they were inside the Fortress and had ascertained that, aside from the "federal agent" Major Voges had left guarding the showroom, the place was deserted, did Shawn feel it necessary to converse.

"Okay, here's what I need you to do," he said as they checked out the main parlor. "Go offer the guard a drink."

"Maybe you'd like me to burn down the police station while I'm at it," Gus said. "Or hack into their databases and change all the names of the criminals."

"First of all," Shawn said, "you know this guy isn't a real fed."

"I know that's what you told me," Gus said. "I have no way of knowing if it's the truth or not, since you're not sharing any actual information with me."

"Well, then," Shawn said, "there's an easy way to find out. Go offer him a drink. If he takes it, he's a rent-a-cop. If he doesn't, he's a fed."

"Or a very good rent-a-cop."

"He's spent days standing outside a doorway with no one to talk to except Officer McNab," Shawn said. "I'll be surprised if he hasn't drained the bar by now."

"Uh-huh," Gus said, wandering toward the nearest open door, which led into the Fortress' cramped office. He took a seat in an ancient swivel chair and felt the leather upholstery decaying into powder beneath him. "And what will you be doing while I'm subverting justice?"

"Stuff," Shawn said. "Followed by things. Then maybe, if I get a chance, more stuff. All of which is essential if we're going to get through our reveal tonight."

Gus lifted his legs up and dropped his heels on the desk, nearly toppling over backward as he did so. The chair wobbled underneath him and he had to fight to keep from collapsing onto the floor, but it was worth straining his calves to let Shawn know exactly how indifferent he was to this plan. To complete the picture, he grabbed a dusty volume from the desk and flipped through it before he answered.

"Our reveal?" Gus said. "You mean one of those scenes where you explain it all, and I get to be amazed along with the rubes?"

"Oh, come on," Shawn said. "You know you want to be a part of this."

Gus leafed through the book, which turned out to be the Fortress' booking calendar, and did his best to look fascinated by what he saw there. He would have whistled a jaunty tune while he pretended to read, but the cloud of dust rising up around him forced him to devote all his bronchial resources to fighting off a coughing fit.

"I'll tell you who did it," Shawn said.

Gus spared him a glance.

"I don't mean right now," Shawn said, "but definitely before everyone else."

Gus slowly turned another page in the volume.

"Please, Gus," Shawn said. "I can't do this without you. Which means that P'tol P'kah will get away with everything."

Part of Gus' brain registered the fact that Shawn was desperate enough to make peace that he was willing to stop pretending he couldn't remember the Martian Magician's stage name. But most of it was too occupied with what his eyes had just seen in the ledger.

"Please?" Shawn said.

Gus eased his feet off the desk, knowing that any sudden movement would probably smash the chair into kindling, and stood up. "Look at this," he said.

Shawn came into the office and took the book. Gus pointed down at the entry. Shawn stared, shocked.

"Do you know what this means?" Shawn said. "You've just cracked this case wide open."

"You said you'd already solved it," Gus said. "And not only that, you said it in a way that strongly suggested you actually meant it this time."

"Not that case," Shawn said. "That one I put to bed ages ago. No, this is a bigger case. An even more mysterious case. It's so huge, it's . . . it's . . . it's *Jaws: The Revenge*."

"You mean . . . ?"

"Exactly," Shawn said. "This time it's personal."

Chapter Twenty-Three

The tank was simple, a glass rectangle ten feet tall and four feet across with steel brackets reinforcing the corners and a metal lid on the top. Amazing how an object that looked so simple could be at the heart of something so complex, Gus thought as he stood next to it, watching the police usher in the people whose presence Shawn had demanded.

From what Gus understood, none of them had come easily. Now that the Higgenbothams had been unanimously accepted into the Little Hills Country Club, Jessica had threatened to turn to her new friends on the board, three of whom were also members of the Santa Barbara City Council. The only thing that brought her to the Fortress was Lassiter's promise that if she didn't come willingly, they'd bring her husband in her place and let him know all about her secret life. Benny Fleck, who had millions riding on the solution, nonetheless demanded that he be allowed to participate via video conference. Chief Vick had to apply personal pressure on Judge Albert Moore to persuade Fleck that his presence was required.

While she was at it, she got Judge Moore to lift the restraining order forbidding Henry Spencer from setting foot inside the Fortress of Magic, which eliminated the only plausible excuse he had for not showing up. Neither Bud Flanek nor Lyle Wheelock had any desire to return to the site of their great humiliation; fortunately, as veterans they both responded to the military presence of U.S. Army major Holly Voges, retired.

For most of the afternoon, the lone holdout was Barnaby Rudge, who seemed to have finally learned the art of the disappearing act. In fact, he was in the one place no one had thought to look—curled up asleep on a couch in the bar of the Fortress of Magic, just across from the comatose form of Major Voges' guard. If one of the uniformed officers hadn't popped in looking for the men's room, they might never have stumbled across him.

Now everyone was assembled in the showroom, and they were all staring up at Gus in eager anticipation. Well, not eager so much as angry, and not anticipation so much as rage, but Gus did allow himself a moment of pleasure at being the center of attention for once in his detective career. And then he allowed himself another moment at the knowledge that as soon as Shawn took the stage, no one would be paying any more attention to him.

But where was Shawn? Why wasn't he here hogging the spotlight? Gus checked his watch, suddenly aware that he'd been standing mute on stage for a good three minutes and the crowd was getting restless.

"I'm sure you're all wondering why we've called you

here tonight," he said finally, feeling a need to fill at least a little of the hostile silence.

"You didn't call us here. You had us dragged by the police," Jessica Higgenbotham said. "If I'd wanted to spend my life being rousted by cops, I would have stuck with the carny life."

"I promise, it's going to be worth all the inconvenience," Gus said, hoping fervently this was true. After all, Shawn had already announced on several occasions that he'd solved the case, only to have Gus point out that he was actually nowhere close. He fought off the terrible feeling that the real reason Shawn hadn't explained the solution to him was that he was afraid Gus would poke holes in this one, too.

There was an ugly murmur running through the crowd. Lassiter had noticed the change in mood as well, and had signaled the uniformed officers to take positions by the exits.

"Let's get on with this, Gus," Henry called. "Where's Shawn?"

Before Gus could answer, Lyle Wheelock spit out a curse. "Maybe he's got to break up another happy couple first."

"Yeah?" Henry said. "Which happy couple was that—the people who were getting married, or the ones who were cheating?"

Benny Fleck marched up to Lassiter and O'Hara. "I am here, Detectives, under duress, having been forced to abandon several key negotiations at a crucial point. I was dragged across state lines for this catastrophe. So I strongly urge you convince me this was worthwhile before my lawyers can come up with a lawsuit that will bankrupt Santa Barbara."

"You may be able to throw your weight around Las Vegas, but the SBPD doesn't play that way," Lassiter said. "Now get back in the front row so you can see."

Fleck glared up at him. If Lassiter was the slightest bit intimidated by the billionaire, Gus couldn't see it.

For the moment, Lassiter had successfully taken control of the crowd, and the muttering had died away. But Gus knew it was only a matter of minutes before the unrest would start again.

Just as Gus was searching for the right words to calm the audience, the houselights dimmed and a spot shone down on the stage. Shawn strode out into the middle of the spotlight and took a deep bow.

No one clapped.

"Where have you been?" Gus whispered furiously.

"You never heard of making an entrance?" Shawn said. "Besides, there were a few last-second details that needed tending to."

"Like what?" Gus said.

"Hey, it's the psycho!" Lyle Wheelock yelled. "He's the one who— Ow!"

"Like that," Shawn said.

Gus peered out into the crowd and could make out a small boy sticking his hand in the air as a superball flew into it.

"Is that Hank Stenberg?" Gus asked.

"The Headhunter himself," Shawn said. "Best crowd control you can buy for less than five bucks."

"Okay, Spencer, time to get going," Lassiter said. "Make it good, make it convincing, but most of all, make it short."

Shawn made another deep bow and waited for the applause to subside, which presented a small problem in that it had never actually started. Gus nudged him and he straightened up.

"Ladies and gentlemen," Shawn intoned, "and police and ex-army majors and carny freaks and anyone I might have left out. We are gathered here tonight to solve a crime."

"Yes, Shawn, we are," O'Hara called out. "We've been gathered here for a long time. So maybe you could start solving."

"Yes, to solve a crime," Shawn started. "And not just any crime, but the worst kind of crime."

"We all know someone was murdered," Lassiter said.

"I'm talking about a theft," Shawn said. "The theft of a young boy's sense of wonder."

Over the course of their detective career, Gus had occasionally entertained the notion that they should cater Shawn's denouements—at least serve a few light hors d'oeuvres, in case the summation ran long. But he was particularly glad there hadn't been food served tonight, as there was little doubt it all would have rained down on them.

Shawn persevered through the boos, hisses, and occasional obscenity. "Two decades ago, a small boy came to the Fortress of Magic, wanting only to be amazed and delighted. But instead of allowing him those few moments of, yes, magic, his father cruelly exposed its practitioners as tricksters, hoaxsters, and frauds, stealing that precious gift of enchantment away forever. And the author of that theft is standing among us right now," he said, leveling the powerful finger of judgment at his father. "Henry Spencer, *j'accuse*."

"If you mean I told you the truth about these phonies, you're welcome," Henry said, then noticed Rudge glaring at him. "Nothing personal."

Rudge gave him a conciliatory bow.

"What you call the truth is nothing more than a fear of being tricked," Shawn said, "a belief that if someone is holding the truth from you, it must be for nefarious purposes."

"Well, of course it is," Henry said.

"And that's exactly the attitude that sent me here in the first place," Shawn said.

Lassiter turned to Henry. "It was your idea for Shawn to come here in the first place? Gee, thanks."

"I was banned from the Fortress for exposing the truth," Henry said.

"Oh, come on, Dad," Shawn said. "You were banned because you arrested the magician who was showing me card tricks for contributing to the delinquency of a minor."

"As if your delinquency needed any more contributions," Henry said.

"Hey!" The voice that rang out was so full of authority, everybody turned in its direction immediately. Major Voges didn't have her gun out, but her bearing was so intimidating, she might as well have. "We're not here to participate in your private psychodrama."

"See?" Lyle said. "I told you he was a psycho."

Shawn gave Hank a hand signal, and the boy hurled the superball at Lyle's head.

"Ow," Lyle said as the ball zipped back into Hank's hand.

"See, they do sting," Shawn said to Gus, then turned back to the audience. "This is exactly where you're wrong, Major Voges. You are all here to participate in our private psychodrama. Because that was key to solving this mystery. You see, it was the cynicism my father imparted to me that kept me from realizing the truth. Now I know you're all wondering, just how cynical is Henry Spencer?"

If noes were bullets, Shawn and Gus would have been flopping on the stage like Bonnie and Clyde.

"I'm glad you asked," Shawn said quickly. "Here's how cynical my father is. He looked at two friends, two old, dear, close friends, and saw something strange. I don't know what sparked his suspicions, but he could tell there was something off about Bud's engagement. And being the cynic that he is, he leapt to the conclusion that Lyle was cheating with Bud's lovely fiancée, Savonia."

"Does this have anything to do with the case?" Gus whispered to Shawn.

Shawn ignored him. "But he'd known these friends for far too long to confront either of them with his suspicion. So he arranged a bachelor party for Bud—but he booked it for the one place he knew he couldn't possibly attend."

"How did you find that out?" Henry said.

Shawn gave him a small smile. "And then he sent me. Do you know why?"

"So he wouldn't have to listen to you anymore?" Rudge called out to mutters of approval.

"Because he knew he'd raised a cynic just like himself," Shawn said. "And he knew that cynic would leap to the same conclusion he did. But without the encumbrance of years of friendship, he'd make the accusation."

"It's not an accusation. It's a fact, for God's sake,"

Henry said. "A blind idiot could see it. Or even my son."

"And I did," Shawn said. "I saw exactly the same thing you saw, because I saw it through your prejudices. But once the prejudice was gone, I could see the truth."

"That's great," Lassiter said. "Glad we wrapped that one up. Let's move on to the murder."

"And the truth wasn't that Lyle was a bad friend," Shawn said. "It was that Bud was a great one. Lyle's wife has been institutionalized with Alzheimer's for years. The marriage is long dead, but he can't divorce her because she'll lose her health insurance and be dumped on the street. Last year he met Savonia and fell in love, only to discover that her visa was running out and she was going to have to leave the country. Bud volunteered to marry her so she could get her green card and live with Lyle."

Everybody turned to stare at Bud and Lyle.

"Is this true?" Henry said.

"We couldn't tell anyone because we were worried about the immigration people," Bud said.

Lyle threw his arms around Bud. "Isn't he the greatest friend ever?"

Shawn took another deep bow. "And with that, ladies and gentlemen, the opening act of this presentation is over. Part two will commence after a brief intermission."

Major Voges marched up to Lassiter and O'Hara. "This is a farce," she said. "If you don't arrest him, I will. And then I'm shutting this ridiculous charade down and taking that tank back to Washington."

"You can have the tank as soon as I'm done with

it," Shawn said. He signaled to Gus, who wheeled the airplane steps out from the wings and locked them into place. Shawn took the first three steps at a bound.

"Stop that man!" Voges shouted, but no one moved. She lunged toward the stage, but O'Hara pulled her back.

"Sorry, Major, but I missed the first show," O'Hara said. "I've got to see this."

Shawn reached the top of the steps, then bent down and flipped the latch on the tank lid open, then slid it closed. He unlatched it again, then pulled the heavy steel lid up.

"Get out of there!" Fleck said. "That belongs to my client."

"Magic belongs to all of us," Shawn said. He gave another deep bow, then stepped off the platform into the tank.

Shawn sunk down to the bottom, then bobbed back up. He floated midway in the tank, his cheeks puffed out with air.

"Get him out of there," Henry said, rushing toward the stage.

Major Voges blocked his way. "No one touches the tank."

"That's my son in there!" Henry said. "He'll drown."

"Which is preferable to what will happen to him once he gets out," Major Voges said.

Henry shoved her out of the way and went to the stage, but before he could climb up, the water in the tank had changed. Before it had been perfectly still. Now it bubbled and frothed like a glass of cheap champagne. As Henry stared, he realized the bubbles were coming from his son's body.

Shawn raised his hands over his head, sending a storm of froth rising to the surface. As the bubbles flew from his fingertips, the crowd saw with a shock that the fingers were shrinking. No, *dissolving*. Within seconds, they were gone down to the first two knuckles, and quickly the hands were reduced to clublike stumps.

Shawn lowered one deformed hand to touch his stomach, and immediately the bubbles began fizzing out of his abdomen. But they didn't rise to the top of the tank. They spun around, as if caught in a whirlpool. And when they cleared, they had eaten a hole clear through Shawn's midsection. Where moments before there had been a blue-checked flannel shirt over a white T, now there was a void. And it was growing in all directions, devouring his chest, his hips, his shoulders. His arms, eaten from both sides, fell off his body and dissolved into bubbles before they hit the tank floor. All that was left was the grinning head floating seven feet over the enormous black boots that still sat at the bottom of the tank.

The bubbles were working on Shawn's chin now. Before they could reach any higher, he opened his mouth as if to speak—or to scream. But what came out wasn't just a blisteringly loud roaring sound. It was light—a blast of pure white light that lit up every corner of the showroom.

Then the light went out, and the room was plunged into darkness.

Chapter Twenty-Four

When the houselights came back on, everyone was staring at the tank, stunned. Even Gus, who'd known what was going to happen, was rendered momentarily speechless by the spectacle.

Henry broke the silence, turning savagely on Fleck. "Where's my son?" he demanded. "What has your machine done to my son?"

The showroom doors flew open and Shawn strolled in. "Was someone looking for me?"

For one brief second, a look of relief washed over Henry's face. But he managed to get his emotions under control quickly and replaced the relieved look with a scowl.

A mournful cry came from the center of the room. "All my life I've been working at my craft," Rudge wailed, "and this punk is able to duplicate the most amazing illusion ever performed without any effort at all."

"There was a little bit of effort," Shawn said. "The backstage door weighs a ton."

"I knew it was all a cheap trick," Jessica Higgenbotham spit. "There was no way P'tol P'kah wasn't a complete fraud."

"How did you get out of the tank?" Lassiter said.

"Look," Shawn said, wringing out his shirt. No water dripped out of it. The cloth was completely dry. "I was never in it."

"But we saw you," Detective O'Hara said.

"Did you?" Shawn said. "Did you really?"

"Yes, Shawn, we all did," Henry said. "Do you want to explain now?"

"Or do we have to beat it out of you?" Lassiter added hopefully.

"Gus!" Shawn called. "Show them."

Gus went over to the tank and picked at the glass where it met the metal frame. Scraping at it with his fingernail, he pried back a thin sheet of clear plastic, much like the sticky protective wrapping on a new iPod screen.

"Get away from that tank," Major Voges commanded. "That information is classified."

"Then we promise not to tell anyone," O'Hara said. "Go on, Shawn."

"It was Augie Balustrade who gave me the clue," Shawn said. "Because he wasn't a crook or a hustler, he really was devoted to his craft. And it personally offended him that P'tol P'kah was perverting it."

Gus stepped away from the tank. "That's why he was clutching a TV remote when he died. To send us a message from beyond the grave."

"What message?" Lassiter said.

"That P'tol P'kah was not only our favorite Martian; he was actually *My Favorite Martian*," Shawn said. "A TV show about a fake alien."

Gus pulled the plastic sheeting off the glass so that it covered only the left half of the tank. Then he ran up the airplane stairs and fiddled with something on the lid. After a second, the thin plastic came alive with the image of Shawn splashing into the tank. The plain glass showed nothing but still water behind it.

"Hey, Henry," Bud shouted. "If you want to get me a wedding present to make up for being such a jerk, I'll take one of those."

"If you flip the latch one way, the lid opens to reveal the water below," Shawn said. "If you flip it again, a panel in the lid slides back and opens a chamber in the back of the tank. You drop down there and step out a hidden door when the lights go out."

"That's not possible," Jessica Higgenbotham said. "We would have heard of this TV technology if it existed."

"Exactly what I said about the dissolving ray," Gus said. "And the answer turns out to be the same. We never hear of it if the government wants to keep it secret."

"And what branch of the government would be in charge of something like this?" Shawn said.

"I do believe that would be the Federal Communications Commission," Gus said.

"Specifically the Office of Engineering and Technology, Equipment Authorization Branch," Shawn added.

Lassiter and O'Hara swiveled toward Major Voges, who stared at them coldly.

"I'm thinking that somewhere out there is a company that's been waiting a long, long time for government approval of their new technology," Shawn said. "Not realizing that the people who were supposed to be testing it had actually put it into use."

"At least they didn't realize it until Augie Balustrade started phoning around, asking if something like that was possible," Gus said. "And when they started to hear rumors, they called the agency in charge. They called Holly Voges."

"And she went to shut him up," Shawn said.

Major Voges glared at Shawn as if she were imagining what he'd look like strapped down to a board waiting for the fire hose.

"Is this true?" O'Hara demanded. "The government organization you work for is the FCC?"

"I never said anything else," she said coldly.

"You certainly implied something else." Lassiter looked like a kid who'd just opened the giant box under the Christmas tree only to discover it contained socks.

"I am not responsible for your assumptions, Detective," Major Voges said, "any more than I am for your psychic's errors in logic."

"I've got errors?" Shawn said.

"He's got logic?" Gus said.

"He got part of the story right," Major Voges said. "We were testing the stick-on TV technology, and it was stolen from our labs. My colleague, Doug Firrell, came under suspicion within the agency. He knew the only way to clear his name was to catch the real thief. Officially he took a leave of absence from the FCC; only I knew what he was really doing."

"Feeling up spacegirls in Las Vegas casinos," Shawn said.

Jessica Higgenbotham wheeled furiously on Major Voges. "That chubby dead creep worked for you?" she spit.

"That's why he knew all about your husband's tele-communications company," Gus said.

"Hold on," Lassiter commanded. "Are you identifying the man we found floating in the tank?"

"Try to keep up, Lassie," Shawn said.

"He was a product tester for the FCC?" O'Hara said. "Then why couldn't we find any record of him in any database?"

"He was working undercover on a delicate issue," Voges said. "I had his identity classified."

"How?" O'Hara said. "You work for the FCC, not Homeland Security."

"Anyone can mark anything classified these days," Shawn said. "It's getting it unclassified that's hard. In fact, I've just had Gus' waist size marked top secret, so if anyone sells him a pair of pants, he's going down."

"Doug was trying to prove P'tol P'kah, whoever he really was, had the stolen technology," Major Voges said. "But the magician figured out who he was. He set up the private show here as a trap and used it to kill Doug, then disappeared."

"From the tank?" Lassiter said. "Didn't he always do that?"

"In a convertible," Shawn said. "There was a police report that night of Shrek driving through downtown Santa Barbara."

"So now we know the identity of the dead man in the

tank," Lassiter said. "We just don't know the identity of the man who put him there."

"Or how he did it," O'Hara said.

"I promise you, I will not stop searching until I find this man," Major Voges said. "Once I take my fallen colleague back to Washington and see to his eternal rest, I will go after his killer."

"Going to be kind of hard to do from a jail cell," Shawn said.

"August Balustrade was dead when I got to his house," Major Voges said. "P'tol P'kah must have gotten to him before I did."

"So you took off your clothes and ran into the street in your underwear," Shawn said.

"I have no idea what you're talking about," Voges said.

Lassiter and O'Hara inched toward Major Voges. She didn't move an inch.

"I think we should continue this at the station," Lassiter said.

"This is ridiculous," Major Voges said. "I was with you at the crime scene. P'tol P'kah set off a bomb to distract the police and he fled. He's still out there while you're stopping me from pursuing him."

"There was an explosion, but there was no bomb," Shawn said.

"Something exploded," Lassiter said. "The neighbors heard it."

"It was P'tol P'kah," Shawn said.

"Wait a minute," Jessica said. "The Martian Magician blew himself up? Why?"

"For the answer to that, we have to return to the definitive work on all things magical," Shawn said. "*The*

Prestige. What that movie teaches us is that it's easy to disappear from a cabinet. What's hard is to reappear across the room, unless you happen to have—"

Gus tugged on Shawn's shirt. "I think you need to say spoiler alert here."

"You need spoiler alerts at a denouement?"

"It's just basic politeness," Gus said.

"Fine," Shawn said. "Spoiler alert. You can't make it look like you're reappearing across the room unless you happen to have a machine for generating clones or a twin brother no one in the world has ever heard about."

"Hey!" Lyle Wheelock looked up from the back of the room, where he, Bud, and Henry had been talking over old times while Shawn explained the case. "You just ruined the movie for me—and it's at the top of my Netflix queue."

"See?" Gus said.

"But the next-best thing to a secret twin is somebody who looks like a secret twin," Shawn said. "And a secret shaft from your apartment closet that leads into the ceiling of the showroom, where I have to imagine there's a secret panel."

"The architect told me that was a laundry chute," Fleck said. "No wonder it had rungs all the way down."

"The only problem is finding someone who looks like a seven-foot-tall Martian," Gus said. "That would seem pretty hard to pull off."

"Unless you had the right tools," Shawn said. "Hey, Lassie, did you ever get around to testing the air in that tank?"

"I did. It was air."

"Not Martian air," Shawn said. "Plain old Earth air."

"Plain old," Lassiter said.

"Why would P'tol P'kah possibly need all those tanks of compressed air?"

Gus had retreated to the back of the stage, and came back carrying the tank that Lassiter's men had left there for them. He took something dark and shriveled out of his pocket, then attached it to the tank's nozzle and turned the valve. There was a loud hissing of escaped air, and Gus removed the now-filled balloon from the tank.

"My million-dollar magician was nothing but a balloon animal?" Fleck said.

"A little more than that," Shawn said. "I'd guess he used a smaller version of the stick-on TV for the face. But he did have one thing in common with every other balloon animal. If he came across a sharp object . . ."

Gus held a pin aloft so that everyone could see it, then jabbed the balloon. It exploded with a bang.

"Which is why you should always wear clean underwear when you commit murder wearing a balloon suit," Shawn said. "I'd guess you planned to run out of the house as P'tol P'kah to support your story that you were chasing down your partner's killer."

Major Voges turned to the doors, but they were blocked by uniformed officers. Before they could move, she'd reached into her purse and pulled out her gun.

Lassiter and O'Hara already had their guns out.

"You can't get away," Lassiter said.

"Don't even think about it," O'Hara said calmly.

"I've already thought about it," Major Voges said.

"And there's no way you can stop me without a bloodbath."

She took two steps backward to the door. Shawn shot his hand up in the air.

"Hank!" Shawn shouted.

A superball flew across the room right into Shawn's palm. In one smooth motion he hurled it back, right at Major Voges' head.

It missed.

"You idiot," she snapped, and turned the gun on him. But before she could fire, the ball slammed into the door behind her, rocketed off, and blasted into the back of her head, knocking her off balance. Lassiter and O'Hara leapt across the room, grabbing her gun, spinning her around, and slapping the cuffs on her.

"That concludes the denouement portion of this evening's events," Shawn said with a bow. "After a brief intermission, maybe we can persuade a special guest to stick knives in her eyeballs."

Shawn and Gus linked hands, took a deep bow, and started to walk off stage.

"Hey!" Henry shouted. "What about the guy in the tank? How did he get in there?"

Shawn stopped at the edge of the stage. "You don't really care about how a magic trick is done, do you, Dad?"

"I care," Benny Fleck said. "I have a right to know."

Shawn sighed heavily. "Say, Gus," he said, "what's the first thing you need to know about any magic trick?"

"When you finally learn the explanation, it's much simpler than you ever could have imagined," Gus said.

"And what's the simplest way Chubby Dead Guy could have gotten into the tank?" Shawn said.

"I don't know, Shawn," Gus said. "What do you think it is?"

"He climbed up those stairs and stepped into it. And you all watched him do it. Because Chubby Dead Guy was not only Doug Firrell, FCC, he was also the Martian Magician."

Chapter Twenty-Five

Shawn and Gus stood outside the Outer Space showroom, watching the exiting crowd, who were clearly stunned by the brilliant illusion they'd just seen. Shawn shook his head in amazement.

"All these people looking like they've just seen a miracle," Shawn said. "If they knew what we know, they'd tear the place to pieces."

"But they never will," Gus said, looking around nervously. "Or Benny Fleck will have us torn to pieces."

"Worse than that," Shawn said. "He'll revoke our lifetime buffet pass."

"Which wouldn't be an issue if you hadn't asked for that instead of cash for solving the case," Gus said.

Because the case was solved. Once Major Voges had been booked for murder, it didn't take long to get the rest of the truth from her. Doug Firrell was an amateur magician who dreamed of going pro, but could never come up with an illusion big enough to take him beyond the children's birthday party circuit. When the stick-on TV technology came through their office for approval, he came up with the idea for P'tol P'kah.

The one drawback to the act was that it required a second person. Firrell turned to his coworker and lover, Holly Voges. She'd been reluctant to join him, but once she saw how eager Benny Fleck was to throw money at them, she became an enthusiastic participant.

But never as enthusiastic as Firrell. And as the act became more popular, he seemed to lose all grasp on reality. She tried to remind him that the technology of the tank had to be approved sooner or later, that they couldn't keep up their double life forever. But he refused to consider giving up the act.

They began to fight, and Firrell began to change. He wasn't the same sweet guy she'd fallen in love with. Instead, he'd become arrogant and smug. The last straw for Voges was when she "materialized" in the showroom to find him groping some tattooed spacegirl.

She'd had enough, and she was putting an end to the act. P'tol P'kah was going to disappear for good, and the two of them were going back to Washington. He begged her to reconsider, and when she wouldn't, he tried to persuade her into letting him continue with a new partner. But she wanted their old lives back. If he didn't give up the act, she was going to reveal the truth and let them both face the consequences.

Finally he agreed. All he wanted in return was the chance to do one show at the Fortress of Magic to amaze his peers before he gave it all up. She had no idea that he'd rather be dead than go back to Washington— or that he really intended to go out like Houdini in a tank of water on stage. But there was no other possible explanation for what happened to him. He must have set the latch so he would plummet into the water instead of the cabinet, and in the seconds when the tank was obscured by the video image, he burst his balloon suit, hid the scraps in the giant boots he left at the bottom, and inhaled a lungful of water. When the police finally drained the tank, they found exactly what she predicted in the boots.

That night she fled, terrified at what had happened. But she was quickly consumed with guilt and realized that she had to protect his secret, his legacy, no matter what it cost her. Even if it meant murdering Augie Balustrade.

She was willing to confess to all of it and spend the rest of her life in prison on one condition—that the truth never be revealed.

That condition was quickly granted by Judge Albert Moore of the Superior Court for the State of California, and Benny Fleck also persuaded him to restrain anyone involved in the case from ever disclosing the secret of the Dissolving Man. He made a quick deal with the owners of the stick-on TV technology for exclusive rights until it was certified for sale by the FCC—a process that was even slower now that half the office involved in its approval was dead and the other half in jail.

All Fleck needed after that was two people to fill the suits. Shawn and Gus declined the offer graciously and Fleck turned to the two magicians nearest him.

Shawn nudged Gus as a cocktail waitress sheathed in silver came out of the showroom. Her arms were bare except for the brightly colored snakes running up and down them. She came over to Shawn and Gus.

"Nice addition, turning up in the showroom as a

cocktail waitress after you get out of the tank," Shawn said.

"I need to keep an eye on Rudge," Jessica said. "He's not too steady coming down from the ceiling. Besides, I like the applause."

"And your husband?" Gus asked.

"I like him, too," Jessica said. "Especially now that I can perform in public without jeopardizing our social standing."

She gave them a smile, then let herself be carried off in the crowd.

"Amazing," Gus said. "That really ended up working out well for everyone."

"Yeah," Shawn said. "It's just like magic."

About the Author

William Rabkin is a two-time Edgar-nominated television writer and producer. He has written for numerous mystery shows, including *Psych* and *Monk*, and served as showrunner on *Diagnosis Murder* and *Martial Law*.

Also Available
in the brand-new series based on
the hit USA Network television show!

PSYCH
A Mind Is a Terrible Thing to Read

by

WILLIAM RABKIN

After the PSYCH detective agency gets some top-notch
publicity, Shawn's high-school nemesis, Dallas Steele,
hires him to help choose his investments. Naturally,
their predictions turn out to be total busts. And the
deceptive Dallas is thrilled that he has completely
discredited and humiliated Shawn once and for all—
until he's found murdered.

But the police have a suspect—found at the scene with
a smoking gun. And she says Shawn took control of her
mind and forced her to do it. After all, he is a psychic...

**Available wherever books are sold or at
penguin.com**

Obsessive.
Compulsive.
Detective.

MONK

The mystery series starring the
brilliant, beloved, and slightly
off-beat sleuth from the USA
Network's hit show!

BURN NOTICE: *THE FIX*

by
TOD GOLDBERG

First in the series based on the critically
acclaimed USA Network television show

Covert spy Michael Westen has found himself
in forced seclusion in Miami—and a little
paranoid. Watched by the FBI, cut off from
intelligence contacts, and with his assets
frozen, Weston is on ice with a warning:
stay there or get "disappeared."

Also Available
Burn Notice: The End Game